In a Moment

SARAH GERDES

RPM Publishing

Seattle, WA

ISBN-10: 154323013X
ISBN-13: 9781543230130

Library of Congress cataloging-in-publication data on file

Printed in the United States of America

First American Edition 2017

Cover design by Lyuben Valevski
http://lv-designs.eu

P.O. Box 841 Coeur d'Alene, ID 83816

In a Moment

PREFACE

"Come on, Lindy, come on!" a voice commanded. "You can do it. Breathe! You can start again. I know you can!" I felt nothing as I hovered above, watching the doctor tape a device around my mouth, the cord stretching to a machine. The upside of having my spirit separated from my body was freedom from the pain I'd experienced during the accident.

My hand received a squeeze and I turned to my Grandfather who had been beside me since my death, moments before.

'Now I'm not so sure I want to return," I admitted. My body was jolting, blood was on my forehead and cheek, my ribs were black. Lines and pricks marked locations where glass had hit and embedded themselves in my skin.

But that was nothing compared to the images I'd seen. The quick, staccato spurts of disjointed visuals scared me more than a damaged body. A woman leaning on her side on a gurney, frozen with grief. Another being held down against her will, her back to me. A man, sitting in an elegant office, torn apart inside but pretending to be in control. A heavy-set woman behind a wall of glass, on the phone, counseling someone in a low, concerned voice. Me, walking beside a man on a beach, the sunset fading as the moon rose on the horizon. The faces were blurred, but the feelings were acutely clear; grief, heartache, pain, but also compassion, joy and love.

The soft, loose skin on Grandfather's cheeks dropped into his lips as his eyes glimmered.

"That's a common feeling when it comes time to reenter the body," he said as though I'd be comforted. I wasn't, and he seemed to know this. "I can tell you that your physical self will be just fine."

"But the inside? My emotions and those who I saw?" He smiled, the hand that was holding mine started to release.

"Come on Lindy!" urged the doctor with such force I looked down at him. A flood of information passed to me from the doctor who feverishly worked on my motionless body. I could sense him using all his known techniques and skills in this moment to bring me back from the dead. He was fighting for my life in a way I though was admirable.

As if sensing my mood, Grandfather squeezed my hand again, his gaze firm and endowed with a faith far greater than what I possessed. "You are necessary. It is part of why you've made your choice."

I wanted to protest that I wasn't strong enough to endure what I saw before me, but didn't have the chance. The warmth of my Grandfather's hand slipped away with his image. That instant, the doctor shouted and I felt a coldness followed by excruciating pain; a million nerve endings manually reconnecting.

"That's it! We have her heartbeat," the doctor said triumphantly. I was lying on the operating room table, looking up at a silhouette of my Grandfather's face.

"Be patient and trust your inner promptings," he said faintly. "The noise of your life will try to down them out, but *listen*," he emphasized. "And Lindy. You will find love again, I promise." As I strained and tried to cry out for him not to leave, another face came into focus; a man with white hair and green eyes.

"That's right. You're getting stronger by the second. In, out, in, out." He kept coaching me, drawing a hand over my eyes as I tried to open them. "Don't try to look now. You will see soon enough."

Pain raced through my body and I heard myself choke, then scream with agony, the point where my eternal self made peace with my physical shell. Gradually, my aching eased into an exhausted, but stable state, the words of my Grandfather echoing in my mind.

"You're going to make it, Lindy," the doctor said confidently, as if he knew what I was going through. "You're right here with us, and you aren't leaving."

I was returning to a world unlike the one I left, and I had asked for it. He said I'd find love *again.* In my haze of pain, I wondered why would I need to find something I already had?

CHAPTER 1

"Well, Lindy Gordon, are you ready to hear what happened?" It was my doctor, Jake Redding, the one who'd been on call during my accident. I nodded, trying to focus on his face. I wondered if his insistence at using my first and last name was to keep reminding me of who I was.

"Please call me Lindy," I said, my voice rough, hoping to reassure him—and myself.

"Of course," he answered politely. "Focus on me so I can watch your eye movement as I speak." I did. The doctor had smooth skin and linen white hair, coarse and thick on the top and the sides, like he'd forgotten his last appointment with the hair dresser.

"To start, a car struck the cab you were in and your head smashed the window. Do you remember that?"

"Not the hit," I answered slowly, starting to move my head.

"Don't," he cautioned, but his advice came too late. A spike shot from my shoulder blade to my temple. "When you came in, you were in pretty bad shape and we wanted to prevent you from going into cardiac arrest. We put you in a blue suit to cool you down, like an ice pack. You had it on from head to toe."

"You refrigerated me?" I asked.

Dr. Redding chuckled. "In a manner of speaking, yes. No one knew how long your brain had been without oxygen, so we attempted to cool it down. It's quite evident you have one that still works."

A functioning brain was good. A working body was better. In a panicked rush, I twitched my fingers, then my toes. I inhaled to speak, and caught myself.

"My chest," I gasped, feeling like I had a boulder sitting on top of me from my sternum up.

"Two of your ribs were cracked, but they will heal. Your body should recover without long-term effects."

Thank you, Lord. Thank you, *thank you.*

"My head," I groaned.

"You hit so hard that technically, you died." He paused.

I had a fleeting image of seeing him, standing over me, working so hard. "You told me to stay with you. To breathe."

"That's right." The doctor held my eyes and to my relief, didn't give me a look as though I'd lost what was left of my mind. "Do you recall much else?"

"My Grandfather," I answered automatically. "He was…I thought he was holding my hand."

"I imagine he was." I glanced around. It was dark outside, black almost, even with streetlights on. It was also quiet, as though it was the dead of night.

"How can you be so sure?"

"When you work in the trauma unit of a city like San Francisco, you see, hear, and experience things that can't be fabricated." He stood, telling me he was going to check my forehead. I winced, and he apologized, but continued working. "Your husband kept vigil during the six hours after you arrived, but then we forced him to leave so you could rest. I liked him, by the way. Anyone with grey hair is a kindred spirit."

I tried to concentrate, worried my mind wasn't functioning. "Grey hair?" It was my doctor's turn to look at me, a concerned expression on his face.

"Yes, Alan. White hair, short, trim and fit looking man." I continued to stare at him. "If he wasn't your husband…" I could see the anxiety on his face, worried he'd allowed an individual in the room that didn't have my approval.

"Yes—no, I mean, it was fine he was here. He's my CFO, not my husband, who is Patrick." I could read the man's face as clearly as if he said the words. He was wondering why Alan was at the hospital instead of Patrick.

"Normally we don't let anyone in who can't produce documentation of their relationship to the victim, but this is the city, and to a degree we take people at their word. In this case, Alan said he didn't know if you were going to live or die, and he wasn't going to leave your side."

Nice of him. I could just see him going toe-to-toe with Dr. Redding. "How do you think Alan knew about the accident?"

Dr. Redding slid the notepad into the pocket of his white smock. "The news. Apparently, you're an important person in this little town of ours. Give me your husband's number and I'll have one of the nurses call him. If we do hear back from him, I'll let the nurses station know he can see you, even if it's during the off hours." The doctor walked to the door and asked if I wanted the lights on or off.

"Dimmed," I told him, "not completely off."

He adjusted the light to my preference, pausing as his fingers rested on the light switch. "I've seen a lot of people die in this hospital, and those who survive usually have good stories to tell. Tomorrow I'll return and see how much you remember."

#

The next day my head still hurt as I focused on Dr. Redding. He'd asked me to recount everything I remembered the entire day of the accident. When he sat beside me, notepad in hand, I was worried of failure before I even began.

The morning began with Patrick teasing me for changing outfits because they were tight, while I'd ribbed him back for spending money on clothes. Granted, he was a vice president of sales at a software company, he spent twice as much as I did, I had a public relations company to run. My attire wasn't discretionary, it was required.

"Not a new wardrobe every quarter," I'd muttered.

After the mini-argument, I'd also been searching for a missing purse or something else. What was it, I tried to remember.

"My watch," I said, relieved. My Rolex was gone and I knew it was around the house—somewhere, along with the purse. When I asked Patrick about them, he blamed the cleaning people. Another argument, but I refrained from telling that part to Dr. Redding, because it led into a third conversation. My mind was blank for a minute, then it came to me. "I received another request from a woman to help her non-profit."

"Do you remember her name?" prompted Dr. Redding. He was vitally interested in the details, no matter how seemingly insignificant. I felt my eyes squint with concentration.

"Yes. Kay Abrahms. Patrick was adamant I not sacrifice a non-profit account for a paying client. Sorry," I said self-consciously, glancing at up at him. "TMI."

He smirked. "I'm not going to record the content," he assured me. "It's the details and quality I'm worried about. What next?"

"I think normal work stuff until I got a boot on my tire late morning. I had to go pay a fine during lunch." That raised another image. "The parking ticket lady," I semi-groaned, a rush of anger heating my cheeks. "I begged her to let me have my car and get the boot off before the end of the day."

"And she refused your request, I take it?" he asked with humor and sympathy.

"It's San Francisco," I said dryly. "On my way out I called Patrick to see if he was in the city, because I thought he said he had a meeting. I wanted to go to have a late lunch," I continued, trying to recall why. "He couldn't. His voice message said the client was running late." I paused, trying to recall what came after. "I listened to a voice message from my brother Charlie."

"Very good!" Dr. Redding said. "Did you call him back?"

"I don't think so," but I couldn't recall why. "I do remember calling my cousin Ann, and another friend Vanessa." The recollections were coming faster now and my talking kept pace. I left messages, reminding Vanessa to avoid this guy we met at a conference and telling Ann I was worried I hadn't heard from her. "Oh! And my banker, Darcy. She'd invited us to an anniversary party of some sort." And on this, I was crystal clear. I declined because Patrick refused to go. He hated events where he didn't know anyone and the objective wasn't closing a new account.

"All of this happened in the cab?"

"The car is when I make a lot of calls." He nodded, gesturing for me to continue. "The cab moved through the intersection, turning onto Market as a trolley cleared the view. Out of the corner of my eye, a red dart zoomed directly toward us. The cab driver didn't see it. I yelled at him to stop and to swerve…and the bus came right for my side. That's it."

The doctor made notes on his paper. As I watched him, I felt dreamy. "My Grandfather…he took me away from all the people. I think my Grandma Ovi was there, and others, but it's blurry." I blinked a few times, trying to clarify the image, but it was gone. "I'm sorry. I hope that doesn't sound silly."

"No need to apologize to me," he said with an easy laugh. "From what my peers in the psychologist ward say, the mind needs to be able to handle what is locked inside, conscious or subconscious. If it can't, it simply chooses to ignore the information that exists until you are ready to accept it. I will say this. You are one lucky woman. Few survive the type of head trauma that you endured without significant lasting damage."

Dr. Redding had been gone only a few minutes when a female nurse in her late fifties entered the room. Her dark, wiry hair was pulled back in a modified French twist, the bun sitting to one side of her neck. She checked the drip hanging from its long, metal pole.

"By the way, your wedding ring had to be cut off right before you were put on ice. It's in the safe waiting for you." I touched the indentation, the ghostly white line on my ring finger visible in the darkened room. It always received more attention than I did.

I'd made it through a horrible accident alive with mind and body intact. I'd been given a second chance at life.

Yes, I was a very lucky woman.

CHAPTER 2

Sunday morning, Patrick's face was the first thing that came into focus.

"Nice to see you," he said softly. In his hand, he held a cup of coffee. His perennially tan face looked a little pale and he had missed a spot or two shaving.

"When did you get here?" I asked, my voice groggy.

"Just a few minutes ago. Coffee's still hot," he said, raising his cup slightly. "Can I get you anything? Some water?" I nodded, my tongue covered with a pasty film that the nurse said was a side effect of the medication I was taking. He gave me a cup and I gratefully took a few sips. "I came by after I got the message last night and stayed for a few hours, but you slept right through it."

"These drugs wipe me out." Which was good. My chest started aching when I tried to inhale a deep breath.

"Dr. Redding seems competent," Patrick remarked. "He told me about the ice."

My husband looked every bit the part of a successful professional, even in his casual, meridian blue Armani sweater. When my cousin Ann, my girlfriend Vanessa and I had first spotted him at a restaurant at The Boulevard down on the waterfront, he'd been having a business meeting and we were having a girl's lunch. After his guest left, he'd walked over, handed me his card, and we had our first date the next week. Six months later, we married in the penthouse suite of the Hoffman Hotel, the affair my wedding gift to him, a no-expense spared event that represented all that I'd come to love about San Francisco—good food, exquisite ambience and fun friends. Today, five years later, the only noticeable difference in the man before me was the slight grey that had appeared above his ears and the softness of his belly. He wore both well, and I still found him as attractive as I did the first time I saw him.

I sipped the water as Patrick related what he'd been told, holding my free hand only by the fingertips, his palm damp.

"Why don't you take your jacket off?" I suggested.

"The doc doesn't want me to stay long." Perplexed, I explained Dr. Redding relaxed the visiting hours just for him, but he shook his head. "I don't want to keep you from getting better."

He sat forward in his chair, crossing his legs, bouncing one on the other. When he noticed me staring, he stopped jiggling. "Sorry, Lindy, I'm just so disgusted at myself for not being here for you the night of the accident. Tell me what happened."

I related the entire sequence of events, from the time I left the house to waking up in the hospital. Patrick alternated running his hands through his hair and rubbing the tips of his fingers on his pants, the linen-cotton blend wrinkling a bit more each time.

"The whole thing makes me want to kill the guy who hit you. And what an idiotic cabby for not swerving in time."

"He couldn't have. He turned but it was all over."

"Just like you to defend the guy," he said. "You're lying here having literally died, and he's roaming around without a scratch on his body."

"Dr. Redding said the other driver did have some injuries."

"But left the hospital that night," he said, continuing to fume. "What planner in his right mind would put a turn lane where buses are waiting to come into the street?"

I encouraged him just to sit and hold my hand. He flapped his palms in the air and I retracted my request. He didn't want me to share in his anxiety. "How did your meeting go?" I asked. After all my trauma, it would be a double tragedy if the reason for him not picking me up had been a failure.

"Brad said we'll receive bonuses for exceeding the numbers."

"That's great," I responded with as much enthusiasm as possible, my breathing shallow.

"It's nothing compared to this," he said, glancing at the IV. I tugged at his top, wanting him closer. He looked great and I told him so.

"Well, I couldn't have you waking up to a frump." He leaned forward, a look of contrition and guilt on his face. He explained his business meeting ran late because the client dickered over the last three percent he wanted off the sales price, his cellphone was off and he didn't know about the accident until the following morning when he listened to the answering machine. Urgent messages had been left by the hospital, Alan and the cops.

"It's okay, Patrick," I consoled him, finding it funny that I was the one doing the comforting.

"It was so stupid of me," he said. Then he went on again about the city planners. I let him rant, his words fading to background noise.

"I could use a hug," I said, extending a limp hand.

Patrick rose, touching my shoulder lightly. "The doctor said to be careful about your upper body since it will take a while for it to heal." When he pressed against my leg, my stomach clenched.

"What's wrong? Do your legs hurt?"

I shook my head. "I feel more nausea than anything. Like being on a wretched sailboat. Must be the drugs they're giving me."

Patrick leaned against the bed, touching a bouquet of lilies and hydrangeas with blossoms the size of cantaloupes. Without asking, he picked up the card and read it. "She's still after you?"

"Who?"

"Kay Abrahms, the woman you said has the children's center over by the Potrero District and wants you to do the work for her center for free."

"It's called pro bono," I interjected.

"Semantics. This one is from her, Adi and John. Who's John?"

"Her son, I believe. A nice thought," I said absently. Something struck me about the bouquet and senders. What was it?

The door opened and Dr. Redding entered. "The recent tests look good. Your heart is like a racehorse, Lindy, but we're not taking any chances. We're going to keep you a few more days." I tried to feel the stitches on my temple through the bandages, but raising my arm pulled at my chest so I dropped it.

"You shouldn't even be able to tell you were ever in an accident, and the cracked ribs didn't puncture the skin so you can still wear your bathing suit." The thought of being impaled by my own bones made me even more nauseous. "Other than the obvious, how are you feeling now?"

"Sick to my stomach."

"Pregnancy will do that." He glanced down at my wide eyes, divining that the news came as a surprise. He turned to Patrick, who sat stone-faced, his hands and eyes motionless.

"Lindy is pregnant?" Patrick asked, his voice flat. The man glanced between the two of us.

"I didn't think to mention it before," apologized the doctor. "It's standard procedure to run a pregnancy test before we prescribe any medications."

"But I've been on the pill for years," I said automatically.

Dr. Redding raised a finger. "Most people aren't aware birth control pills expire. That's why they are only given out a few months at a time. Also, alcohol and some recreational drugs have been known to interfere with its effectivity. Of course, fate can also play a role."

Unbelievable. It was a halo on the misfortune of the accident. "Any idea of how far along I am?"

"According to the hormone levels, I guess month three or four. But it's only that, a guess. I'm no OB."

As Dr. Redding left, he told Patrick that the pills were going knock me out, his subtle way of encouraging we end the conversation. After the door shut, Patrick leaned towards me. "Well, what are we going to do?"

"Okay, I've had zero time to think about this life-changing event, but off the top of my head, I'll continue to work. I'll figure out a transition plan for the day-to-day work with Alan and the other managers, who have been leading the client accounts for years anyway. Your job won't be affected in the slightest, until after the baby is born, when sleep might become an issue." I started to smile but then saw his face.

"No," he said, interrupting me, his face anxious. "I didn't mean about work. I meant about your pregnancy."

"I've just started to answer you," I said calmly. "There is nothing to do but eat healthy and watch the baby grow."

"We can't have a child Lindy. Not now."

"Look," I started, mustering as much humor as possible. "It's not like we were planning on doing this, not until we purchased a house, but we've saved more than enough for that, so it's fate taking control, as the doctor said."

He stood, arms folded, staring me in the eye. "It's stupidity, Lindy. Not fate."

"Don't even go there, Patrick. I've been consistent about birth control and you know it." It was true. I shrugged, the lilt back in my voice. "Couples face unplanned pregnancies all the time and make it through."

"We have a lot of choices," he continued, the tenor of his voice changing to consultative, as though he were the hired expert talking reason to the belligerent client. "It's not our time, Lindy. Not now. We have another five or six weeks before it can be taken care of."

I jerked my hand away. "What you're suggesting isn't an option," I whispered, fighting back tears of anger.

A knock at the door was followed by a nurse who politely noted the time.

Patrick bent over me, whispering in my ear. "Look, we're dealing with a lot," he said. "Get some sleep."

I nodded, gulping down the air that had stuck in my throat. "Please call mom and dad, and also Charlie and Ann when you can. And Alan," I added as an afterthought. He agreed, giving me a kiss on the forehead.

The pills fell like rocks going down a barren hill as I swallowed. The man I loved, the man I married, was asking me to destroy a part of us.

CHAPTER 3

One week after the accident, I came home from the hospital. The rooms of the one-floor flat were warm and I went to the sliding glass doors to open them but stopped the moment I felt the pressure from my hand go to my arm then pull on my ribs. I had no idea how much I used my chest and mid-section before now. I stood there, looking down below me. The view was a rare one; unobstructed by trees or buildings, stretching from the top of Noe Valley looking over the colored rooftops of the homes below that spread like stepping stones down to the Mission District.

I had a whole new appreciation for what was before me.

It was just before ten, but the morning fog had already risen, revealing a neighborhood defined by the thin rim of homes overlooking art deco galleries, Asian food restaurants and hair salons. To the left was Capitol Hill, Russian Hill, Cow Hollow and the Presidio, each subsequent community more expensive than the last.

I'd be back to work starting on Monday and I was looking forward to it. The silence on the topic of my belly was oppressive.

"I can see your ribs now," Patrick remarked as he unrolled the bandage that circled my chest, his face changing from autumn pale to wintergreen as I lifted my arms. Between sleeping and the pain medication that curbed my appetite, I'd lost another ten pounds. He finished applying the bandage and left. I stayed in the bathroom, observing myself. I noticed the skin on my face was a shade lighter than my tan Coach bag, a bit sun weathered, with a few crows feet in the corner of my eyes and some vertical lines above my lips if I pushed them together.

I patted my cheeks. Somewhere underneath this layer was an attractive person who used to regularly get compared to a tall Eva Mendes, the actress. A thick lock of brown hair fell across my cheek, curling under my chin. It could be my imagination, but my hair appeared lush, the amber highlights mixing with the brown as it did its best to cover my shoulders.

Joining Patrick in the kitchen, I scanned the counters and the dining room. "I don't suppose you found the brown purse that went missing before the accident?" I asked, recalling my conversation with Dr. Redding, and the argument I'd had with Patrick the morning I was hit.

"No, and I called the Prada store to make sure." Leave it to Patrick to mention the brand. Before I met him, I was brand clueless. I bought what I liked and what fit, as long as it was classic and well made. Once I mentioned to Ann and Vanessa that Patrick was my personal style director and Vanessa quipped Patrick did it for the appreciative stares, not the quality of the goods.

"You're a trophy, face it," she said.

I'd rolled my eyes. "Patrick loves me no matter what I wear or how heavy I am," I'd responded at the time. As Patrick finished his cup of coffee, I wondered about those words. Heavier, yes, pregnant, maybe not so much. Our sex life had taken a hiatus over the last few months, which I attributed to our off-cycle work patterns, not my pant size.

"Take a look at that get-well card," he said, pointing to the wall. Propped against it was a poster, covered with small handprints and scribbled, illegible names. I could see from my position it was from Kay Abrahms as well. "I'm glad you took my advice and turned her down, but if I recall correctly, you also turned down another potential client that same week, one that was paying."

"That was John, her son."

"One in the same?" he said, biting an apple. "Huh. Well, whatever. Tell me again why you wouldn't take the project on?"

I pursed my lips at him. "Because corporate public relations and crisis communications are two very different things," I reminded him. "One is company launches and product introduction with all the basic, non-scandalous new hires and partnership announcements. Crisis communications is a niche market. Big issues, major damage to stocks, the pace is intense and failing to address the crisis in a timely manner can make or break a company."

"Companies in a desperate situation will pay dearly for help."

I nodded. "Yep, but I want to have a life and honestly I don't need that kind of stress." The few people I knew in the business were adrenaline junkies and single, the all-nighters and constant travel brutal on relationships.

"Crisis' probably pay really, really well," he mumbled, turning away, taking the card with him.

"Like I said, I want a life, not discussing why a new building cracked when we had a slight earthquake."

"That's what this John wanted you for?"

I laughed. "Yep, well, sort of. His family owns the building, but another construction firm built it. They were both in some hot water and he wanted PR help." Patrick gave me a look that I interpreted as not understanding my rejection. "It all worked out, because I followed the story. It wasn't structural, but cosmetic. The press had made it out to be more than it was, so their regular PR agency took care of it with a few on-site interviews."

"Did you ever follow up with the guy, just to keep you in mind for the future?" I inhaled deeply, shaking my head, ending the discussion.

"Go the office," I encouraged him, joining him by the front door. "I'm going to catch up on email."

"Do that, and check up on Alan. Make sure he hasn't stolen the company while you were in the hospital. It's probably why he stood vigil over you."

"Sure. I can just see Alan plotting the takeover as he hovered above my swollen face, looking down over his steel-framed glasses." It was a ridiculous image. Maybe Patrick was suffering from residual guilt he felt about not being at the hospital. The thought gave me a simple pleasure. He should feel bad.

I nudged him with my hip. "Go on." When he left, I went back to bed, nestling under the covers as the cats pawed the comforter, kneading their own comfort zones. Getting a second chance at life had minimized the anxiety I used to feel at the notion of facing Patrick's displeasure.

An image of my Grandfather's face came to, and consciously or not, I felt my unborn child was the reason I was still alive.

My optimistic outlook continued throughout the weekend and increased when Patrick didn't bring up the pregnancy. In fact, he went out of his way to go out and pick me up an order of meatloaf and potatoes from Fog City, explaining his elongated time away on a few errands he had to run, including the dry cleaners and post office. I'd not minded. I'd fallen asleep with Remus my black cat joining me, his purring near my neck as good as a lullaby.

Monday at 6 a.m., my chest felt fifty percent better, only hurting when I over extended myself. Patrick was by the door, briefcase in hand, anxious to leave. I'd delayed us because I spent extra time looking for my chocolate-colored sheepskin coat I'd purchased at Barney's the year prior and which had inexplicably gone missing.

"It better not be with my purse and watch," I muttered. Fall had officially arrived, misty, wet, fog dense and bone-chilling. Patrick heard my statement, reminding me he'd taken it to the dry cleaners before the accident.

"Sorry I haven't picked it up yet. I'll do it next time I'm in." I took my black trench out of the closet, grateful for the fuzzy liner, getting us on our way. With luck, I'd have at least 45 minutes to go through my emails before the rest of the group arrived.

#

"Surprise!!"

A flash to my right confirmed that Samantha had captured my shock with her digital camera. The reception area was draped with streamers from the ceiling, and the floor of my office was covered with balloons. Alan held a box of Krispy Kreme doughnuts. Eng-kee, Anita and the others wore buttons with my photo and name at the bottom.

This wasn't a welcome-back party. It was a national political convention.

"You only come back to life once," Sam said, relieving me of my briefcase. "We couldn't help ourselves."

"I'm sorry, Lindy," Alan said, with a broad smile that confirmed he didn't feel an ounce of regret. He opened the box and encouraged me to take a glazed donut while it was still warm. "Aren't you supposed to be pasty and grey after being at the hospital?"

"And fat from the hospital food?" Sam added, scoping me from top to bottom. "I want to die, too, if I can come back looking like someone on a magazine cover."

"Raises for all!" I said happily, ignoring the pang as I lifted the donut to my mouth. The group asked about the wounds, the recovery and we all ate doughnuts until the phones started ringing. Two hours later, I wandered by Samantha's desk, stretching my wrists. The ligaments on the top of them were tight, unused to typing.

"Are you actually loitering?" Sam asked without looking up. I peered over the privacy ledge of her desk. The 25-year-old UC Berkeley graduate's appearance was more Starbucks barista than corporate executive assistant.

"Stretching isn't loitering," I replied. Today her purple-and-black hair was pulled back into a tight bun, revealing her multi-pierced ears, complete with a black javelin on one side and an orange and purple hoop on the other. The fuchsia liner around her eyes matched her lipstick and complimented the earrings. At least she was color coordinated.

"Any word from Monson while I was out?"

"No, but Alan might have news" she answered, squinting in the late-morning sunlight. "The latest bill I sent out was up to forty-thousand, not including interest." And it's not getting any smaller, I thought to myself.

"Since you're here, I do have something for you. While you were out, I dug up some information on Kay Abrahms, on the off chance you got Patrick to change his mind about. Did you know that she was from a prominent family and she married Adi Abrahms, as in—the Abrahms family who owns half the real estate in this town. They moved into a large home in Seacliff and had four children and all seemed perfect until her youngest son was kidnapped right off his bike in front of her home. A neighbor saw the whole thing."

The last part of her revelation took my breath away. I stopped stretching and placed my elbows on the counter top. "Did they ever find him?"

Sam shook her head. "But it was that event that caused her to establish the center for kids who have no place to go afterschool, to get them off the streets. Here," she said, handing me another print out. "They have a daughter and two sons who still live in the area. One of which you have met, I understand."

As she spoke, I gazed at the picture. It was John alright. He was the opposite of Patrick, light brown hair with blond on the top, a few lines at the corner of his eyes, but the kind that were caused by sun, not stress. His gazed was straight into the camera, as though he'd been caught off guard and had been in the middle of a conversation.

"Is he that handsome in person?" Sam asked a lilt in her voice.

"More so, and I think he's single too, though maybe a little old for you. How do you know I met him?"

"Because I spoke to him on the phone last week. He requested a meeting with you."

"What for?"

"Perhaps he's going to ask you about his mom's project. He's going to show up in about five minutes." My stupefied stare was interrupted by the dinging of the elevator to my right. Sam's eyes brightened and she shrugged. "You were saying that we needed another account in order to take on Kay's center, so when he called, I did what you would do: I took advantage of the opportunity."

"Thanks for not telling me," I said pleasantly, adjusting the paperwork on the counter, pulling my stomach muscles inward to stop the nervous contractions.

"Don't mention it," she quipped, unrepentant.

The next moment, John Abrahms was in front of me. Faded jeans, dark blue sports coat and an open-collared shirt, his relaxed confidence consistent with his manner at the San Francisco Museum of Modern Art. He and the modern structure were alike in many ways, sleek and contemporary, but solidly built and unbending.

"Good afternoon," he said pleasantly, glancing at me with a smile. Gracious, I thought instantly. Much more so than I deserved after declining to take his company on as a client, although, that part wasn't what I regretted. It was how I'd communicated the rejection that had nagged at me ever since.

"A pleasure," I said politely, extending my hand. "We just happened to be here chatting and you—"

"Arrived early," Sam finished for me, walking around the deck to introduce herself. John impressed me by not registering the javelin in Sam's left ear or the hoop in her nose.

"Thank you for arranging this," he said to Sam, shaking her hand. Turning back to me, he took in my face in an investigatory way. "You don't appear to have been in a car accident. From the way it was written up, I didn't know if you would look like the walking dead." His dry tone struck me and I laughed, taking a seat, offering him the window.

"Take the good side," I offered. "Guests always get the best view, at least on the first visit."

"So if you take me as a client, only brick walls?"

"Exactly, but that presupposes the outcome of this conversation, but typically, me or the team will go to the client." Something about his look told me that such a visit wouldn't entirely be unwelcome, and I felt an uncomfortable spread to my neck. Although the bantering was good natured and professional, a part of me knew my emotions weren't as smooth as I sounded. The moment he'd approached me at the Gala months before, I'd felt insecure, causing me to turn down his client project in a manner far harsher than was necessary. *Furthermore, had I been single, I probably wouldn't have denied the project.*

"Great, because I'm here to ask you to be on my radio show."

Of all the things I'd been expecting, an offer for publicity wasn't one of them. "Radio show? I thought your profession was real estate." Had he gotten fired over the incident with the building? He must have divined my concern because he cracked a smile.

"It still is, but I'm on the commercial side, which is rewarding but sometimes rather dry. I started a radio station a few years ago that began as a hobby and is now something more."

"So you're not launching the station but you want me on it nonetheless? I'm confused."

He gave me an inquisitive smile. "Your PR agency only takes on start-ups and sometimes those entities who aren't given a chance to succeed and yet somehow, they do. I think you and your firm play a big part in that. Plus, you are never personally profiled in the press, a rarity in this town of extroverts. I might get an insight into your world no one else has yet seen." The heat from my neck now shot down my spine.

"This is what almost dying got me. A shot at my fifteen minutes of radio fame."

He moved a disobedient lock of sandy blond hair from his forehead, pushing it back and to the side. It fell over, and he repeated the movement. "You didn't have to be so dramatic to get attention."

I raised an eyebrow skeptically. "Seriously John. You're telling me the reason for the visit isn't your mom?"

"Is it wrong to try a ploy to get your time for her center?" he asked. The almost playful way he asked the question caused me to stare longer at his hazel eyes than I normally would have. I brought it down a notch, in both my expression and tone of voice. General bantering during a discussion was appropriate, but it didn't need to be more than that.

"Look," I said, leaning forward, then feeling pain, stopped, pausing for a second. He noticed, and his countenance changed instantly.

"Are you okay?" he asked, concern in his voice. Behind him, I saw Sam raise her head again. I shook mine, and she nodded.

"Yes, I think so." I stared at him, hand on my side as I breathed through the discomfort. "Sorry," I whispered. "Just a few, ah, after effects of the accident." He had leaned forward, one hand already across the table as if to help me.

"Are you sure?" When I nodded a yes, he leaned back, but only halfway. "Maybe this isn't the right time."

"You didn't cause me any pain," I said, trying to smile. After a few moments, I sat back. "The truth is, we aren't in the position to take on a non-paying entity until we can get another client, maybe two."

"The truth is," John said, his voice kind, "I'm not sure you should be here, at the office, so soon after the accident." It wasn't his words that struck me, but his tone. It was full of caring that should have come from Patrick, and hadn't. "So what if I find you a paying client or two? Then will you take on the center?"

"You don't give up, do you?"

He pushed his lips out at the challenge. "Does a gallery or restaurant opening count as a new product launch?"

I considered his comment. "It does."

"Good, then we have might have more to discuss in the near future. Now that the business topic is over, are you really okay?"

Patrick always told me I couldn't lie if my life depended on it, and for some reason I didn't want John to think me dishonest, which he might if I dodged his question.

"In confidence, I do have some internal issues, but they will pass in time," I answered, purposefully rising.

"Don't overdo it okay? And I appreciate knowing you're open to new clients." He shook my hand, smiled and left.

"That was decent," Sam remarked, her eyes barely glancing up from her screen.

"What part?"

"The conversation and the way he acted toward you." My eyes narrowed as I smiled but said not a word as I walked away. Now and then it didn't hurt to have a client that was both engaging and attractive. Of course, he wasn't a client, and from his comments, wouldn't become so. But perhaps I'd be able to chat with him every now and then as he referred other entities to me with legitimate needs. With his family connections, I could easily see him sitting on the boards of privately-held companies, and those likely had money to hire us for an actual project. It would allow us take on Kay's organization without charge and Patrick couldn't complain. Everyone would be happy.

Once or twice during the afternoon, I looked up at Sam. She continually fielded calls, assisted clients who needed a person tracked down or a document template sent over. All the while she handled the staff's questions, and diligently completed the tasks I gave her.

After lunch, I stopped by her office on the way back from the kitchen.

"Sam, our client roster could change with short notice. Why don't you take the first step by calling Kay to schedule a meeting?"

"You think John might come through with a client or two?" I was right. She'd overheard the entire exchange through the thin walls.

I nodded. "Furthermore, while we don't need the press and we can't be bought, he doesn't strike me as a man who makes flippant promises.

Besides, conversations are free. If that comes to pass, we'll need a liaison and project manager with the center. Do you think you could pull double-duty for a time, just in case?" Sam was left momentarily speechless then gave a little squeak of delight.

Little things, little changes, I thought sitting down. I glanced up and out of the windows. I liked what my near death experience had done to me.

CHAPTER 4

That night, I had my first dream.

An old, withered hand pulled me through a translucent, white sheet of light, willing me to follow through to the other side.

A face came into focus.

"Grandfather?" His big, crooked smile cracked his face into wrinkles, rippling like a wave on the ocean.

"Welcome back, Lindy." Grandpa opened his arms to encircle me. When he stepped back, happiness glistened from the corner of his eyes. "You have others waiting to see you as well."

Beyond him stood my Grandmother Ovi, who died when I was fourteen. Her shoulder-length, white hair was thick and luxurious, the way it was before the cancer took it in clumps. As I leaned towards her for a hug, the aroma of my favorite molasses cookies hovered over her faint, yet present. She gave me another squeeze and hurried off before I could say a word. My great-uncle Andrew, towering at nearly a foot above my 5'8 frame, looked every bit the 94 he was when he died. He bent over, placing a kiss on my forehead before making way for another person I remembered fondly.

"Mr. Bennett?" He'd been my eighth-grade Spanish teacher at Walker Middle School. His smile was broad and lopsided, his hair still in the wild comb-over, the same mid-50's paunch overhanging his skinny legs.

"You can call me Frank now, Lindy." He'd been my favorite teacher, always taking the time to answer my questions and tolerating me passing notes to my friends. One day while I was in the gym I'd heard sirens. He'd had a heart attack and died on the way to the hospital. I'd never seen him again. "You grew up to be as pretty on the outside as you were on the inside," he remarked, and I smiled. "What are you now? Late twenties?"

"Thirty-one," I answered, pleased. He embraced me again before he moved on. Most of the dead I could see were elderly, although a group of teenagers passed by. A bus crash? They ignored their elders in death as they probably had in life.

"Why is everyone rushing around?" I asked my Grandfather.

"A world is swirling around us, and we're constantly working. You'll see."

I thought of myself as a religious person. I believed in God. But I never thought about the afterlife as anything more than good or bad, heaven or hell. I never thought about what one actually did in either place, as if there was something to do.

He paused before an ornate door. "We'll start here the next time you visit."

The following day at work, a knock was preceded by Alan entering my office, interrupting my tenth replay of the dream from the night before. It had been floating in and out of my mind, feeling real in a strange way.

I'd mentioned it to Patrick that morning, who suggested rather sarcastically I was having notions of the afterlife that didn't exist. "Except in science fiction books or by those crazy religious freaks." I'd nodded, thinking his point had some merit. Who knew what the subconscious kept inside that came out only in the quiet of a dream state?

"Still no sign of life from Monson," Alan said, disgust in his voice. Alan didn't have the flair or vitality of a salesperson, but clients liked his straight-shooting style, as did the employees.

He set a balance sheet front of me. The accounts receivable report showed nearly a $100,000, $40,000 of it from Monson. No single account should be worth nearly half the revenue, but I'd let it happen.

"Consider these minor cash-flow issues helpful growth experiences," I said, not too worried. We had a line of credit to cover any unforeseen lags in client payments.

"I call it the life of an entrepreneur," he said dryly. "Something I'm glad to revert back to you. Remember our deal when you hired me? You bring in the money and I'll count it. And on that note, I want to sue Monson. The New York Times article is on the edge of running and we can use it as a lever."

"Force his hand?" Alan nodded. He was asking me to kill the story we'd pitched unless the man paid up.

"Lindy, he went on a cruise to celebrate the last piece we got him in Fortune. Payment to us? Nope. Boat ride for a hundred people, of course."

I gnawed the inside of my cheek. I stopped when I remembered my aesthetician said that habit was causing my smile lines to prematurely deepen.

"Maybe someone else footed the bill?" I suggested, feeling like Charlotte holding on to her web of hope in a windstorm.

The three lines on Alan's forehead, one representing each decade of his 30 years in finance, pushed together. His thin, angular face was set in a concerned mold, his full lips pressed. I'd never been sure of Alan's nationality, although I guessed Eastern European from his arched, thick eyebrows, flat ears and light-brown eyes, pierced with intelligence. His cashmere sweater stretched perfectly across his chest and hung loose at his waist. Alan's figure was a testament to his triathlon training and a rigorous weight training routine. The combination dropped ten years off his age.

He tightened his lips. A ray of light hit the brick wall on the inside of my office, bouncing off the bay and shining between The Transamerica Pyramid Building and the Embarcadero Mall.

"It's what he would do if the shoe were on the other foot," Alan said.

I nodded, but felt uneasy. This wasn't normal behavior for Monson, a self-made millionaire with a track record of successful manufacturing businesses a page long. After a long look at Alan, my advisor and the financial arm of the company, I acquiesced. "Have Henry draft a letter dropping the account with a time limit for payment."

Alan nodded approvingly. "You've kept the faith with this guy for a long time."

I'd kept hope alive, was what I'd done.

The word hope made me think of Patrick. I was hoping his heart and mind would open up to having a baby. I was hoping he'd give me a big hug when I got home tonight, with a bunch of flowers and have dinner made. I was hoping he'd do all the things that a soon-to-be-father would do for his wife of five years.

I glanced up. Alan was observing me. Alan hadn't had hope that I would return from the hospital. But he'd acted as though I would, and he'd kept the company going in my absence. It suddenly occurred to me I'd been holding him down in the same way I'd been doing with Sam.

"Now I have another item that needs discussing," I began, the thought forming a moment before I said the words. "I believe the timing is right to structure the business from a sole proprietor to an LLC."

Alan blinked a few times. "You're thinking of bringing in a partner?" Inside, a bubble of giddiness threatened to crack a smile on my face, but I nodded solemnly.

"I've found the right person, too."

"Okay." He coughed, recovering his brisk tone. He opened his tablet, maintaining his professionalism. I could practically hear the engines turning in his mind. He had to be thinking that he'd finally had the chance to prove himself but I'd completely overlooked him as the first candidate. "Do I know the person?"

"Intimately." His fingers stopped, an intense look on his face. "No. It's not Patrick." A brief wave of relief broke his frown. I would have laughed but the instantaneous reaction gave me a pang of regret. "But he's extremely bright, came out of finance and services, and has worked in the technology field for about fifteen years. Lots of fun, too. Peers and subordinates rave about him."

"Sounds like a good fit. When do you want the start-date to be?"

"Well," I said slowly. "Assuming he accepts, I'd like him to start tomorrow."

"Are you saying you haven't offered him the role yet, but we're drawing up the paperwork anyway?"

"Yep. I think I know this guy pretty well." My eyes purposefully wandered to the window. "I mean, am I wrong? Don't you want to move into your new role immediately?" I slid my eyes back to him, forcing my lips flat.

"You are an evil woman." His lips were level, but his eyes were bright and lively.

I grinned. "I couldn't help it. Beyond how you handled everything while I was gone, you hung out at the hospital when no one else was around."

"Don't go doing this out of guilt."

"You know me better than that. But while I'm in the mood for changes, what do you think of me shifting to working on books and on-line templates that we could sell on the Internet? You know, taking the documents we use for launching a product or going out on a press tour and making them into templates. Instead of hiring us, which many small companies can't do, they could buy the template for a few bucks, insert their information step-by-step and be self-guided."

Alan tilted his head in remembrance. "And thereby save tens of thousands of dollars. I liked it when you first brought it up a year ago, and still do. But if I'm not mistaken, Patrick hated the idea."

"I think it was because he didn't want me to take on another project that was going to keep me out of the house. I could think of worse things for a spouse to say." Alan's facial expression told me that he disagreed with some part of my statement, but he didn't clarify which one. "And the reason for bringing this up now is a very good one." Alan leaned back, his hands on the armrests as if to steady himself, eyes wide. "There's really no good way to say this, so I'll just come out with it. I'm pregnant. And to preempt you, I'm not kidding. I found out in the hospital."

I told him about the blood tests, the doctor who assumed Patrick and I knew, and the indelicacy of the moment.

"Are you — is it, okay?" Nodding, I explained I'd been a bit more tired than usual, uninterested in breakfast. "You shouldn't be traveling too much, or stressing out." He sounded like my mother and I told him so.

"Another reason for the products. As the pregnancy progresses, and then maternity leave, I see myself gradually shifting my time to less client engagement and more consultation."

"And that's why me becoming a partner made sense." His phone rang and I checked my email as he took the call. Moments later, he had a grin that threatened to crack his face in half.

"Well, fortune is on our side. Our former client GeorgiaLiman has filed to go public."

My pulse slowed one beat then skyrocketed. "Seriously?"

"The news just hit the wire."

I floated through the rest of the afternoon, feeling like this was a divine balance. My pregnancy and issues with Patrick were on one end of the see-saw, while the opportunity for bringing our proven methodologies for creating media attention and associated revenue for small companies were on the other end. The bonus was GeorgiaLiman going public, an event that would make life easier for so many of my staff members, some of who weren't all that long out of graduate school.

Life did have a balance. I'd just have to find mine, like the kind I had prior to the accident.

Or maybe the balance I thought I had, but didn't.

CHAPTER 5

I waited until just before the day was done to call Patrick. I relayed how well Alan had been working with clients and also about John dropping by, summarizing his well-intentioned ploy to give me publicity as a means to get me to take on Kay's account.

"You don't think it's a problem that Alan's working directly with key customers?" Patrick asked.

"No. Not at all. The transition of him including client relations in addition to finance is a natural one."

"And what's with Kay's son having the balls to approach you directly?" Patrick asked. "Wasn't your no at the Museum of Modern Art enough for him?"

"I guess I wasn't rude enough." Patrick agreed, completely oblivious to my sarcasm.

"I'm working late tonight," he said abruptly. "Meetings in the valley." Convenient. Regardless if it was real or not, I'd enjoy the alone time.

Just before I rose from my desk to leave, the phone rang through on my land line. Seeing the number, I picked up.

"Ann, how are you?" I asked, happy to hear her voice. "Have you been out of town or something?"

"What are you talking about? I've called and left a million messages on your cell phone. I called Patrick but no word from him as well." I was momentarily speechless.

"Ann, something must be wrong with my phone. I haven't received any messages from you, or really anyone for that matter. I was beginning to wonder if I had a friend in the world. Patrick hasn't said a word."

"Patrick has hated me since shortly after you got married, but we won't digress into that right now. Tomorrow night," she said forcefully. "Your place. I'll feed Jared and the kids and be at your house before six so we can be by ourselves." I agreed and hung up.

On the way home I picked up a to-go order from Fog City Diner and ate my crab cakes and banana bread pudding alone. Before I went to bed, I checked my phone messages again, thinking about Ann's comment. Not a single message from her, Vanessa, Mom, Dad or Charlie, all of whom I'd asked Patrick to call. One by one, I dialed their numbers, receiving nothing but voice mails. Loneliness prompted me to have another slice of bread pudding, but the sugar was unable to give me the emotional pick-me-up I so desired.

Wednesday Patrick was up and gone before I rose, which left me standing in the bedroom in an all-consuming moment of frustration. I had to get my car from the impound and Patrick was to have been my ride.

One cab ride later, I admitted to myself it worked out for the best. I wanted the mental acuity to focus on the backlog of items sitting in my in-box and ended up getting quite a bit of work done. Not long after arriving at the office, Patrick sent me a text, informing me of another dinner in the valley.

Really? I wondered to myself. Convenient. Time away from me meant no opportunity to talk about uncomfortable subjects.

When Ann came over, we ate dinner on the patio under the heat lamps. I summarized the chain of events, listening to her gasps and an occasional "ow."

"Tell me again why Patrick wasn't at the hospital?"

"He didn't know about it until the next morning. Apparently, he had a late meeting and turned his cell off like he always does."

"Well, that doesn't excuse him for not calling me the moment he saw you! And you? Why didn't you call me and ask for help? I could have been doing your laundry or bringing you food." She sounded as disgusted with me as she was with Patrick. "The cat boxes were probably overflowing and the dishes were piled up. And don't tell me Patrick's doing it, because I'll know you're lying."

I laughed, admitting she was right about Patrick. "You have your husband and children and your baby to worry about." At that, she stopped and looked down. Only then did I realize she looked a little smaller in the middle, but I thought it was her shirt camouflaging her belly.

"Can we go inside?" Once we were settled on the couch, a throw over our legs, she opened up.

"About two weeks after my six-month checkup, I noticed the baby hadn't been kicking. By noon I called the nurse. She said to push the baby around, get him moving, since he might be asleep. I tried everything. At 2 p.m. she said to come in. She put the stethoscope to my belly, said nothing, but then called the doctor in. He hooked me up to the ultrasound and we looked at it together. There was no heartbeat. Nothing."

My heart felt like it had stopped, gripped with the hand of grief I saw on her face.

Tears filled Ann's eyes and she nodded. "It happened sometime during the night, they don't know when. I wanted to die, Lindy. If the baby inside me was going to be taken, I wanted to be taken too."

I pressed my lips together and swallowed against the rising tide of sorrow. Then an image—a woman, on a gurney, turned on her side, her head faced away from me. It was one of the visuals I'd had when Dr. Redding was trying to keep me alive. It matched what Ann was telling me now.

"I'm so sorry, Ann," I whispered, my voice hoarse. "We don't have to keep talking about it."

"No, it feels better to get it out. Maybe I'm in denial, but honestly I feel like this was meant to happen, for whatever horrid reason." She paused, collected herself and started again, brighter. "Are you okay?" I shifted in my chair. Telling someone who has just lost a child that you are going to have one might hurt.

"I have some news, but I don't want to hurt your feelings." My cousin cocked her head and then she leaned forward.

"Are you pregnant?" she whispered. I nodded my head while biting my lip. Ann let out a yip of excitement and gave me a big hug. I promised to make her a bigger part of my life from that time forward, with or without Patrick's support.

I was already in bed and half-asleep later that night when Patrick came in the bedroom. I didn't have the energy to bring up Ann, or the fact that he'd not called her. The mystery of my phone not taking her calls hadn't been solved before she left and I made a note to talk to Alan about it. He could figure out my phone when I couldn't.

The following day, I had my appointment with Dr. Redding. He removed the remaining stitches from my forehead, reminding me to continue sleeping on my back until the bruises were gone. The attending nurse teased Dr. Redding about the personal attention I was receiving.

"It was recently pointed out that I was lacking an emotional connection to my patients," he remarked dryly, casting a glance to the nurse.

"You seem to be doing fine with me," I'd said thoughtfully, feeling the tips of his fingers as he applied a small bandage. I couldn't help comparing his world to my own. He has patients, I have clients. When I had a task, it's all that mattered to me, not what occurred yesterday or what was going on tomorrow. Did I come across the same way; focused but emotionless, saving the patient but ignoring the person?

"I'd like to see you in another few weeks," said Dr. Redding, stepping back, scanning me top to bottom with and inquisitive look. "You are healing just fine, but I'd like to run another full checkup to be on the safe side. Besides, I've noticed that most patients who experience death for even a short time have their lives dramatically altered in the first thirty days or not at all."

"You have no idea," I said quietly, meeting his eyes as I heard the door open behind me, signaling that our appointment was finished.

In the parking lot, I called Patrick and left him a message that all was well, and that I'd stop by the post office to get our mail on the way back. I'd been missing a stack of magazines and wanted good bathtub reading. By the time he called me back, telling me he'd do it, I'd already been.

I was in the living room, enjoying the oranges of the setting sun on the bay when Patrick arrived home. In my hand was a package, the return address from Canada. The handwriting on the note was a distinctive cursive, the blue ink from a thick-nibbed fountain pen.

I saved this for you Lindy. We had it buffed and a new strap put on for your wrist. It's yours, if you'll have it. I love you, Dad.

Sliding my fingers into the drawstring bag, I felt a smooth metal band. It was a watch. I stared at the vintage Omega Seamaster, the rounded face of the men's stainless steel and gold version was in perfect condition, the corners etched with the fine indentations of wear.

I reread the note: *If you'll have it.*

Patrick saw me holding the note and the watch. "You're not going to wear that, are you?" An unconcealed edge in his voice told me he didn't have an interest in the object.

"It's a classic," I half-mumbled to myself. An image of John came to me. I doubt he'd be so snobby as to imply the watch had no value. And Sam? She'd tell me it was retro.

I checked the date on the package. Dad had sent it the week before my accident. "Did you call Dad's cell?"

"Of course. Like I said, no answer and the account said the voice mail account wasn't set up." I groaned. I'd repeatedly told him to get the darn thing set up when he first got it—not long before we stopped speaking to one another—requiring that he actually pick up. Given our estrangement and by association, Patrick, who was the cause, it was not entirely surprising

Dad didn't take the call. He probably took one look at the caller ID and walked away.

The sigh that escaped felt as heavy as the history with my father. The push and pull between a headstrong, determined daughter and a selfish, self-made man who were too much alike.

Maybe forgiveness is why I'm here. That's four reasons now. First I thought I was here because I was pregnant. Then it was to help Sam and Alan progress. Those things could be, and were being rectified. Dad, on the other hand, required an actual conversation.

"Can we have a talk this weekend, Patrick? When we have some time to relax for a real discussion?" I intended to raise the prospect of moving outside the city, closer to his work, perhaps a more reasonable option than asking he give up the second bedroom that was his dedicated music room.

"I'm out at the off-site team-building activity in Sonoma, remember?"

"Oh, right." He'd told me about this a month ago and I'd forgotten.

"What time will you be back?"

"It's really late Friday night—you will probably be in bed, then overnight on Saturday. I should be home Sunday afternoon, maybe earlier if we finish up."

"You know, most companies have team-building outings during the week. Why are yours always on the weekends?"

"Look, if you aren't up for me going and want me to stay here with you, I'll cancel. They'll understand." It was what I wanted him to say, but he'd be irritable that he missed it, and the conversation I planned would be that much harder.

"Absolutely not. Go and get stuff done. But I want to go to Fog City on Sunday." Patrick suggested we try someplace different for a change, maybe in the Sunset District. I shook my head. Fog City was where I wanted to eat. Besides, I wanted Doug and Stacy to see how good I looked before I started gaining back the weight I had just lost.

Patrick told me he was going to work in the second bedroom for a few hours and I went to our bedroom, making a straight line for the pull-out drawer under the bed. I knelt and retrieved box. A lock of hair from my first haircut, a little shoe I'd made out of clay in third grade, year books, a few letters, my ski passes. Down at the bottom, in the very back, I found what I was seeking. I curled my fingers around it, feeling the leather. My Grandfather had given it to me as an early graduation gift my senior year and was in the same condition as when he gave it to me, scratch free and shiny.

Two hours later, my eyes burned. I set the Bible on the end table and turned out the light, an uncomfortable feeling that if I'd opened it once or twice before now, I wouldn't be sleeping alone.

CHAPTER 6

The white door opened and Grandfather walked me into an open space defined by rows and rows of pedestals. Each one had a book on top, in varying thicknesses; some were slender while others resembled encyclopedias the width of an outstretched hand. A few didn't appear to have any pages at all.

As we walked down the nearest row, golden letters streamed onto pages as though an invisible hand were inscribing the words. When a page was full, it turned over, with the writing starting again at the top.

"Each book represents an individual's time on earth," Grandfather explained. "The pages contain the actions of the person." My heart pounded. A flash of regrettable actions filled my mind like a bullet train in a dark tunnel. The time I took a pair of fake turquoise-and-silver earrings from a drugstore on a dare; making out with my best friend's boyfriend. Thankfully I'd done nothing like that in years, living the past two decades as a relatively responsible, honest adult. "We use the books to refresh our memories about what we need to work on."

"Not really helpful when a person must be dead to read it," I observed, thinking it odd my dry sarcasm came through in my dream.

Grandfather tilted his head slightly. "Sometimes. This is a dream for you, but your eternal self is very real, just as the information in those books is real."

"You mean…?" I left the question hanging.

"Yes. Just like in the Book of Revelations, but it's also in the Quran, Torah and other books of enlightenment across cultures. All people deserve the right to the knowledge."

Maybe that was the reason I was dreaming about this. Tonight I'd opened the Bible and read. My subconscious was coming out again.

As he spoke, hundreds of books kept appearing on pedestals while just as many books closed. One book near us shut without a sound. A cover and one or two pages was all that represented the life of the person inside. Was it a baby? How much of a person's life did one page represent? I contemplated the possibilities as the book lifted off the pedestal, passing above the others, moving to our left.

"Now it goes into the archives," Grandfather said, motioning for us to follow the floating book.

Unlike the quiet, empty serenity of the first room, the archives were crowded to capacity. People stood in groups of two or three reading individual books, others were alone, reading in quiet contemplation. I gulped.

"Can anyone read about my life?"

"Once you're here, the books are open to everyone." He patted my arm. "The mistakes you took care of were erased. Those you didn't do anything about remain on the page. That," he winked, "and the good things."

Every last deed recorded in gold calligraphy. I hoped these would be balanced by my good actions, like the time I was driving away from a store and discovered a cashier had overlooked an item. I returned and paid for it.

Grandfather led me to a book in the corner, two rows back. It stood alone, the area around it vacant of onlookers. The cover was in my favorite hues of blue and green, the colors that shimmer in shallow, tropical waters. How could a static book reflect the shapes and colors of an ever-moving, changing sea floor? I was about to find out. My Grandfather looked at me then opened the cover to the final page from the book of my life.

All morning long, the dream replayed in my mind. I wish I'd seen what was in my book! How cool would that have been, even if was only a dream. Maybe I'd see things from a totally different perspective.

It was Friday, exactly two weeks after the accident. Over a bowl of cereal, I brought up the topic of Alan, unable to stop from praising his ability to move the company along. In the process, I slipped in that I'd made the promotion official and also related my plans to start the product line. While I wasn't expecting him to be elated, I was fishing for some level of support.

Patrick's fingers turned white around the coffee mug. "Did it ever occur to you to have a conversation with me about it before you went off and made it legal?"

I cocked my head, stymied. "How does changing his role from a chief financial officer to a partner impact you, or us, for that matter?"

"Percentage of ownership in the business, that's how," he answered, his cheeks drawn, his voice flat. I ignored his look and processed the response. It came from left field. Only in the cases of divorce did percentage of ownership matter, and in California, a fifty-fifty state, only when it applied to joint assets.

"Ownership?" I repeated, incredulous. "You've maintained your stock is one hundred percent yours, no matter what happened, all the while reiterating that my company is mine, from the time we were dating, then engaged and for the last five years. It's "clean," I said, putting the word in air quotes, mimicking his words. "What's mine is mine, and yours is yours, the way you've always wanted it."

He quickly picked up the mug, the black liquid slopping over the side, coating the lapel of his jacket. Furious, he took the jacket off, marching down the hall to the bedroom. I followed him, continuing to speak.

"I'm rewarding a very capable, deserving person, Patrick. Why aren't you more supportive?"

"Because you go and give away a chunk of the very company you created, leaving yourself vulnerable to Alan. What next?" he turned abruptly. "You're going to start reading the Bible and give everything away?"

So, he'd noticed the book on the night stand either this morning or last night when he came to bed. It didn't matter. His thoughts regarding what I chose to read was irrelevant.

"You're just mad I didn't take your advice," I said objectively, unable to keep the lilt of humor out of my voice. His attitude about Alan was absurd.

"Of course I am!" he exploded.

I suddenly realized I needed to put new will in place. If anything happened to me, I didn't want Patrick ousting Alan or shutting down the business.

I was two steps behind him, stalking him back to the kitchen. "As Alan takes over the day-to-day client operations, I can focus on products. That way I'll have the flexibility to work from home when I want."

"You don't need to be home," he argued. "All you have to say is you miscarried and continue on."

With that one statement, I took on the protective instincts of a lion in the wilderness.

"I'll be home around six tonight and we can talk about it then," I said flatly, turning towards the door.

He grabbed my arm. "There's nothing to talk about, Lindy," he said. "I'm not having this baby."

"You're right," I responded, shrugging him off, gritting my teeth. "You're not."

Leaving him with his mouth open, I returned to the bedroom, slamming the door. I heard the sound of him trotting down the outside stairs and the garage door open.

Not possible, I mentally shouted to myself, my breathing uneven. Flashes of our life to this point appeared like a slideshow projected in front of me. At a park, talking of having two kids, a boy and a girl, moving from downtown to the South Bay or up in Sausalito, closer to the mountains.

That was before we were married.

I threw my stuff in my car, trying to remember the last time we had spoken of kids. One, two years ago? Or was it right after we were married?

Preoccupied with my worries, I downshifted into second on the steep hill when a black and white dog darted into my peripheral vision. I slammed on the brakes, swerved to the right, just missing a trashcan. The pug darted under the car and onto the sidewalk, where it came to a stop, yipping at me.

Stifling a frightened expletive, I recognized the dog as Bondo, far from home and obviously now frantic.

I looked at the time on my watch. I'd never make the conference call Alan had set up with a prospect based on the East Coast. I vacillated between rushing to make the meeting and rescuing the cute little pug. Then I remembered Patrick's recent comment about his hope the dog would get run over and stop its incessant barking. I'd replied the owner would simply replace it with a new one, further irritating him.

I sighed, dithering. Patrick hadn't started out minding dogs, but over the last few years, his desire for quiet and the solitary confines of his stereo increasing in direct correlation to his patience level with outside distractions.

I got out my phone. "Alan? Is it really critical I'm on this call or am I right in saying you are just being nice?" When he laughed I knew I'd been spot on. "You're superb on your own. I'm going to go save a dog."

After resisting several calls, Bondo finally came toward me. I placed him on the passenger seat hoping to heaven he was car trained. I flipped the car around and moments later pulled into our neighbors' driveway. His owner wasn't going to be happy to see it was me who retrieved him. Holding Bondo in my arms, I rang the doorbell and after waiting five minutes, gave up. I scribbled my name and number on a piece of paper, wedging it in the doorjamb where he'd see it, and got back in the car.

"Guess you're going to be my shadow today," I told Bondo. I arrived at the office, the pug in my left arm, purse slung over my shoulder.

Samantha cooed in delight at my furry package as I looked her over. She had her hair down, parted to one side. The nose ring was absent, as were the black rings around her upper and lower eyelids. A pale, neutral color on her lips touched off a natural rosy glow on her cheeks.

"Do I see actual heels?" In the twelve months she'd been on staff, I'd never seen her in anything other than flats.

"We have the meeting with Kay today, remember?"

"I think you look beautiful and Bondo approves."

"Are we going to keep him?" Sam asked rubbing the back of his neck, his rumbles of appreciation echoing down the hall.

"Only for the day. The owner wasn't home and I didn't want him getting run over. I'll keep him in my office with the door closed so he won't bother the team."

The owner, I sighed, turning towards my office. Another person Patrick had alienated. The morning before the accident, he and I had been on the porch, overlooking the bay as he drank his coffee. We'd seen Bondo running through the backyard of a home down the hillside, above Noe Valley where we lived. A man had come out to retrieve the animal, scooping him up in his arms like a baby. Patrick had made a disparaging remark about animal and gone inside. The man loved to give parties, and the music often drifted upwards, to our home. Had we actually been invited, perhaps he wouldn't have minded so much. But we weren't, and Patrick thought it his responsibility to call the cops. It took him two times to learn that the police officers of San Francisco had better things to do than chase down noise complaints.

Bondo broke free of my hold, diving for the floor before racing toward the conference room. There he inspected the legs of the table, zipping to the bookshelf and then around to Sam's desk.

"I think we should let him run around," Sam suggested, as if we had a choice. "The worst place he'll end up is in the bathroom."

Bondo darted down the hall. Surprised, happy voices called out welcomes to the new companion, taking turns vying for Bondo's attention. I was standing at Sam's desk, reviewing the agenda she'd prepared for the meeting with Kay when Alan walked up.

"You okay?" he asked, holding the dog in his arms. "You look pale."

"Physically, I'm fine." Either my voice or expression caught his attention, for he tipped his head towards my office. I took the lead, sitting down my desk, expecting him to join me, but he hesitated at the door. "Coming or going?" I asked him, an attempt at humor.

"Well, normally you would ask me if I had something to do and then I'd leave. This confirms something is up."

"I really say that?" He nodded, and I waved him in, more disturbed at his comment than what I was about to disclose. After he shut the door and sat, I gave him the news.

"Patrick wants me to get an abortion," I said without fanfare.

Alan's face flushed, a pinkish-red moving up his neck to his hairline. His lips twitched, bound by the conflict over a professional barrier he wasn't comfortable crossing.

"You want to take the day off?"

"Leaving here won't accomplish anything," I replied. Since hyperventilating in my bedroom, I'd gotten a firm lasso around my emotions. "Bondo will keep us occupied, and I'm going to be meeting with Kay shortly."

Alan continued to stare at me, a worried expression plain on his face. "You're a lot calmer than someone else would be in your shoes."

"Speaking of shoes, did you see what Sam is wearing today?"

"As unbelievable as her hair," he said, taking the hint. "Suggesting her as the program coordinator is a great idea. She's fired up."

Alan rubbed his knuckle against the dog's flat face, between the chin and cheek. Bondo flattened his ears in appreciation, his tail wagging so furiously it slapped against Alan's forearm. "Snorts like all get-out. Want him?"

"Sure," I said, opening my arms.

"So..." Alan drawled. "Is something else up?"

"What makes you ask? Wasn't one bomb enough for day?"

"You brought a dog to work. And we are taking on Kay Abrahms' center, our first non-paying account since you founded this company, and I saw the outline for products on the printer."

Alan's observation was another sorry statement on my interpersonal skills. Bondo thrust his chin toward my chest, the soft nuzzle causing a twinge of pain, not all of it physical.

"Are you suggesting that I'm a different woman?"

"It doesn't take a genius to draw the conclusion you are back from the dead and perhaps feeling a little more charitable than normal."

"I was uncharitable before?"

Alan cocked an eye at me. "No, actually you are incredibly generous. You gave all of us some of the personal stock you had in your clients, even GeorgiaLiman. But generally speaking, I'd characterize you as all-business."

"Maybe I needed a wake-up call to make me more human."

"I'm not sure," he answered. "No human I know of would be so calm sitting here, pregnant and on the verge of being a single mother. They would be breaking down. That's pretty all-business to me."

"Who said I was going to be single?" Alan's expression was a mixture of disbelief and regret.

"Lindy, you are a smart, pragmatic woman," he began, his words purposeful and firm. "Patrick has effectively issued an ultimatum: it's him or the baby. You are showing no intention of backing down. Do you expect him to just wake up one of these days and say he's on board?"

I reluctantly nodded. That's exactly what I thought.

Alan blew out a whiff of air through thin lips. "What's your favorite phrase?"

"Hope is not a strategy," I said, my voice flat.

"Correct. As your new partner, might I suggest you prepare yourself for the worst while you expect the best? That way you aren't caught off guard."

It was too late for that, I wanted to tell him. Of all the scenarios I'd envisioned since waking up in the hospital, being alone—for real—as a single mother, hadn't been one of them.

CHAPTER 7

The South Potrero Youth Center was on a flat stretch of former landfill covered with row houses, storage facilities and tenement buildings. It was a pale-green cement block of a building covered with street art, the colorful illustrations depicting life on this side of Potrero Hill, far from the pristine homes of Cow Hollow or the views seen from the marina. Inside the youth center, a moldy smell accompanied the heat in the reception area.

A man in his early 20s greeted us, extending a well-worn clipboard to Sam. "Visitors sign in, please."

"I pulled in behind a white pickup if that's okay."

"No worries. No one leaves for lunch." He gestured for us take a seat on the chairs lined against the wall. "I'll let Kay know you're here." We'd just finished filling out the passes when Kay appeared.

"I'm so glad you could make it, Lindy," she said, embracing me warmly as though I were an old friend. She gave no indication of knowing about my conversation with John, and I guessed she'd be mildly upset if she'd been made aware about his not-so-subtle offer. I introduced her to Sam.

"Let's go find an empty space to chat."

She led us down a hallway to where a two older women making phone calls while working on ancient computers. Patrick would grimace with disdain if he saw the state of this facility.

Kay described the fundraising efforts led by volunteers, and how the kids waited for hours to work on the computers, the rows of devices donated by local software companies. A small room full of books served as a reading room. A purple Barney beanbag with a green patch lounged in front of a French-country-print loveseat. "The local shelter is willing to trade some furniture for things we need, like this couch."

We moved on from the small room to an open area. "This is where we eat and put on plays," Kay explained. "Fabricland donates returned materials, and what we don't use, we give to the art center." Storage bins overflowed with scrap materials and beside it sat a bookshelf with paint and brushes. Two easels leaned against the wall, the leg of one held together with duct tape.

She pulled down a chair from the stack along the wall while Sam and I did the same, joining Kay at a round table. "We've gotten by for years through creative horse trading, but we're out of time. In sixty days, we'll close. The owner of this building has never wanted to sell, but now, they don't even want to lease to us."

"Let me guess," I interjected. "They want to tear it down and build condos?"

"Anything will pay more than a non-profit." The area had views of the south bay, home to Saturday sailboat racing, the blue towers of office buildings gleaming even now through the dirty gymnasium windows. "The voices of parents barely able to afford to live in this part of San Francisco aren't as loud as the interests of developers looking to flatten the buildings, especially a mile down from the Giants' stadium."

"Could you gather investors and buy out the owner of this building and the ones on either side or write a check yourself?" Sam asked bluntly.

"If it was only the money, perhaps," answered Kay with grace. "The problem is I'm not going to be around forever. This organization needs an entity that's invested in seeing it succeed for decades, not months or a few years."

"You now need a strong public relations campaign to create pressure against tearing this down in favor of condos," I surmised.

"That, and perhaps turn up an angel who's currently hiding under a rock somewhere."

Just then we were interrupted by a young man who pushed his way through the door, using his shoulder to wedge it open as he cradled a large, outdated computer protectively in his arms. His chestnut-colored hair had streaks of sun-kissed blond at the edges, touching the tops of his ears. Freckles dotted the back of his neck, ending at a pronounced, curved line that followed the rim of his T-shirt.

He stopped, mid-push, seeing that he'd interrupted a meeting. Kay motioned him in, introducing us as she walked him to a location in the corner of the room.

"I knew you'd come through, Greyson," Kay said, patting him on the shoulder and offering to take the newer-looking flat-screen monitor. Greyson wiped his hands on his khaki pants, extending one to me as Kay told us he was a pre-med student at the University of California San Francisco Medical Center.

"And you find time to work here?" I asked.

"I volunteer," he answered. "I spent a lot of time here growing up and Kay's like my adopted Grandma."

"Over there, on top is fine," Kay directed, unbundling the cord. Greyson was a half-hand taller than Kay, and his shoulders were only slightly wider, his tan, tone arms visible underneath his casual t-shirt.

Sam asked how he finds parking around here and at med school.

"I like taking the trolley," he told her.

A noise like a herd of stampeding buffalos rumbled through the doors.

"Get ready. School's out," Kay announced.

As the kids came through the hallway and into the gym, they dropped their bags on the floor by the chairs and ran toward their preferred activities. Several came over to Kay, giving her happy bear hugs and showing her report cards or school assignments.

"Where would they all go if the center closes?" Sam asked, her voice lowered.

"The streets. A lot of them are latchkey kids. The closest YMCA is down on Market Street and caters to the adult professional crowd, not the at-risk group. Parents can't get off work to come home, so these kids will be wandering around, at home alone or getting into trouble."

I thought of all the reasons why the public relations aspect of this was would be appealing to the media. Big corporations wanting to displace the kids and Kay's own personal story lent itself to communicating her bigger objective of making the prospective buyers back down.

Kay interrupted my thoughts. "So what do you think, Lindy? Is this something you can work on?"

Rule number one for a public relations firm was to work with profitable companies, followed by rule number two, never work with nonprofits. On top of her needs, I had my own life that included contending with Patrick and a pregnancy. All these concerns flashed through me in an instant.

Even so the media coverage might change hearts and it was worth a try. I already knew what I was going to do, told her yes, we'd take on the project.

On the drive back to the office, Sam couldn't stop talking about the project. "We're not that invested in the community ourselves, are we, unless you count our annual donation to the Chamber of Commerce? It seems to me," she continued, before I could get in a word, "that if we're perceived as a caring agency, we will differentiate ourselves in a positive way."

By the time we were in the elevator, Sam had almost convinced me the entire project would be fun, as she called it. "And the more clients we get, the more money comes in our doors. That would cover the costs of our nonprofit work, right?" Sam asked abruptly as the doors opened and we walked into the foyer.

I paused by her desk. "Sam, the only way this will work is if you take the lead, not me." She'd been the receptionist, executive assistant and all-around sponge in black eyeliner, absorbing the subtleties of operating a public relations firm. Sam chirped out her delight and default acceptance of the task. "I'll take that as a yes. Just promise you'll help me write the classified ad for someone as qualified as you to take your place at the front desk, because if this goes where I think it will, you won't be there for long."

Sam rose, giving me a hug. "Do you think I'll be making many on-site visits?"

"I don't think the trolley goes that way, but maybe Greyson can correct me on that one."

Later that afternoon, I sent a text to Patrick; a reminder about the appointment with the OB/GYN. His reply was fast and short.

I'm not bothering neither should you

I deleted his text. He would change his mind. I remembered when my brother Charlie's girlfriend became pregnant. He freaked out and went into denial for almost six months until she started to show. Then he got excited and by the time the baby was born, he seemed more energized and enthusiastic than she was. Of course, by that time they were married, and he was having a family. Patrick just needed...perspective. Mine had changed, dramatically. So would his.

As I sat alone in the waiting room of Dr. Michael Kustin's office, the preeminent OB/GYN for high-risk pregnancies and those with infertility problems, I turned my attention to the waiting area. The dark wood and soft suede chairs were staggered in twos around the room, separated by square end tables. Brushed copper lamps with soft dual-tone shades provided subdued lighting, the overhead illumination from recessed lighting more fit for a high-end bar than a doctor's office.

The man across from me flipped through BusinessWeek as the woman next to him rubbed his neck. To my left, a woman in a beautiful sari, orange and red flowers on her top, peered down at her sandals. The man with her wore a tailored shirt and slacks. Gold bracelets around her wrists rested against his gold watch.

I glanced at the clock. Thirty minutes past the time of my appointment. Alan couldn't stay at the office forever and Bondo needed to be returned. I prayed for tolerance and patience.

The door opened with a snap and a woman emerged, her face a lifeless grey. The man wasn't much better, as much as he tried to maintain an appearance of control. An even stronger silence fell on the room as they left.

Instead of blaming the doctor's appointment desk for squeezing in too many patients back to back, I should be considering alternative reasons for a delay. Not everyone was having their dreams of a pregnancy realized.

I took out the demand letter for Monson. My stomach hurt as I read and re-read it. Two times I wrote the lines to Alan telling him the document would be signed and on his desk this evening, and two times I deleted the message. What was stopping me?

Pausing in confusion, I sent a text to Ann.

In my OB appointment, alone

Next time ask me to come- I'll be your stand-in husband

Not long after that, my name was called. The thin white paper covering the examination table crinkled beneath me as I sat down on it. On the ceiling was a picture of a newborn, its small, delicate eyes closed, and thick, dark lashes forming a line resembling two smiles on either side of a flat pug nose.

Dr. Kustin entered, and in his thick Australian accent, apologized for the delay. He informed me the samples I'd given were being analyzed and that he'd reviewed the documentation provided by Dr. Redding. To begin, he had a few questions for me. How often did I travel? How many hours a day were I on my feet? What did I do to relax? I answered, attempting to keep my irritation to a minimum. None of the questions had to do with my pregnancy and I had a company to run.

He remained standing while I spoke, his large, wide frame made even wider as he folded his arms across his chest. Bushy white eyebrows furrowed, creasing his tan skin as now and then he asked me to elaborate. Finally, he sat down on the round stool next to the examining table.

A knock at the door was followed by a nurse. "Doctor, here are the blood sample results," she said, giving him the paperwork. Kustin grunted.

"Problems?" I asked.

"We should know more in a minute," he said I eased myself down on the table, grimacing once at a sharp pain. "Still hurts quite a bit, I imagine." He placed a strong hand behind my upper back, his nurse placing hers below my lower back. Then he turned on the ultrasound and asked me to relax.

He moved the ultrasound wand around with one hand, his other on the keyboard, pointing and clicking as the screen captured a moment in time. "I'm measuring right now," he said. The screen was clear enough to see a sack with a peanut inside.

"Look here," he said, pointing to the monitor. "I'm estimating you are at week 10, which means your baby is eight weeks old and the embryo has officially become a fetus." My heart jumped. "Let's see now, the heart is almost developed. Maybe we can hear it."

He turned a dial. The sound came through loud and clear. It was very fast, sounding irregular, as if it was bumping over itself. I looked at his face for a reaction. Instead of concern, I felt him adjusting the wand inside me, switching the screen from a 3-D view to a flat view. I inhaled sharply from relief and fear. We both heard two distinct heartbeats.

"I thought so. Twins," he said with satisfaction. "It's why Dr. Redding thought you were further along than you are."

I forced myself to breathe through the tightening in my throat, dizzy with a complex set of feelings. I was excited to hear the news after years of wanting to become pregnant. But twins? That was more than I could handle.

"But this black here? That's blood. Too much of it is going to cause the body to push out the babies. You'll have a self-induced abortion." He turned the screen off and sat back.

"Are you are prepared to do what it's going to take to have the children?"

"Absolutely."

"You've got to increase the thickness of the uterine wall. Travel is out. Lifting, bending and all those things you take for granted and do a hundred times a day are also out, as well as exercising. It all creates pressure on the uterus. You will go on progesterone and I'd recommend you start eating spinach and eggs in the morning. The spinach causes the stomach muscles to relax and the egg whites will provide the protein you need."

"So much for hot dogs and ice cream," I quipped.

"Don't worry. You'll get plenty of that in too. Taking the progesterone is going to prevent your brain from realizing you're full of food."

"Okay, I got it," I said breathlessly. As long as I knew the ground rules, I could adjust my life accordingly.

"Now, before you get dressed, I have one more thing for you to think about. Do you know much about zebras?" he asked, the question causing my lips to part. What in the world… "When zebras are being chased across the Serengeti, with lions nipping at their heels, they don't get pregnant. The body doesn't allow it. Instinctively, the zebra knows carrying a child on the run can't be sustained. At some level, that female zebra knows it will be slowed down and die, or a calf will be born and quickly eaten. Mind you, the zebra is fulfilling her instinct to mate. Her body just doesn't allow conception."

This was the craziest thing I'd ever heard from a physician, but he was talking with such conviction that I couldn't help but listen.

"What I'm saying is the body knows when it can get pregnant, just like the zebra. Follow me? From what you've described, your life has been like that zebra's, seventeen-hour days for nine years, am I right?" He barely paused for my acknowledgement. "You said your travel slowed down about four months ago and the body figured it was in a safe environment to become pregnant, like that zebra. But you're still running a business, with every intention of running full tilt until the day you give birth."

"Well it does seem to make sense."

He wagged his finger at me. "Not if you want to keep the children. I'm speaking to you as I do with all the women who come into my office, who tell me about lives that would make an emergency room physician tired, and then they wonder why things aren't working out so well. This is the only way for someone like you to hear me. I lay out the realities and let you decide. I'm your doctor, but most of the responsibility is on your shoulders, not mine."

When I emerged into the waiting room, I turned to the appointment desk, oblivious to the others in the room.

I'm having twins. I needed drugs. I was going to be eating enough for a tribe. I was a zebra in the Serengeti who took a pause and got pregnant.

I hoped the dizziness passed before I started driving.

In my car, I sent a text to Ann. It was one word. *Twins.* I got an immediate call back, with Ann talking over and under my answers, barely allowing herself time to ask one question before she had another.

"What did Patrick say?"

"He doesn't know yet."

"Give me a heads up when you're going to drop the news and I'll be your back-up plan." I promised and hung up, lingering on the thought that requiring a back-up plan for my family was disturbing.

CHAPTER 8

On the way to my car, I was conscious of every step I took. Not knowing what constituted strain on my abdomen, suddenly every movement seemed to use my midsection: putting my purse on the passenger seat, taking my blazer off, laying it on the backseat. I bent my knees in an attempt to avoid bending my middle. The act was unnatural, but I'd get used to it. Just as I'd learn to love spinach and egg whites.

By the time I arrived back at the office, it was a quarter past 6. Alan was in the kitchen, feeding Bondo Fritos and part of a sandwich. He was the only person left in the office.

"How'd it go?" he asked me. As much as I wanted to keep the information to myself, I had to tell him.

"You know how I told you the emergency room doctor told me that my life was either going to be back to normal thirty days post-accident or be completely different? Well, let me just say this. It can't get any more different." He looked at me expectantly. "Twins," I blurted.

Bondo's snorting punctuated the silence until it was broken by Alan's chuckling. "Never do anything halfway, do you? What'd Patrick say when you told him?"

"Haven't yet," I answered, staring at Bondo taking a bite of stale pastrami sandwich. I didn't need telepathy to know I was being watched. "Right now I've got to get this little guy home."

Twenty minutes later, I pulled up in front of Bondo's home. Ringing the doorbell produced the sound of footsteps. I saw the curtain pull back and the face of a man peered out before the door opened.

"Bondo!" he exclaimed, his voice full of love.

I released Bondo into his arms and couldn't help but notice the muscle rippling under his striped, short-sleeved oxford shirt. I'd seen it before, as well as the tailored herringbone pants that were doing nothing to hide his muscular thighs.

As they loved on one another, I looked around, appreciating the green-and-grey stamped pavement. Small archways of climbing roses lined the path to the front door, the flowers carefully cut above stems with five leaves, a trick my grandmother taught me just before she passed away.

"Jackson Matthews," he said, stretching out his hand with the introduction. "Where did you find Bondo?" His hand was warm, thick with calluses at the base of each finger.

"A few blocks south, roaming in the flower plants. I nearly hit him with my car. I'm Lindy. We live above you," I said, turning and pointing. "A few houses up." Our deck with the barbecue grill was clearly visible from the driveway.

His demeanor changed once he made the connection. He withdrew his hand, as though a disease had jumped from my fingers to his. Sure enough, Alan and Ann weren't the only people Patrick had managed to alienate.

"I left a note on your door," I said, attempting to bridge the gap that had opened between us. "Bondo is adorable. I was worried he'd get run over or stolen so I thought it was better to take him with me."

"I didn't see a note," he said blankly.

I looked around the small lawn. The trashcans were set out, standing beside recycle boxes. Wedged in between two empty blue plastic containers was a yellow piece of paper. Taking my time, I bent, making sure to use my knees, to pick up my note.

"The wind must have gotten it," I said, walking back to him. "By the way, is that shirt from Billy Blue? I got one for my husband this spring. Brushed cotton like that is wonderful for this weather." I had no problem using a bit of flattery to thaw the guy out.

"It is," he smiled, my comment having the intended effect on his attitude. "With you bending like that, you should see a chiropractor."

"What I have won't be that easy to treat." Over his shoulder, I saw golden candelabra on a marble-topped credenza in the entryway foyer. The curved legs looked 17th century, though I wasn't a furniture expert. My knowledge was strictly from the pages of Architectural Digest.

"I should warn you that the entire staff at my office fell in love with him. When I got back from an afternoon appointment, an associate was giving him a pastrami sandwich. I'm just glad it wasn't Krispy Kremes."

"You took him to work?"

"I had no choice. My two cats wouldn't have been too good with him."

"Was Bondo okay? I mean, he didn't have an accident in front of the boss, did he?"

"I own the company, so it was like a free day for the team and Bondo was perfect. The only worry we had was if he was going to take the elevator down to the first floor." Jackson laughed. "Take care of yourself and Bondo," I said, giving the back of Bondo's ear a final rub.

Jackson watched me place my hand on the back of the seat as I got in my car, putting one leg in before sitting, then lifting the other. "You want the name of a good chiropractor?" he asked, a hint of concern in his voice. I shook my head.

"My doctor just told me I'm having twins. The condition is temporary."

His eyes told me I'd given him way too much information. "That's some news."

A man's voice called from the doorway. Jackson turned, waved, motioning the other man to come out to join us. In an instant, I knew at least one of the reasons Patrick called the cops when they had parties, and it had nothing to do with the noise factor.

"Ronnie, meet Lindy. She rescued Bondo this morning and had him all day at the office. No — don't get out," Jackson said, placing a hand on my shoulder. "She just learned she's having twins," Jackson said by way of explanation.

"Congratulations," Ronnie said, his voice thick and deep. The r rolled slightly, the t spoken with a clear emphasis and enunciation.

"Singer, or do you have an exotic background?" I asked, taking in his broad shoulders and deep chest.

His eyebrows rose approvingly. "Opera. Though I dabble in the jazz department for extra cash. You have a good ear."

"No, I can't take any credit. I grew up going to opera, symphonies, lots and lots of concerts. My mom's a classically trained pianist."

"Then you saw 'Madame Butterfly' last year?"

"Unfortunately no. My husband loves strings, not arias. I haven't been in a few years."

"I'll tell you what. You saved little Bondo here. Anytime you want to come to the opera house, I'll get you some great tickets."

Thanking him, I put on my seat belt. "My sister had twins. You shouldn't be moving at all," Ronnie said. He looked at Jackson for confirmation.

"I know, but I've got to get home somehow. I'll feed my cats and then gear up for telling my husband the news."

"They live up there," said Jackson, pointing to our balcony apartment.

"Really?" asked Ronnie, as surprised as Jackson was.

Thanks again, Patrick, I thought miserably. "I'm sorry about my husband calling the cops. He's a light sleeper and has this thing about noise. The good news is that the cops don't pay attention to him anymore." The men shared a smirk. "I'll give you a tip. Have a party Saturday night. Patrick won't be home." I winked and shut the car door. They both seemed like decent individuals who certainly bestowed as much caring and affection on their dog as I did my cats. Certainly more than Patrick did, even in his best of moods.

That night, I turned off the lights at eleven, wondering if Patrick's off-site included a comedy club or other entertainment. The last time I'd joined him for a retreat, it had been at the Ritz-Carlton in Half-Moon Bay and his company had brought in a stand-up act who was playing in the city the following weekend. How long ago was that? Eighteen months?

Remus lumbered onto me, this time followed by Romulus, his brother, curling his two tone body down by my feet. Soon I drifted away.

Grandfather stood beside me as he looked at my book of life, waiting patiently as though the last dream had never ended.

"It's here for you to read," Grandfather said.

"But I am alive," I said, knowing this was a dream and that my physical body was lying in bed. "Why do I want read about what's already happened?" The future was far more interesting, but that hadn't yet occurred.

A smile pushed up his wrinkled cheeks, crinkling the corners of his eyes like an accordion.

"Perspective," he said. "The last day of our life can be very enlightening."

Realizing we weren't going to leave until I did as he wanted, I reluctantly looked down.

I skimmed several paragraphs of my life, reading the emails I'd written that morning, along with accounts of the phone calls common to the life of the CEO of a small business.

I scanned the page until I saw Patrick's name, going slower. I was intrigued with the replay of our life together, although the recollections weren't positive.

"What about merging your taxes with Patrick's?" Bruce, my accountant asked. "It would mean a big tax break for you this year."

"You've been telling me this for five years, Bruce. And I'm sure it's great advice. But Patrick feels strongly he wants our tax returns separate. So, I've got my S-corporation and he has his own tax forms. You know how it goes Bruce, you're married. You choose battles worth fighting."

"I'm not in a position to judge. Maybe next year," he finished, his tone conciliatory.

My finger scrolled down the page. Sam was in my office, pointing out the window. It was still the last day of my life, the morning of the accident. I read about myself watching a member of the San Francisco parking police locking a gigantic, yellow, metal boot on the front, left tire of my car. I'd let too many tickets amass and now I had to pay up.

"Does that make two times or three?" Samantha asked in the way only a twenty-five-year-old could.

"Three, but who's counting?" I asked, biting my fingernail.

"I was kidding, Lindy," she said, responding to my sour tone.

"Sorry, Sam. Going to City Hall is the last thing I want to do right now."

"The whole Monson thing is a real bummer," she observed, offering me a piece of gum, squinting in the late morning sunlight. "Read this before you go. It will make you feel better." She handed me a small envelope. The card was heavy, the return address on the back of the envelope printed in raised, formal cursive, the color a soft lavender.

"Thinking of you and all that your organization could do for our youth center. Perhaps you would reconsider? Have a wonderful day. Kay."

I sighed. "If I could have one Kay Abrahms for every Monson, life would be a lot better."

The page in my book of life turned over and I paused to look at my Grandfather.

"You are starting to listen, Lindy." I nodded, grateful. What I was reading took place two weeks before, and since then, I'd taken action with Kay. It felt good to think I was making progress on my own.

He gestured my attention back to the page.

"Lindy, it's Jacob from Chanel. Your watch arrived in today's shipment. It's boxed, wrapped and ready for you to pick up." I'd spent an outrageous amount of money for a watch I'd been wanting for a year and for no good reason, other than it was a shiny object I thought was attractive. I promised myself to save more and spend less of my income in the future.

Spotting a cab on the corner I waved my hand in the air. I jumped in and said, "City Hall, please."

The street signs dotting the side roads of Market came and went, just like my family, I mused. I couldn't help thinking about Mom and Dad. I hadn't talked with Mom since their wedding anniversary, eight months ago, and Dad far longer. I took a deep breath. I'd give her a call later today, after work.

The cab slowed to a halt, allowing for a trolley to pass in front of us, across Market. The avenue was crammed with out-of-towners wandering around the shopping district. No doubt half of them were from the convention taking place over at the Moscone Center. Seeing them reminded me of another call I'd put off.

"Hi Vanessa. I got your message regarding that guy from the conference on Wednesday. Okay, he's gorgeous, and even though he says he's single, he still seems slimy. You asked for my opinion, there it is. I'm sorry I didn't call and tell you earlier. Call me later."

As I continued to scan down my page, it seemed I didn't notice much other than my cell phone. According to my book, I didn't pay much attention to the streets or even the town I lived in. I'd become blasé, my mind singularly focused on succeeding to the exclusion of all around me.

Grandfather touched my forearm, love and compassion in his eyes. "A different lens, isn't it?" I only nodded, disturbed by what I'd seen. "That is all for now."

CHAPTER 9

At quarter past 10 on Saturday morning, the Eastern sun streamed through the window, hitting my legs. Both cats were lounging on the bed with me, splayed out, their bellies elongated to capture as much of the warmth as possible.

Patrick had been invisible, coming home late last night. Only the vibration of the garage door under the bedroom told me he'd actually been in the house. He must have slept on the couch in the living room and was gone before I got up. If only he displayed a fraction of the enthusiasm John had shone in my office, or even the first time I met him.

Enthusiasm, or interest?

Rolling back the duvet cover, I turned on my side, propping myself up with my elbow as I sat up straight. It would be good for my ego to think that a man of John's looks could possibly be flirting with a woman like me, a married, slightly overweight one at that, but not realistic.

"Realistic is getting my prescription filled," I muttered to myself.

My stomach grumbled and I made a breakfast of egg whites, hating the texture and taste until I added salsa. I compared Patrick's absence to what I thought the 'normal situation' would be for newly pregnant couples. I imagined the husband at home, doting on his expectant wife, taking the day off, proudly stating it was family time.

But no, I sighed, making my way back to bed, avoiding thoughts of him and our situation.

Lying in the half-light, I thought of my conversation with Alan and his perspective about my office behavior. That couldn't have been me, thinking of my phone calls and interactions with others. *Wasn't me.* Well, but then again, it was and perhaps still is. I thought of Alan and how he conducted himself with others. He was focused and all-business while at the office. It didn't make him a bad person, just professional. The question was whether or not this alternative view of reality was going to remain, or if I was going to change it.

I'm already changing it, I thought, closing my eyes. I cared about people and sent good thoughts in the direction of someone in need. I expected that my friends did the same with me; those in my inner circle connected and elastic like a rubber band, sometimes it stretched when we weren't close or contracted when we were, but it never broke.

Restless, I got out of bed, wanting to take a shower, hoping the hot beats of water would eliminate my self-doubt. As I tilted my head back under the hot water, I went through my checklist of friends and family. Ann: I rarely saw her or her family, even before the accident. It had been over a year since I'd seen Charlie, and I only talked with him maybe once or twice a month. The last conversation with mom had been eight months prior on her wedding anniversary and with my Dad had been even longer. They'd been financially stretched for money for so long….

With a towel still on the top of my head, I went into the living room. Gazing out over the rooftops below me, I thought further of my father and the watch I'd purchased. I'd wanted it, and completely, totally didn't need it. My parents on the other hand…

Two seconds later, I called the shop and had the funds put back into my account, apologizing to the manager.

"Don't worry in the least," said Jacob. "I have three other customers who are on a waitlist." A feeling of nervous joy coursed through me.

Vanessa was next on my list. I'd seen her a few days before the accident and left her a message. I could see her today. *If she's home.* Vanessa's lifestyle of retail fashion kept her on the road so much, I never knew if she was in town from one week to the next, but I called anyway.

"Of course I'm in town, but not for long." She offered to pick me up before I asked and forty minutes later, she stepped out of her Lexus convertible. I was waiting at the bottom of my steps, smiling enviously at her figure. She was the epitome of San Francisco glamour, wearing a blue-and-black wrap cashmere top, black leggings, suede booties and a retro poncho.

Thanks to her parent's import business, Vanessa grew up knowing most of the owners of high retail boutiques in the city. As a teenager, she worked at Barney's, where she so impressed the manager with her taste and flair that she got an assistant buyer's position before she left for college. While attending NYU, she also managed a Chanel boutique, moving from merchandising to senior buyer as easily as switching majors. With her camera-ready confidence and three-inch heels, she was boosted to a model-ready 5-11 and traveled to and from the runway shows in Europe to New York as easily and glamorously as though she were one of them.

"Just another Saturday dress-down day?" I teased. She smiled and gave me a hug, but left her glasses on.

Once we were in the car, I pinched the protruding bones of her right knee. "And have you lost weight in the last few weeks?"

"Some," she replied. Her voice didn't have its usual bounce but I attributed this to jet lag. "You look like you've lost weight too," she said, giving me an approving look. "Do you have something new in your life you haven't shared with me?"

"Yes, but I'm not telling until lunch."

The first stop was the bank. I sent a wire to my father, who would be surprised and rightly so. It wasn't the amount he'd asked me to loan him a year earlier. It was double plus some interest, twelve-thousand, the exact amount I'd paid for the watch. I hoped it went a little ways to make up for my idiocy in siding with Patrick who believed that a man old enough to make and lose a small fortune didn't deserve help. Who was I to have judged my father and his decisions? I had no idea what he'd been going through and should have stopped long enough to consider what might have brought him to a point of asking his estranged daughter to help him out.

Then we hit the bookstore. Vanessa headed in a different direction, telling me she needed to search for a specific title. I found the pregnancy section, pouring over the rows of books. I must have looked lost as I stood vacillating with my hand outstretched.

"Go with 'The Pregnancy Bible,'" said a man walking by. "We have three kids and my wife swears by it."

"Thanks," I replied. I flipped through the thick book, marveling at the pictures of the little black dot, morphing from a peanut to a seahorse. I turned to eight weeks. Sure enough, fingers and toes were nearly formed.

Vanessa scared me, peering over my shoulder. "Doing some research, or do you have something to tell me?"

"Both," I said coyly. She gave me a tremendous hug. "What about you?" I asked, indicating several books in her arms. She partially covered the title of the book with her hands, but I saw the words Recovering and Rape. "Let's get out of here," I whispered.

We went to Demoine's off Chestnut Street. It was far enough from the main shopping strip for the tourists to miss it, and quiet enough at the lunch hour that we could have a private conversation.

"It was the guy we met at the conference on Wednesday, do you remember him?" I did. He was drop-dead handsome but gave off bad vibes in an undefinable way. "You called and left me a message, saying that even though he was gorgeous you had a bad feeling or something. I didn't listen." He'd asked her out, and she'd suggested going to Guyma's in Tiburon. "We even had the tamales you always order," she said. He'd expressed an interest in seeing her new house and offered to drive. At the door, he gave her the keys, and once they'd stepped inside, he'd pinned her from behind.

"I don't really remember the rest of it," she said, raising her water for a drink. "My therapist says I've blocked it out."

"Do you think he'll be caught? I mean, you know his name. Who he works for," I said, my feelings of remorse and distress turning to anger. Had I told her earlier, maybe she would have been less inclined to have gone out with him. I felt sick.

"It's not your fault or responsibility," she told me, sitting up a few inches. "Besides, I'm so headstrong, like I said, I would have done it anyway."

Her words gave me no comfort. I still should have called the day before, not after. "I can give a description," I offered. "We go straight up to his booth at the next trade and arrest him on the spot."

She shook her head no. "He said he had a girlfriend, though they were in the process of breaking up."

"So?" I hissed back. "Men and women who commit murders have spouses. Did you call the police?"

"I called the rape crisis center and talked to a woman. She told me to go to the hospital and get tested."

"Did you?"

"Yes. Arlene, the counselor from the center went with me. My parents advised against the police getting involved." She caught herself, hesitating. "They said…I'd invited it by bringing him over to my unfinished home in Sausalito."

"You didn't ask for this!"

"Arlene said it's a common family reaction from parents or boyfriends who can't deal with the situation so they blame the victim."

"Vanessa," I leaned forward to touch her hand. "You can't let him get away with this."

Tears flooded her eyes. "I can't do it, Lindy. I can't go to court and see him again. I just can't."

"What about the next person he does this to?" I asked fiercely. "You could be one more person in a long line. You need to be the last. If his soon-to-be-ex-girlfriend knew what he was doing, she'd throw him out or turn him in. For that matter, his whole story could be a fabrication he uses to lull women into an unsuspecting sense of security."

"I hadn't thought of that," she said quietly.

I leaned forward, earnest and intent. "As your friend, I'm begging you, to track this man down and make sure this doesn't happen again."

Vanessa nodded reluctantly. She put her hand to her forehead, hiding her eyes. I reached over, touching her free hand. I held it tight. We were silent for a few moments before she composed herself.

"Now, can you tell me what's behind the pregnancy book?" she asked.

"Well," I began, "I'm almost nine weeks. I'm hoping for a boy and a girl."

"Twins?" she whispered. I was starting to get a perverse sense of enjoyment each time I delivered the news to someone for the first time.

Her demeanor changed and I knew what was coming next. "I never thought Patrick was the kid type," she said. Vanessa and Patrick had been at odds from the moment they met, not dissimilar from Ann, but more--obvious. I blamed it on their similar personalities. Now my analysis seemed naïve. She had seen something I hadn't, long ago.

"I thought I'd get better informed before hitting him with the news."

"Just leave the pregnancy book on the table or something, open to the section on twins," she said, a wicked look in her eyes. "Hey," she said, leaning toward me, her eyes gleaming with fun. "I've got an idea. One of the best maternity shops is less than two blocks from here. Let's go get some clothes for you."

"Not now."

"If not now, when?" she persisted, a little life of color returning to her cheeks. "No," she said, cutting off my protest. "This is going to be my gift to you, and if you don't let me, I'll just show up on your doorstep with a bunch of bags."

Seeing her joyful smile, I set aside my pride and agreed to let her spoil me.

Vanessa expertly picked out the latest trends in dresses, shirts, shorts and slacks, throwing in some sun hats and scarves, both of us laughing when a saleswoman had me strap a fake bump on my belly and wear a puffed up bras that would simulate the eventual size of my chest. The laughter continued on our way to the flower mart to get her bouquet, then diminished as we arrived outside the rape crisis center.

"You don't have to come in," Vanessa said, subdued now but not depressed. "I won't be very long."

But I insisted. My heart was full of gratitude for what a complete stranger had done for Vanessa. I wanted to meet Arlene at least, even if I didn't have much to say.

Vanessa dropped me off and I waited in front of the door for her to park. Vanessa joined me and we went inside.

"Arlene! I wanted you to have these," Vanessa said, hurrying toward a woman at a desk and handing her the bouquet of lilies.

"Thank you so much," the woman whispered, obviously moved, standing to give Vanessa a hug.

When she pulled away and I got a look at her face, I was stunned. She was the parking ticket lady. It was she who had refused to release my car over the weekend so I had to take the cab and ended up getting hit.

All my anger at the role she had played in my current situation started up, then eased back down. It wasn't just her fault; I'd not paid the tickets. Patrick hadn't been available. She was just the last straw that made my present situation inevitable.

"Hi Arlene, I'm Lindy," I said quietly, extending my hand, knowing that she'd already recognized me. Arlene returned my shake without a word. Her cool response didn't bother me. She didn't know me for who I really was any more than I'd seen beyond her rough exterior.

"Lindy insisted on coming in with me to meet you."

"Really?" Arlene questioned, skepticism rich in her voice. "Did you have a life-changing experience?"

"Actually, I did. I was in an accident right after I saw you. The day you counseled Vanessa," I said without fanfare. "I just wanted to see the woman who helped Vanessa and say thanks."

The woman's craggy face softened. It was like I was seeing her for the first time.

"You were the friend in the hospital?" she asked me, incredulous. Acknowledging she'd heard of my situation, she wrapped a big arm around Vanessa again. "This girl's going to be okay," Arlene said in her gruff manner, which no longer put me off.

"Lindy is the one who helped me make the decision to be here," Vanessa said, her voice gaining strength as she looked at me.

"I met the guy. If it's helpful, I can give a description." Arlene got a fire in her eyes. She asked Vanessa to sit down as she got a notepad.

Later, when we pulled into my garage, Patrick's car was already inside. He was home early.

"Do you want me to leave the new clothes in the car?" Vanessa asked softly. Even without me telling Vanessa my worries about Patrick, she'd guessed. My father always said that what usually needs to be done most is what a person wants to do the least. What I wanted least was to go in the door with my arms full of bags of maternity clothes.

"It'll be ok," I said, hoping I didn't sound as doubtful as I felt. We hugged, and I promised to call if I needed anything.

"I'm gone for a week, but I always have my phone." I waved as she drove away.

"Patrick?" I called, walking down the hallway, my hands full of bags on either side. Fortunately, it wasn't far and they weren't overly heavy. He emerged from the music room, a pop tart in his hand.

"We ended early," he said, eyeing the bag that read Baby Chic Boutique. I continued to the bedroom, dropping the bags by the bed then sitting. Patrick pulled out a maternity bra, holding it like a slithering snake at arm's length from his body. "Aren't getting ahead of yourself?" he asked, throwing the bra on the bed.

"These were a gift from Vanessa."

He lifted up a dress, glancing at the price tag. "A lot of money for a dress that may never be worn."

"That's a risk she was willing to take," I responded, refusing to take the bait. He left the room and I heard him opening and closing the fridge. After a few minutes, I joined him in the living room. He was staring out the patio windows, a glass of wine in his hand.

I sat down on the white couch, under my favorite chalk drawing of a San Francisco roofline.

"Remus, come here," I called to my black cat. "I saw the OB/GYN. Good news, bad news," I chattered on nervously as Patrick took another drink. "The good news is that I'm at a little more than nine weeks and they are fine. The bad news is I've got internal bleeding but it's manageable. He gave me a prescription and told me to stop exercising."

Patrick turned toward me, his face red. "They?" he repeated. I scrunched my lips to keep from crying at his look. He gave me only silence, and the silence was deafening.

"Do you have anything to say?" I asked finally, the question emerging as a plea.

He turned his back to me, opened the patio door and walked outside. He leaned against the railing, gazing out at the city. Carefully lifting Remus off my lap, I joined him on the deck. The lights of the Bay Bridge were now reflecting off the water, the sunset casting an orange on the hills beyond Berkeley.

"I can stay in the second bedroom so you won't miss out on any sleep," I offered. He remained stone-faced, glaring straight ahead. I followed his gaze, and saw Jackson and Ronnie waving at me. I waved back, smiling.

"For as smart as you are, you can still be delusional. No matter how many times I tell you, you're not listening, so let me say it again. I don't want children. Not now. Maybe not ever. Period." He abruptly turned and went back inside the house.

A sob caught in the base of my throat, momentarily choking off the air. This wasn't happening.

By the time I joined him, he was grabbing his coat. I didn't want to ask him where he was going, but couldn't help myself.

"Out," he answered flatly. "Don't wait up."

"But Patrick, we have to talk about next steps."

"I gave you the only option. Here's another: you can give them up for adoption, but don't expect me to wait around for the birth, because I won't."

CHAPTER 10

After he left, an emotional paralysis confined me to my chair. I couldn't call Vanessa—it was too humiliating. Ann? Yes, I'd promised to call her, but what was her 'back-up plan' going to amount to? Still, I promised.

The news of twins went over badly- we will talk later

I could see the text had been delivered and I guessed she was wondering what to write that wouldn't compound my agony. Finally, it came.

I'm here for you whenever you need me

It was the best thing she could have written.

John's smiling, tan face framed by his unkempt, blond hair appeared in my mind's eye. Why in the world had I thought of him?

Because I'm already envisioning what a future without Patrick would look like, as Alan had predicted. No adoption. Just me and my children.

Too upset to eat, I went back into the bedroom, looking at the sacks of clothes, another maternity bra half in, half out of the bag. In the midst of it, I reached for my phone. First I called my dad and a recording said it was no longer in service. Then I tried Charlie, but his phone went directly to voice mail.

With an icepack on my forehead, I turned on soft music, pulled my warm comforter over me and closed my eyes.

I found myself sitting in the middle of a white room that could best be described as a box. The chair I sat in was also white, as were the walls and floors. The room had no windows or moldings, nothing but an austere shell with a single door. A second later, it opened and in walked my Grandmother Ovi. She wore an ankle-length white dress with gold trim around the collar and wrists. Her eyes found mine and never left. Her face exuded compassion, a trait she acquired from years of living with an unfaithful husband. It was also full of love, her eyes brimming with the memories of a life fulfilled by the purpose given to her by raising children.

She continued walking until she was almost an arm's length away from me, close enough for me to see every wrinkle on her lined face, but not near enough where I could touch her.

"You must leave him," she said quietly, though her voice was as strong as if it had physically touched me. Her message wasn't accompanied by an outstretched arm or tender hug. She repeated her message again, turned and walked out of the room.

I'd not had time to digest the strange encounter, when the door opened again. This time it was Aunt Mamee. Her grey hair shone as she shuffled towards me befitting her ninety-three years when she passed. She came across the floor just as my grandmother had done, stopped where Grandmother had and said clearly, "You must leave him."

There was only one "him" in my life; the man I was living with, married to and who had fathered my unborn children.

The dream did not end with my Aunt. She was followed by other female relatives, all who had important roles in my life. Each one said the same words. "You must leave him."

When the door shut for the last time, I sat in my white chair, unable to move, feeling as though all the strength of my body had left along with the hope that I'd been clinging on to. After many moments, the silence told me I'd heard all that was meant for me. It was time to wake up.

The cats complained as I moved. It was black outside and the clock read 11:12 p.m. The vivid dream replayed itself over and over.

It's my fears and paranoia about Patrick cutting through my defenseless subconscious.

It took a while, but I eventually went back to sleep, looking forward to a peaceful and dreamless experience.

During the night, the dream repeated itself again. When I woke, a strange, unearthly feeling of serenity accompanied the soberness of what I was experiencing. I felt as though a part of my reality had been left within that dream.

I made my way into the living room. Patrick was on the couch reading a book. It was cloudy outside, and he had the fireplace on, the flickers of light bouncing from the gold-rimmed glass coffee table to the large, gold-leaf-framed pastels and watercolors. I sat on the embroidered loveseat, delicately woven by master craftsman in 17th-century Europe, a treasure I'd found at Jamison's.

"Do you love me?" It was all I could think to ask. I hoped he would furrow his brows, curl his lips and give me a look like I had a screw loose.

Patrick looked me straight in the eye. "No." The word and delivery were so jolting my chest constricted. With effort, a second question came to mind. One I didn't want to ask, but I had to. It was now or never.

"Did you ever love me?"

"I'm not sure." The wall of emotional security I'd fabricated and held on to during our time together started to disintegrate.

"Do you think I'm attractive?"

"I did, at one time." Down to the ground went my image of who I was, splayed out in bits and pieces. It dawned on me that his rejection was not just about having children. The other part was about me. He didn't want to be *with me*.

I don't remember what words were said after that because Patrick did most of the talking. Last night, he'd consulted an attorney who told him a Costa Rican divorce could be issued immediately, while California divorce papers were simultaneously filed. All he wanted was his clothes, music, one cat and a piece of art we'd purchased together in Sonoma. Those items and a piece of paper releasing him from any obligation to pay the costs of raising the children in return for giving up his rights. I'd be free to travel with the children, remarry, move to another state and send them to church.

"If you sign, I'll forgo any claim I have on your business." But he'd never wanted a part of my business, so his bargaining chip was stupid.

"You're not a shareholder, Patrick."

"California is a communal property state," he responded objectively as though we were debating on where to eat breakfast. "What you earned over the last five years was stock in half a dozen technology companies. Half of that is legally mine." The GeorgiaLiman stock came to mind first, Alan's words second. Be pragmatic, he'd counseled. In other words, face the situation and deal with it.

"Draw up the paperwork." My words were barely audible.

Patrick began packing the moment the conversation ended. I called Vanessa who came over to pick me up. He didn't come out of the bedroom when the doorbell rang and I didn't tell him I was leaving.

Once at Vanessa's parents' home on the Marina waterfront, we sat by the pool until the evening sun set. We talked about Patrick and the what-ifs of my future life until the subject was exhausted. At seven forty, Patrick sent me a text message to say he was out.

When I arrived back home, silence greeted me. The master closet was three-quarters empty but the furniture remained. I called for our cats, knowing he was going to take one, though he didn't say which. Remus, my black cat came out from behind the couch, looking like a lost soul. It was a tender mercy, as he was my favorite of the two. He slunk around, as if he had noticed and felt the emptiness as much as I did.

I fell asleep with Remus curled against my stomach, my arm draped around him. I considered what had happened in the last eight hours. The dream had been just that, a dream, but in it had been enough of a trigger to cause me to ask a simple question; one to which Patrick could have said many things.

The dream forced me to a point of closure. Another blessing, although awful to experience and hell on my life. If Alan ever asked, I'd be honest. Had it not been for the dream, I would have held onto Patrick, tightly and irrationally, until he pushed me away.

We were still standing beside my pedestal, as if we'd never left it and I had the distinct impression some of the men and women reading the pages were relatives or loved ones, looking down on another's life, praying fervently for their welfare.

"I don't think I want to see anymore," I told Grandfather, my fragile state manifesting itself by a weak voice. Knowing my dreams were having a very real impact on my life scared me.

"Are you sure?" The question, so soft and love-filled, resonated within my bones.

"Why am I having these dreams with you now? Is it because I died?"

"For you, yes."

"But not everyone?" I pressed. I had a very real surge of jealousy when he nodded. In my lifetime I had asked for help a lot of times and got nothing in return. "But help doesn't always come," I said with frustration.

"Ah. Sometimes an answer is a long time in coming, and when it does come, those who are impatient are closed off from hearing the answer, especially if it's not what they'd hoped for."

"I'd been praying about Patrick," I said, closing my mouth the moment the words were out. I did get an answer, just not what I wanted.

"And sometimes, prayers given by others are heard and delivered by friends or relatives. In some cases, complete strangers. One must be sensitive to the input."

Grandfather flipped the pages of my book and I looked down. I was 18 and stayed too late at my boyfriend's house. Dad told me to be home by midnight and it was already 12:30 a.m. I raced out of the house and into my car and was about to throw it into reverse when my boyfriend stopped me.

"Wait," my boyfriend said, pulling my seatbelt in place. I harped at him, irritated at the delay. He ignored me, ensuring it was tight and I was secure before he let me leave. Seconds later, speeding down the gravel road, I took the sharp corner too fast. The back of my four-door Volkswagen Jetta slid out, flipping the car on its hood. When I awoke, my boyfriend was peering at me. I was hanging upside down from the roof like a bat, the seatbelt suspending me in midair. The lid of the car was crushed, the vehicle wedged in an irrigation ditch with water a foot deep. My boyfriend's dad later said I'd have drowned if I didn't have my belt on.

"Look here," Grandfather said. He flipped to one page earlier. It was my father, on bended knee, audibly praying for his daughter. I hadn't called and he was worried. He was praying for my safety.

I looked at my Grandfather. "That was you?" I asked.

"I came just as you got in the car. I was whispering for you to put on your seat belt. You were so preoccupied, you couldn't listen. Your boyfriend, on the other hand, was receptive to the prompting."

"I was so worried dad was going to be mad. My boyfriend, what was his name? Brandt Severson? He was more aware and sensitive than me." Grandfather nodded. "What would have happened if my dad hadn't said a prayer?"

"I can't say for sure. Death. Paralysis. I don't know. Some things aren't supposed to be prevented. That's where free will and choice come in to play, and it's the way we learn and grow."

I looked at him intently. "You were here all the time but I was too blind to see it."

"Blind isn't only a physical state," he said informatively. "It's mental and emotional. One must have the right view on life to be receptive." I scrunched the corner of my mouth. Although I wasn't perfect, and had been very focused on business. I thought I had a positive, open view of the world.

"We're going to take a journey, Lindy, to visit those you encountered during your last day on earth. Perhaps then you will see what I mean."

A curtain of light appeared, draping itself from an invisible hanger high above us down to our feet. He took my hand and we stepped through the veil.

CHAPTER 11

Soft gusts rolled off the sea, up and over the cliffs south of the Golden Gate Bridge, through the homes lining the western ridge of the seaside cliff. Feeling the familiar temperature of the air and smelling the sea salt was strange, as though I were still a part of Earth.

"Being outside your body doesn't mean you don't feel the physical sensations," Grandfather said in my ear as though I'd spoken my question aloud.

The white dome of the Palace of the Legion of Honor sparkled, its neoclassical pillars and majestic open square nestled on a plateau between the water and the city. A black stretch Hummer limousine slowly made its way around the large round reflecting pool, stopping in front of the columned entrance. Teenagers emerged from the vehicle, the girls in formal dresses, the young men in tuxes, making their way to the far edge of the lawn where they all posed for photos.

We continued on, following the breeze, until we reached Sea Cliff, an area where third- and fourth-generation San Franciscans lived in massive multi-story homes and where their wealth, derived from banking and real estate, contributed to making this the costliest place to live in the United States. Sea Cliff was always my choice when I took solitary drives after my disagreements with Patrick. Why, I wondered, had I not seen those disagreements for what they were, arguments over fundamental philosophies regarding money, individuality versus teamwork and partnership and the future? As I watched the mansions below me, rimmed by carefully pruned plants and the elegant, old cars parked in the driveways, the answer came to me. I was living in the moment, in the bright light of a successful company, an apartment overlooking the city and going out with my handsome husband with individuals who were like him—attractive and successful, also enjoying the moment. With each year that went by, my internal pull towards things of substance, like a home outside town, shared bank accounts and the unthinkable notion of a dog and children, were like splinters in our relationship; at first they were an irritant, but festered and grew, ultimately exploding, needing to be excised like a topical disease.

On this afternoon, however, the quiet street was disrupted by noise coming from a cream-colored house with three-story-high pillars flanking the entranceway. Children ran around the large lawn while two adults sat in swinging chairs on the veranda. Then, from the front door emerged Kay Abrahms. She made her way down the steps, extending a plate of cupcakes to her husband, Adi, whom I'd met at the charity event.

Kay placed herself next to a pre-teen girl, who took a cupcake from the tray. Kay's simple, shirt-sleeved cotton dress hung loose beneath a red baker's apron, hanging down just below her thick calves. Her modest slip-ons looked more Naturalizer than Chanel, hugging her swollen feet.

"Mom, did the city commissioner finally give you the permit?" A man's voice caught my attention. I couldn't refrain from taking in every aspect of John. Leaning against a pillar, he wore fitted, black jeans, his T-shirt under a blue V-neck sweater that nicely profiled his trim waist and defined arms. In this environment, free from employees, prospective clients or those to impress, he was…even more impressive. Striking, really.

Kay set the tray down, peeling the paper off a cupcake before taking a bite and shooting her son a wink.

"Does the name Lindy Gordon ring a bell?"

"Sure," John replied, pushing up his sleeves, revealing the absence of a watch or a wedding ring.

"I'm hoping to get her to spend a bit of her time at the center."

"She will stretch your bank account to the max if the way she dresses is any indication."

"That's why your mother's trying to convince her to take it pro bono," Adi said, giving his son a skeptical look.

"Seriously, Mother, what do you need a PR person like her for?"

"She may come across as tough, John, but she's representing clients who aren't always in the best of situations."

"I'm not sure 'tough' is the word I'd describe her so much as rude."

"She dogged him," said the young girl with smirk on her face. John gave his daughter a loving, yet irritated look like she had betrayed a secret.

"Attempted to talk to her," John corrected. "She turned me down, rather rudely, I might add."

"Maybe you should have dressed better," interjected Janaye callously.

"You can't charm every lady who crosses your path," Adi teased.

"I wasn't coming on to her, Dad. I was trying to start a professional conversation but she declined and then took off in the other direction." I cringed at the memory. I did walk away, just like he said I had, but the reasons had nothing to do with him. John continued. "Mom, you could pick a dozen people in our circle who have the same attributes as someone like her."

"Dad, get over it," his daughter said without the slightest hint of sympathy. "Just because you didn't see the wedding ring on her finger until after she started walking away doesn't mean other women aren't out there. You need to start dating again."

Surveying the little bodies before her, Kay nodded her head, counting.

"Adi, I don't see Mila. Where's Mila?" With that question, the smiles dropped and all activity ceased. The two men immediately left the veranda and the children stopped their games to engage in a hunt for the missing girl. Kay walked along the wide hedge bordering the property, peering in and out of the oversized blue-and-purple hydrangea, calling anxiously for her granddaughter. John quickly walked along the fencing at the lower perimeter of the property, shaded with trimmed evergreen bushes.

"Found her!" came the call of Adi's voice at the western side of the house. Soon Adi and a young girl who couldn't have been more than eight, came toward the group, the look on her face unconcerned. "She was in the tree house reading a book," he said to Kay.

"Want me, Grandma?" asked the blond-haired girl, adjusting her glasses with one hand and holding a copy of Professor Branestawm in the other.

Kay smiled weakly. "I had cupcakes and we wanted to make sure you had one. That must be an awfully good book." Mila took a bite, nodding. "I'll go in and get some more," said Kay, as the children resumed their fun as if nothing had happened.

Grandfather and I followed Kay into the kitchen then up the stairs to the second floor, stopping outside a closed door. Taking a deep breath, she went inside. The walls of the large room were painted an ocean blue, with white upper and lower moldings that conformed to the formality of the house. The twin bed was covered with a white-and-blue striped comforter, with red-and-white pillows coordinated to match the throw blanket hanging over the footboard. On the nightstand were a boating journal, Boy Scout awards and a sports trophy. Kay picked up the trophy, rubbing her finger along the base, wiping off the dust.

"I thought I might find you here," a voice said from the doorway. Kay looked over her shoulder, giving her husband a loving smile, though it failed to mask the sadness in her eyes.

She continued dusting the trophy, tracing the lines of the little golden car from the top of the hood down over the car rims. "He was the same age as Mila is now, you know."

Adi came to her and squeezed her shoulders. "Who's safe and sound as we speak." Each looked at the trophy for another moment before she placed it back on the table. The noise from shouting children drew her to the window. Adi joined her, this time linking his arm through hers.

"With your permission, I'm going to look for another gardener. Today showed me what a few months does to our hedges."

"Sure. If you tell me the real reason behind asking Lindy Gordon to help out the center."

"Honestly, I can't tell you why I asked her. Maybe I see a bit of a younger me in her." Kay replaced the trophy on the nightstand and gave the room one last look. Adi shut the door behind them and followed his wife downstairs.

We remained in the room after they'd gone and I felt depleted, like a balloon with the air expelled. Patrick hadn't wanted me to take on the account, and I'd been too afraid to stand up to him. Me, my fear, not his own agenda, should have been dealt with.

From the hills on the coast to downtown, we stood between the two faces of San Francisco: the majestic Opera House, its marble columns facing the square's lovely fountain where couples with children played during the day, and the Tenderloin district, famous for the gentleman's clubs on O'Farrell Street as well as its drug scene of home of prostitutes and the homeless.

Grandfather slowed. A large shadow on the ground preceded a woman who shoved a man to the side.

"Excuse me," she said to the man brusquely. "I'm late."

"Whatever, lady. You're going the wrong way. McDonald's is down the street."

The woman turned around. "I'll try to leave you some food." The man ignored her, but my gut churned. It was Arlene.

I glanced past her at the battered metal door of a building. A single strip of paint curled off it. RAPE CRISIS CENTER said a sign on the door. She pulled it open with a tug just as a young, stylishly dressed Asian woman also entered, her eyes bloodshot, her cheeks swollen and red. Behind her was a female police officer.

"This will only take a few hours," the policewoman said, placing a hand on the Asian woman's shoulder. "I'll be with you the entire time." Before I could hear the rest of the conversation, Grandfather led us through the doorway. Arlene showed her identification, opened a can of Coke and made her way to a small cubicle in the back of the office.

"Busy day, Arlene. Convention last night."

"Glad you called me in, then."

"I don't know how you do it," said her cubicle partner, shaking her head in admiration. "Take people's money during the day, putting up with their whining for eight hours, and then you make time to come here and counsel victims."

Arlene put on her headset and took a sip of Coke. "Tell you how. I preserve my energy for people who actually need it You should see the imbeciles who show up at the hall for hours on end trying to justify their existence by writing a check."

"Pick up line two, Arlene," the receptionist called from across the room.

"Got it!" she answered.

Rather than using the demanding, irritating tone I was familiar with, Arlene adapted a kind, gentle voice as she told the caller it was going to be okay, that she had found a safe haven from her experience. The lines of her face softened, compassion filling the deep crevasse between her eyebrows; an emotional Botox taking years off her life. I felt Arlene's strength extend into the room as her words of support wrapped around the caller, protecting and comforting her in her moment of anguish.

"I know it's going to be hard, but you can do it. You have to see a doctor." Arlene scribbled on her notepad. "I know, honey. Yes, it's got to be done. You don't want this to happen to someone else…" Arlene put the phone on hold, swore profusely before she clicked over to the activate button, her voice once again exuding reassurance.

"Listen to me, now. You have people who care. No, it wasn't your fault. Just because you didn't listen to someone doesn't mean a thing. Do you have a friend? Someone you can talk to? No honey, I'm sure that's not the case. That's not your worry at this moment. We can get the guy, but you have to be strong. My name's Arlene. You come down here right now and I'll be here with the police officer. After that, we'll go to the hospital together. That's right. No, it's not a burden. I'll be right by your side. The doctor? It will be a female. She's one of the best. She's the one who treated me when I was raped. You're welcome. You call me anytime between now and then. See you soon."

"I've got an officer on the way," called her co-worker the moment Arlene ended the call.

"Another call on line two, Arlene," the receptionist said. "I got it," she said, abruptly turning away from her conversation. Grandfather asked me if I'd seen enough. I had.

CHAPTER 12

When I arrived at the office Monday morning, I went straight to work, ignoring the notion of telling Alan about Patrick. That he didn't love me, had dumped me and moved out was something I could keep to myself for a few hours longer. Shame and humiliation could wait.

At nine-thirty, my head was down when Alan walked in, said hello and slid a piece of paper under my face. It was list of transactions from Fog City Diner.

"Tell me if you notice anything odd about the highlighted items," Alan said, his voice tight.

"Too many crab cakes?" I glanced briefly at the itemized list, uninterested. I was tired and hungry at the same time. Thanks to the pills Dr. Kustin prescribed, I'd eaten myself silly, making eight egg whites, four pieces of toast and two glasses of milk. I knew I was full before the eggs were half-gone, but my stomach was telling my mind it was still empty. Beyond that, I'd had three hours of self-loathing, induced by the dream-reality of seeing Kay and John and Arlene. I knew the reason I'd been privileged to see parts of the last day of my life was for my betterment, but it felt like a hammer was being pounded into a bruise called my ego.

"Seriously, Lindy. What do you see?" Alan asked. His tone was severe, and I dutifully examined the highlighted items.

"Why are there two transactions on the same day? And what are all these night charges? We never go there at night."

"I checked back six months before calling Fog City accounting," he said impatiently. "Landen said he had an authorized signature and sent over the originals. So, I have to take this on the chin. I got sloppy."

"Okay, tell me. Do I have a clone out there or what?"

"The signature is Patrick's. He had his signature on file as an authorized individual." He handed me a stack of receipts in a folder. Patrick might not want his own children, and my friends didn't like him, but he had always been honest. That much I was sure about.

"There must be some mistake. I've never given him authorization to use the company account."

"It was Patrick. Somehow he had all the business tax ID information, filled out the forms, sent it in the mail—"

"The mail?"

"Yeah, they had sent a confirmation to your home address. I'm assuming you didn't see anything?" The mail. I fought the urge to close my eyes. "And according to eyewitnesses —"

"Who?"

"Doug, Paul and Stacy. He's been there with the same person. A woman in her late twenties. A blond, not a brunette with auburn highlights."

"Not me, in other words." Alan mashed his lips to prevent an audible sound.

I'd made a habit of inputting Patrick's schedule in my computer. That way I could time my own departure from the office or from the gym and be home in time to make dinner for him. I looked at the dates on Alan's list and checked them against my own calendar. Sure enough, the timing of the bills at Fog City matched the windows when Patrick was "at meetings." And that was just for the last month.

I placed my hand on the front of my forehead, pretending to think, all the while shielding my eyes. This can't be happening.

"I'm so sorry, Lindy. I didn't want to bring this up until I knew for sure what was going on. I needed the weekend to hear back from everyone. Then I took preventative measures. This morning, I informed all the managers at Fog City by phone and in writing that Patrick is no longer authorized on the account."

"When was the last transaction?" I asked out loud, not wanting to hear the answer, but needing closure.

"Sunday night, but he was there Saturday night as well."

The night I told him we were having twins he'd gone to have dinner with another woman. Then after he left me, he had another celebratory dinner, knowing I wouldn't leave the house.

If I thought Patrick leaving me was the worst that could happen, I was wrong.

Alan left me to my misery. The hammer had become an anvil and it was pounding in my head as well as my chest. I'd read about post-traumatic stress disorder and wondered if the combination of head trauma and my own subconscious were colluding to make me crazy.

The dream with the white room wasn't real. It was a dream. But the different scenes I'd witnessed last night…

I tried my best to concentrate until lunch, when I planned to walk out for a break. A courier showed up just as I was getting my coat. He wore a suit, not a delivery uniform, and announced to Sam he had a package for me to review and sign. I came out and greeted him.

"I'm being paid to wait," he said helpfully. I tore off the top, scanning the contents. The first page was a cover letter from an attorney, announcing the filing of the divorce papers for both Costa Rica and the State of California. An attached list itemized what Patrick took, and a corresponding page noted my acknowledgment. The last page was a document releasing Patrick from all obligations associated with his biological children, as well as a waiver for parental rights.

"Why don't you take a seat in the conference room?" I suggested to the courier. "I need my attorney to review this."

"Tell me it's a check from Monson," Sam whispered as soon as the door shut. She knew the rest of my life, why hold this back?

"Divorce papers," I answered, keeping my eyes focused on the papers. "Patrick moved out yesterday."

"What?" she asked, and I caught a mix of compassion and anger flash in her eyes. "When you're pregnant?" Though her voice registered disgust, I detected relief and maybe even happiness.

"With twins, in fact." Sam put her hand to her mouth. I hadn't told her that part. "Would you mind ordering me up some lunch from Fog City?" The food was still good, even though it would be slightly tainted with his memory. And at least I'd know where this bill was coming from.

"Sure. If you have time later, I'll give you the update on what's happened with Kay."

I called my corporate attorney who told me to fax over the documentation. In less than 10 minutes he called me back.

"Just get your signature notarized, make two copies, and send one to me so I can track it until it's final." The Costa Rican divorce was immediate, the California one a formality and back-up. "But on the off-chance either if you want to get remarried, I'd err on the cautious side and wait for the six months for the California divorce to be finalized." As if I was going to be needing that.

I walked downstairs to the insurance firm to get the paperwork notarized. When I returned, Sam told me I had a call holding. In my office, I picked up the phone.

"Lindy Embry."

"Hi, it's John Abrahms."

"Hi John," I replied, grateful to have my emotional clouds part with a ray of sunshine. "Do you have a new client for me or have you found someone else to be on your radio show?"

"Neither," he said coldly. "You can answer a question. Why did you put your husband on me?"

"Husband, you mean Patrick?" I asked, confused. I was already starting to mentally refer to him as my *former husband.* "What do you mean 'put on you?' I have no idea what you are talking about."

"I got a call at the station, suggesting that we were giving away interviews or profiles in return for favors to associated businesses." I felt my chest collapse, the air sucking out my ability to respond. "I don't even have the words to describe how pathetic---"

"John," I interrupted forcefully, nausea and nerves making me bold. "You have to believe me. I told Patrick about you being here with humor, and not at all in a derogatory way."

"Sure you did," he said sarcastically.

"John, if I were offended, I never would have gone over to Kay's that Friday, nor would we have accepted the project. I simply don't operate that way, as a professional or a person."

"But you still thought I'd give you radio play?"

"Of course not!" I said indignantly. "I have no desire to be on the air and certainly wouldn't want myself or you to be tainted by any hint of that idea. Such a thing would do neither of good but a great deal of harm."

"They why would Patrick come after me with a dagger in his hand?"

"I truly don't know," I said, almost in tears, though my voice remained relatively even. "He's—we've been under some serious stress and I guess…"

"He took it out on me? Is that what you're suggesting?" John asked, his tone hard.

"I don't know what he was doing," I admitted. "We aren't even…" I said, stopping when my eyes blurred with tears of shame.

"Look," he said forcefully, talking over my last words. "I'm not going to have a circular discussion. Please, if you've started work on the center, drop it. I don't need or want your kind of help."

"John, that's not right. We can do so much for that center."

"Not anymore."

The moment the phone went down I swiveled my chair to the window, facing the street. I didn't want Sam to witness my misery. It wasn't enough for Patrick to reveal he didn't love me or think I was attractive, or that he'd been carrying on with another woman. He was going to make sure that my chances for impressing another male were ruined, even someone I'd only talked to in person twice.

I could barely concentrate until the attorney approved the paperwork. Sam knocked lightly on the door, then put the paperwork in front of me.

"The notary is in the small conference room." I thanked her, pressed my fingers at the corners of my eyes to wipe away the tears and finished signing the documentation to end my marriage.

That evening, I stayed up as late as possible, not wanting to fall asleep. I didn't want more information. I wasn't sure I could handle it.

Yet sleep did come, and with it, my Grandfather.

We were in the corridor of a hospital's surgical unit. A doctor rushed by, attending to an emergency call that was coming over the loudspeaker. He hurried through the heavy, soundproof door to the operating room and the corridor became silent except for the soft pulsing beat from the monitors at the nurse's station in the center of the U-shaped lobby. The attending nurse was the same woman who had attended to me while I was in the hospital.

Standing in the hallway, I felt a presence behind me. I turned and saw a woman lying on a gurney, her back to me. She was covered by a thin, white sheet, an IV inserted in her forearm, her bump pronounced with the extended belly button raising the sheet. She gulped air softly — the sound of a crying female who didn't want to be heard.

The nurse at the desk looked over at the patient. She stopped typing on the computer to bring her a box of tissues, placing it on the metal stand near the woman's head. Taking a sheet, she blotted the corners of the woman's eyes.

"I'll leave these here for you, honey. The doctor might be a while."

"Can't my husband come in?" The nurse touched her forehead, telling her only medical personnel were allowed. My heart skipped a beat as I recognized my cousin Ann's voice. I had intended to call her the day of the accident but ignored the small voice. I felt sick, the urge to turn away losing out to the necessity of watching.

Dr. Redding walked out of the elevator heading straight for the nurses' station. "Where's Lacy?" he demanded curtly, looking around. The nurse looked up.

"In surgery. An emergency C-section." Dr. Redding cursed, and it sounded strange coming from him. "She's got several surgeries backed up," the nurse mentioned. "You won't get any of her time for the next few hours."

Reaching over the desk, Dr. Redding grabbed the phone, snorting. "Thanks for your professional opinion." The nurse kept her eyes lowered though her cheeks turned blotchy red. "Steve? Jake here. You said I had Lacy for the afternoon to work on the grant proposal. Our deadline is 5 P.M. Couldn't someone else have taken her surgeries? One more baby isn't going to make or break the world. Fine," he said with forced acquiescence, "but if we don't get this grant, it's not my problem."

"Doctor, please," the nurse admonished him as she accepted the outstretched phone. He glanced over his shoulder at the gurney, then back, his face unemotional. With hands that quavered on the desk, the older woman stood.

"Your Harvard degree gets you time with the director of the hospital," she hissed, her words barely above a whisper, "and your looks give you a pass with your patients, but on this floor, doctors get paid to care. The woman lying on the gurney was told this morning that her baby was dead," she continued. "Since you don't actually practice medicine on low profile births but wait for the high-profile trauma patients that get you the most press, you wouldn't remember a dead baby has to be delivered naturally. A lifeless child of six months is passing through her. A child that probably had a name, perhaps had clothes waiting at home along with a nursery, and little brothers and sisters expecting a sibling. A child that will come out dead. But go ahead. Talk as loud as you want. After all, nothing is as important as your grant."

The nurse's chest heaved and she sat down, staring at the computer screen in front of her. Ann's head was turned away, her glazed eyes staring at the grey wall. The white blanket rippled intermittently as her body shook underneath.

Dr. Redding stood speechless, the nurse's verbal slapping having its intended effect. He walked straight down the hallway, got in the elevator and left.

"Wait," Grandfather said to me, touching my arm. It wasn't long before the elevator opened, and the doctor emerged. His walk had a discordant feel, as though he was battling himself forward with contrition and back with pride, each step harder than the last. When he reached Ann, Dr. Redding spoke in a clinical manner.

"How are you feeling?" Ann didn't respond, nor did she react when the man's tanned hand rested on her shoulder. "I'm Dr. Redding. Are you in physical pain?" Ann's eyes remained closed. "How can I help you?" he asked with stilted concern. He hovered for a moment more before he turned and left again, this time down the hall, in the other direction.

Once he'd gone, the nurse hurried to Ann's side. "I'll go tell your husband you're with me. Then I'm right across the hall at the station, honey, okay?" The doors opened and shut when she left, leaving the hallway quiet again, until the sound of creaking wheels grew loud.

Dr. Redding returned, pushing a metal stool to Ann's side. He glanced up and down the corridor. "Sorry about that. I had to grab a chair," he said, apologizing. "My feet get sore standing all day running up and down stairs. I …. I understand you have kids. Several. You could probably tell me all about going up and down the stairs and standing too much, huh?" Ann said nothing. "My name's Jake." He looked at her swollen belly first, then lifted her wrist. "I'll just take your pulse."

He turned her hand over, preparing to hold her arm. Before he could make it, her fingers curled around his wrist in a tight grip. She turned her head to face him, her eyes still shut. She drew his hand toward her face, burying her tears in it. Dr. Redding was stunned, but made no attempt to move away.

Time went by differently when I was on the other side. I felt like I watched my cousin for only a few minutes, but the clock told me it was more than an hour. Dr. Redding never moved, his hand her lifeline, his watchful eyes never leaving her. The phone rang and the nurse, who had returned long before and had remained silently watching, answered. Her voice was low and respectful.

"Dr. Redding," she called, "the room is being prepped now. Dr. McLean will be down shortly." The doctor looked up and politely thanked her, conveying a silent apology. Shortly afterward, the operating room door opened and two nurses and a female physician came out. Dr. McLean's eyebrows raised when she saw Dr. Redding sitting by her patient.

"We're almost ready for you, Ann," she said, touching her head. My cousin opened her eyes, showing the deep blue pupils surrounded by red lightning bolts.

"I can't be alone," she pleaded.

"I'm sorry," the female physician replied. "Only the medical staff is allowed in surgery."

"I'll stay with you," Dr. Redding offered.

"That's really generous of you, Dr. Stevens," said Ann's doctor, the tone indicating she didn't believe his offer sincere, "but this isn't a short surgery."

"That's all right. I've got time on my schedule."

"Ann, you asked for full anesthesia," Dr. McLean said. "You won't be able to feel his hand." Ann looked at Dr. Redding, and I saw him give a squeeze.

"I'll be here," he told Ann, then looked at the other doctor. She nodded her acceptance.

Four people walked beside the gurney down the hall. A fifth person, a young man dressed in white, walked on the other side of Dr. Redding, his hand on Ann's arm. When he passed in front of us he looked up for a moment and I saw his face. He shared the same strong jaw line and thick, dark hair of Ann. His attention returned to her as he accompanied the gurney as it proceeded through the double doors.

"Was Ann's unborn son walking beside the gurney?" I asked quietly.

"Yes. He was in her womb for those months and gained a physical body. That was all his time accounted for on this Earth. Even though he's on the other side, he came back to give her comfort, to give her the knowledge they will be together again as a family."

"Why isn't he a baby?" Grandfather smiled.

"We choose the age at which to remain. Some of us want to be at the age where we had the most wisdom, like me. Others, like that young man, never grew old, and he chose to be in his mid-twenties form."

As I passed through the veil again, my heart flooded with regret for what could have been. I spent years working my way up the corporate ladder and then started my own business. Clients paid put me up at five-star hotels and chauffeured me to and from meetings, but Ann had something that had eluded me my entire adult life. She had a family.

"You don't ever stop having feelings, Lindy, even after you arrive," Grandfather. "You carry them with you through the veil. Joy, sadness, anger, regret." It was like I had been living a life inside a dirty glass, not seeing things clearly. "That's why we are all so busy up here. We are helping others work through unresolved issues and the associated emotions."

I bet he'd like to hang out with Grandmother, but she was off running some other errand, maybe helping a relative like me.

"We derive great joy when our work results in an act on the other side. Think about all the times you were moved to stop and visit a friend, send a note or prepare a meal for someone in need," he suggested. "Was it really your impulse or was it a prompting? Sometimes our work consists of nothing more than a thought, but the person must decide whether or not to act on it. That's free will. It becomes easier the more earnestly and eagerly the recipient listens."

"Do the impressions get stronger depending on our actions?"

"Sure, just like a muscle responds to increased workouts. It remembers, making the next act easier. Following the little promptings makes it easier to recognize them in the future." And presumably, once a person hears the promptings—whatever form that takes—requires good interpretation skills to know what the promptings are all about. I recalled times when I'd been in a meeting, stymied by a problem until a solution came into my mind.

"Didn't my intelligence count for anything?"

He laughed reassuringly. "Of course. Remember what your mother taught you?"

"Absolutely." Her inner musician put her little sayings to rhythm. "Prepare for the test, hope for the best and let God do the rest." I guess it stuck.

"It would have been good if you'd have taken that same approach when you were making other big decisions in your life," Grandfather said. He was referring about one specific subject, of course. Men. I hadn't prayed about whether I should marry Patrick. It wasn't because the thought hadn't crossed my mind, but I'd always been too busy, too distracted or both. Deep down I'd known then just as I knew now that I'd been afraid the answer would not be what I wanted to hear.

CHAPTER 13

Tuesday, my thoughts were on Patrick spending thousands of my company's dollars on lunches and dinners. While my accountant, attorney and Alan went back and forth regarding legal alternatives with Patrick, I called Ann with another update.

"Unreal," was all she could get out. "But then, not so much."

"You can say I told you so, again."

"Why would I do that?"

"Because I deserve it."

"How do you figure?" she countered, her tone belligerent, the one a person uses in defense of another. "He was, and still is, tall, dark, handsome and intelligent, and don't forget that there was a time when he treated you like a princess. We all saw it."

"Right," I agreed. "Until about five minutes after we were married---"

"And he got what he wanted," she finished for me. "Now we just know what in addition to all those great traits, he's dishonest, amoral and unethical. You think you deserve what you are getting? He might land in jail, and it would be fitting."

Later that afternoon, Alan came into my office.

"It's not worth it," he summarized. The attorney said it was too large for small claims court but not large enough for a lawsuit. "It will take at least fifteen grand to litigate, and that's not including damages, which is subjective."

"So we might barely break even, or lose money depending on legal fees." Alan eyes held mine as he agreed. "So we chalk this up to my stupidity. The only bright spot on the horizon is that the expenditures can be counted as a write-off."

"You've got dark circles, Lindy," Alan observed with a touch of concern. "Don't let this ass drag you down any more than he has."

"I'll work on that."

Alan's departure was met with Sam's appearance at the door. "I forgot to tell you," she began. "Kay is wondering if you know anyone who could help around the center. Landscaping and odd jobs. She needs someone over 21 who speaks Spanish and English to manage the other part-time help."

"Really? When did you speak with her?"

"She called about an hour ago." The dream…Kay's conversation with Adi. It was real.

"Lindy, why aren't you backing away from the center? No one in their right mind would do what you are doing. Not after the debacle with John. What a mess!" she muttered.

"Yes, it is a mess, thanks to Patrick," I agreed, my voice subdued. "But I should have gone with my gut and taken on the account months ago when Kay first contacted me."

For the next hour, the notion of my dreams being real consumed me. I went from doubt to acceptance then embracing the possibilities. I went through what else had been on my mind the day of my accident for the hundredth time. One name came up very clearly. It was unresolved to be sure, it was an issue, and it sure as hell inspired emotions.

Monson.

The afternoon sun streamed in through my western window. I reached for the phone to call him and my stomach immediately clenched.

Okay, I'm listening, as if a gut-churning sensation meant no.

From the bottom drawer, I pulled out my stationery. The off-white linen card stock with raised, light purple lettering was a far cry from our corporate letterhead with blazing red type and impersonal square logo. No churning manifested itself, so I proceeded.

Holding the pen in my hand, I hesitated. Slowly at first, I started to write, until the page was filled with a message completely at odds with what I'd intended to say.

Dear Monson,

I hope this note finds you and your family well. When we last spoke, we had a good laugh, joking about the upcoming launch of the new product, your fishing trip to Bear Lake and your daughter's 13th birthday.

It's been nearly six weeks since that conversation — far too long. I've been through an ordeal, an accident that put me in the hospital, and while there I found out I'm pregnant with twins. If that weren't all, I'm going to be a single mom. How the world turns!

All that is to say that I'll be stepping back from day-to-day operations on certain accounts to focus on less physically demanding activities. Alan Harrison will be your primary contact at the agency from this point forward, though I'll always welcome a call. I do miss talking to you.

Warmly,
Lindy

As I placed the letter in the outgoing mailbox, I felt better. Sam said she'd drop by the post office on the way to the trolley.

"Anyone else riding that trolley?" I asked. Just because my world was falling apart didn't mean I couldn't pay more attention to others. Sam gave me a shy smile, completely at odds with her appearance, and I thought she might have been flattered I was asking about her personal life.

"Yes, Greyson just happened to be on the trolley."

"And you happened to be going the same way," I teased. "I love it when life works out like that."

Just before five, Alan nocked on my door and came in, sitting down across from me. "Got your email about the letter to Monson. Why the change of heart?"

It took the courage gained from witnessing far-worse experiences of others to answer his question with conviction. "All I can tell you is that each time I started to sign the demand letter or make a call, I felt sick about it. And it's not nervous sick, Alan. It's the type that comes from the gut, that says- don't do it."

He squinted at me. "At this point, I'm unwilling do go against your premonitions."

The sun was setting behind the blue-grey of the crooked mountains of Whistler, British Columbia, the thin air searing my lungs. Grandfather stood beside me by the river rock fireplace in the small ski lodge. Mhen my mother stepped out of the bedroom in an elegant but worn silk chenille bathrobe. Her long brown hair was styled in an updated Grace Kelly look. Her thin frame and drawn skin likely from stress, not exercise. Mom always said she hated to sweat and would rather eat less than work out. Over the past 10 years, she'd been saved the decision. My father's part ownership in a medical equipment device company lost its margins when the competition outsourced overseas. Then his plastics factory lost profitability with the double hit of federal regulations and cheap manufacturing in China. He poured money into real estate but the developers went bankrupt, the result of overzealous construction projects at the wrong time, too few buyers and a softening market.

Dad stood at the other end of the fireplace as regally as if he were in a chateau. His taut face and angular jaw line were the envy of men a quarter of his years, his forehead showed barely a trace of wrinkles, his off-white cable knit sweater a reminder of his beginnings on the shores of southern Spain, where his own father toiled as a fisherman.

Mother went to the closet and lifted a box off an upper shelf. I recognized it as her fine jewelry case. It was empty. "We don't have much left for the children," my mother said.

"We have one thing," Dad replied. He walked to the hope chest at the foot of the bed. Removing pieces of clothing one by one, my dad pulled a small, wooden box from the bottom of the trunk. "I'd forgotten about this until the other day." Mom's eyebrows arched and then dropped, as if to mask disappointment. He took a watch from the box. "I was thinking about this for Lindy."

Mom smiled in recognition. "We were in Paris." She placed her hand on my father's arm, her voice warning him off the subject. "She might have other watches far more expensive, or trendy."

"You're saying she won't wear this?" He rotated it in his hands. "Why should she?" he asked, regret in his voice. "It's what I taught her. Only the newest, the trendiest and most expensive. All three of my worst habits."

"Don't be so hard on yourself," my mother told him.

He rubbed the face of the watch absently. "When Lindy was 16, she asked me if she could wear this watch to school one day. Just begged me. I said no. I was afraid she'd lose it or someone would steal it."

"At an all-girls' Catholic school?"

"I know," he said with regret, rubbing a smudge off the link with his wide thumb. "Once during Charlie's senior year, he asked to wear a jacket for a date and I wouldn't let him. He yelled. We both yelled. I never thought another thing about it until years later, we were at his apartment and Lindy was still in high school. Lindy asked Charlie to wear a sweatshirt. It looked ten years old, but that was the style she wanted. Anyway, Charlie wouldn't let her." Dad stopped talking, his words choking on the other. "That's my legacy, Vivian. Instead of a car or a home that's passed to my children, it's my selfishness." He bowed his head in his hands. My mother put her arm around him, rubbing his back. "I was terrible before her wedding you know. I told her not to marry that guy," Dad said. "She hasn't forgiven me for saying what I did."

My mother sighed. "You didn't trust him. Neither did I. I still don't." My dad slid his hands down from his face. "Is there something else you're not telling me?" she asked.

He hesitated for a moment, and then nodded. "I called Lindy for help. I knew Patrick had made a good bonus with his sales job and her business had boomed. I figured she'd have five grand to spare."

"You didn't tell her what we'd gone through, did you?"

"Not all of it, and I'm glad I didn't. She grilled me. Asking me what I was going to do with it, when she'd get it back. My daughter, whom I'd given everything to her whole life, turned me down for a few thousand dollars. I was in such a state of shock I could barely speak."

"What did you do?"

"I told her it wasn't that big of a deal and I had other ideas. She seemed relieved. I haven't called her since. That was when we started selling the family jewelry." He sighed heavily. "I hated her for the past few years, Vivian. Simply despised my own daughter, but I still couldn't bring myself to get rid of the watch. But after a few months, I realized she wasn't the one I was angry with. It was me. I was so focused on providing that I ignored you. Ignored the kids."

"You treated them a lot better than you were treated by your parents," my mother said, trying to comfort him the best she could. Dad stood and went over to the fire, the light from it outlining his frame.

"Where does the blame stop, Vivian? First I blamed my parents, then I shifted the blame to God, which was cowardly. He didn't make me work outside or be away on the weekends. And I couldn't blame you. You've held this family together through it all." He stopped, and my mother shook her head, as if she were unsure whether to comfort him or to agree. "I finally ran out of excuses. That was the moment I stopped hating Lindy. I had to forgive her and go on, even if she never changed. Then I could love her like my little girl again."

He took a few breaths, collecting himself. "Then we got the bill for the back taxes on this cabin. The one, single thing we have left that we own outright. I couldn't tell you we were going to lose it, too."

"Are we?" she asked. He gazed around the room, as if searching for an answer.

"Possibly. I called the tax office, was up front and honest about my situation. The woman was sympathetic and gave me an extra thirty days. Then they start proceedings. So we really have about 90 days to come up with the money."

"Did you call Lindy?" He shook his head.

"I'm not going to ask her for money again. And Charlie's in no position to help us. In the meantime," he brightened, changing the subject, "I have another business possibility. Markus told me about a man who has a few patents to his name. He doesn't know what to do with them and is willing to do a joint venture. It's in genetics or something."

"Don't tell me it's cloning an animal?"

"Who knows? Markus is getting me the details as we speak. Could be nothing. Could be something. We'll see."

"Why not?" she said, rewarding him with the smile of the long-suffering but still full of trust. The look was not one I'd seen her give him in life. "You've done everything else."

Dad paused, looking down at the watch. "Do you really think she won't wear it?"

Mom patted his arm. "Over the last year, you've changed a lot. Maybe she has, too. The only way to know is to give it to her and find out."

#

"You look terrible," Sam said Wednesday morning.

"It's a lack of sleep, but I promise you, I feel better inside than my appearance suggests."

Back in my office, I attended to the business before me, making enough headway where I felt I could spare ten minutes. Then I dialed Kay. She was mildly surprised at the call, expressing joy and concern about my pregnancy and finally shock when I revealed the abrupt separation and divorce from Patrick.

"Good Lord Lindy. I think you need a vacation, not a pro bono contract."

I nodded to myself. "I was afraid you'd say that, but I didn't call looking to get out of the contract or alarm you. It's actually about your son… Is there way you can communicate to John that the incident with Patrick was not of my doing, without revealing the divorce and the other circumstances? It's all so…humiliating."

The woman clucked sympathetically, then half-chuckled. "I could have spared you the trouble of relating all this," she started, "because we already had a conversation. Not long after he spoke with you I got a visit. John was adamant that I not work with you."

"What did you say?"

"I told him to mind his own business." We shared a laugh. "It will all work out," she concluded. "When one isn't in possession of all the facts, for whatever reason, they rush to judgment."

Didn't I know it.

CHAPTER 14

Yet, I was listening, I thought, giving an upward glance to my Grandfather. Of course, he could be sitting beside me, in front of me or maybe nowhere near me, focusing on other people, living or dead. The notion gave me a feeling of calm, an emotion I'd felt very little of lately.

By twelve, I was midway through a turkey sandwich when Alan appeared at my door.

"Lindy," Alan said, "we need to talk." The look on his face was the same as when he told me about Patrick, but more intense. He shut the door and sat down directly in front of me, papers on his lap.

"Sure," I said with an enforced calm. Alan handed me a printout, a page covered with figures.

"Darcy's assistant just called me. Our accounts have been frozen. Savings and checking. Read."

As I read, he explained to me he'd gone online to shuffle money from one account to another. When it didn't work, he'd called the branch and was told the accounts were on an IRS hold.

"IRS?"

"As of nine this morning, we have no control over anything. While I try to figure this out, you might want to check your personal accounts. If it has something to do with Patrick, all your accounts will be shut down, too, including credit cards; standard operating procedure in the state of California depending on the infraction, and at this point, I don't put anything past him."

"Patrick? It couldn't be."

Alan eyes glinted with anger. "A person is rarely dishonest in one area of life and honest in all the others."

My chest felt so tight I hunched forward. The babies. I forced myself to lean back and breathe. Nothing was worth losing these babies. "What does this mean to us?"

"We have payroll in six days. I've done some calculating and we have thirty grand in equity on the building you own in Berkeley and I've got $10,000 in savings. It's just enough to cover payroll."

"Absolutely not," I told him. "No way you are going to bail out the company because of my idiotic, former husband."

"Would you rather not meet payroll? Besides," Alan continued. "As a partner it doesn't mean I enjoy the benefits when times are good and suck it up when they are bad. The bigger issue is all of our other bills that will come due by the end of the month."

"How do we know this won't be resolved and freed up in a few days?"

"Because I called Bruce. He said in the thirty-plus years of dealing with the IRS, an investigation always takes thirty days to close out, even if the issue is technically resolved in days."

"Thirty days?" I repeated, my voice a ghostly whisper. He nodded. There was no way we'd make it more than a few weeks. "I reverse my earlier opinion. Draw on the equity and I'll take your ten. I'll take care of the rest," I said, though I wasn't quite sure how. I called my banker Darcy and then the credit card companies. Both confirmed the accounts had been locked down. My stockbroker told me my accounts were on a no-sale hold. I had only the money in my wallet, about a hundred bucks.

How could this be happening to me?

I forced myself to stop that line of thought. I'd have a pity-party later. I had assets. Artwork, jewelry, some furniture. Some of the antique shops might pay well for those items.

I started with the owner of a well-known pawnshop located off Columbus Street. He kindly suggested I talk to a broker or antiques dealer in the area. "You'll get more money," he said.

I thanked him for his suggestion and was about to make another call when the phone rang. It was my accountant, Bruce.

"Patrick hasn't filed an income tax return in six years," he informed me. "He owes more than $60,000 in taxes, plus interest and penalties that notch it up to over $300,000." I caught my breath. "Lindy, was Patrick a signer on any bank accounts?"

"No. Never has been. On Monday, Alan discovered he was using our business account at Fog City without our permission or authorization." Bruce didn't think the Fog City transactions would be seen as evidence by the IRS as long as his name wasn't on anything else.

"Lindy, I've already provided the IRS documentation showing a clear separation for the business along with your last seven years of tax returns validating a separation of accounts. But we may not be able to get around the last five years of taxes he owes."

"What?" I practically shouted. It was the ultimate irony that Patrick had purposefully excluded me from his financial world, and now I was taking the brunt of his complete lack of responsibility.

"I know, I know," Bruce began, "but the way the IRS works is this: if, at the time the IRS issues its order while the couple is still co-habiting, both are liable. Lindy, you're legally liable because you are living under the same roof at the time the IRS put the hold on the accounts."

I nearly cried out in relief. Today was Wednesday. He'd left Sunday. The divorce paperwork was signed Monday.

Bruce couldn't believe it. "Fax me the documentation right now. I'll call the IRS as soon as we hang up. Do you have anyone who can vouch for him moving out?" I told him about Vanessa. What I didn't tell him about was the miracle of a dream that was now saving the rest of my life from utter devastation. "Give me Vanessa's information and don't move from your desk. Even with this news, we aren't in the clear yet."

You must leave him.

My hand was still shaking when I placed the phone in the cradle. *Thank you, Lord.* I'd rather lose everything and start over than to be under someone else's mountain of debt.

"Okay," Bruce began when he called back, as though the conversation hadn't ended. "Here it is. The IRS accepts you aren't an accomplice in Patrick's dishonesty. But that doesn't mean they can forgo all the protocols. Once they go over the stack of documents I've sent, your case will be closed, but the account freeze won't be lifted for another month."

I hung up and immediately buzzed Alan to update him. Once I told him my news, he gave me his. "We can postpone everything but the big three: the 401(k), the quarterly healthcare and the liability insurance premiums," he said.

I thought of cash-inducing strategies.

"Do what you can to get a two-week extension on all the other bills. We've never been late on a single bill and I'll talk to anyone personally if need be."

"Well," he said, rubbing the top of his head nervously. "You keep saying everything is going to be all right. The one bright spot is that GeorgiaLiman is still going public, but the transfer won't take place in enough time to help us out for this payroll or even maybe months' end."

GeorgiaLiman. Patrick hadn't known about it. Now the paperwork was signed and he couldn't go after it. Neither could the IRS.

Thank you, again.

The car was still three-quarters full of gas and I'd reluctantly agreed with Alan's suggestion to take advantage of the account at Fog City to keep me fed for lunch and dinner, swinging by for a pick-up on the way home. Before I settled down on the couch, the doorbell rang. It was Marina, my housecleaner. Two thoughts struck me: the first was that I didn't have the money to pay her and would have to ask her to come back in a month. The second was that it wasn't Saturday. She shouldn't be here at all. Feeling better that I wouldn't be out of pocket any money, I opened the door.

"This is a surprise. How are you, Marina?"

"Fine, Mrs. Gordon. Just fine." From her darting eyes looking past me, it was clear she wasn't. Her hands were shaking and her warm brown skin looked faded. She glanced over my shoulder, down the hallway again, agitated. After I told her we were alone, I invited her in but she declined. She stayed put, watching me, her eyes welled up with tears.

"Mrs. Gordon," she began with a rush, looking down at the ground. "A few months ago, I was desperate for money. Your watch was lying on the bathroom floor by the tub, and I took it, selling it to help pay bills. When I went to buy it back from the pawnshop, it was gone, so I bought another one just like it. Here it is." She handed me the watch. It looked brand new and had paperwork to go with it. "I'll understand if you fire me. Just please don't tell the police." Before I had a chance to respond, she was turning to go.

"Wait, Marina. What's been happening?" I asked. She had to have a good reason to resort to theft.

"We were broke. We had hospital bills to pay and the rent. We just don't make enough money."

"Don't all your clients pay you like we do?" Her lower lip quivered. She was holding back. "Marina, what is it?"

"He took money from the counter each time you weren't looking, making it less than what we were owed."

"He — Patrick?" I felt the blood drain from my head. Alan was right. Character traits affect all aspects of a person's life, not just one.

"He'd always take the tip money as well."

I swallowed. "How long, Marina?" She looked down at her hands. Her tan skin bore several spots of grey on the top, evidence of working with hard solvents. Grease marks had not yet been removed from her wrists, and a red-soaked bandage above her thumb needed changing. "Marina?" I repeated.

"Almost 9 months."

It amounted to over a thousand dollars. Marina looked down the hallway, then back at me.

"Patrick isn't here anymore, and won't be coming back."

"I'm sorry," Marina said, but we both knew she wasn't. "Mrs. Gordon, I didn't come here asking for more money. I came hoping for your forgiveness. His dishonesty doesn't excuse mine."

A swell of hot shame gushed upward from the base of my neck, creeping into my skull, resting at the back of my head. It wasn't my fault Marina's money was stolen, and I knew desperate people did desperate things. Marina wouldn't have taken the watch had she not witnessed Patrick's example of dishonesty.

"Then we both want to make amends, starting with me. I can't give you the money he took today, but I will soon. I promise you that." Then a thought struck me. "Has your husband found a full-time job yet?" She shook her head and my heart beat faster. I told her that I might have something for Oliver to consider.

At seven, Remus was on my lap and I was ignoring the cries of hunger from my cramping stomach. I now knew the difference between a stress-induced pain and that constant, incessant hunger caused by the progesterone.

It had been a long, horrid three days, and the week was only half-over. The revelation of Patrick's illegal usage of our corporate account at Fog City, the revelation of a mistress, divorce papers, frozen bank accounts and the cherry on the top of a turd ice cream sandwich, Patrick stealing from our housekeeper was a horror story. I'm all for learning life's lessons, but do they have to come all at once?

The doorbell rang again and I could see two figures on my landing.

"Coming," I yelled, rising up slowly, turning on more lights as I ventured to the front door.

"Hi," I said, touching my hair self-consciously. Jackson stood beside Ronnie who glanced inside. "Don't tell me you lost Bondo again?" It broke the ice and I invited the men in. Ronnie was reluctant and I pre-empted the question as I'd done with Marina. "I'm alone, so come join me as I sit down."

Jackson sat adjacent to me while Ronnie walked to the sliding glass doors. "What a great view," he enthused, and I told him he was welcome to go outside. As he strolled around the deck, Jackson admired the artwork on the walls. The light from the bay glanced off his shirt, a woven square pattern of greens, and a perfect contrast with dark-blue cashmere sport coat.

"How's Bondo?" I asked politely, wondering what other surprises I was in for today.

"Tearing up the place, as usual," Jackson replied, giving me a warm smile. "He needs a playmate, or a person at home with him."

"It's dog attention deficit disorder," Ronnie interjected, joining Jackson on the couch. "Great pieces," he added, nodding appreciatively at my favorite watercolor above my head. "What's missing here?" he asked, pointing at a spot on the wall with a hook but no picture.

"I had an original mixed art bowl with intricate gold-leaf lining, and a really great pattern from inlaid cloth, but clearly Patrick decided it was the one piece he couldn't live without. Well, that, and one of my cats. But I'm sure you didn't come by to hear about the drama in my life."

"He's gone? For good?" Jackson asked, hope and skepticism mixed in his lilting eyebrow and voice.

"He moved out Sunday night. Divorce papers signed Monday." I didn't bother to temper either tone or content of my response. Ronnie leaned forward, his elbows on his knees, fingers clasped.

"Well, the reason we are here is to apologize to you for being judgmental jerks about Bondo. It was very kind of you to take care of him. Without your care, Bondo would have been run over and we'd be devastated." Jackson put a hand on Ronnie's shoulder. "Now knowing what you must have been dealing with on Friday, then finding out about the twins — it was that day, right? — then having to deal with our issues that were … how shall we say, misdirected. So shall we let bygones be bygones and now just be friends?"

"Deal. I could really use some right now."

Ronnie eyed my piano. "You play?" I nodded. "Mind?"

"Take it away." Ronnie sat down at the baby grand and started playing a jazz piece, in the vein of David Brubeck, and then effortlessly transitioned to classical.

"Show off," Jackson said, admiration and love in his voice. Ronnie grinned and kept playing a few more minutes then stopped.

"Not a bad instrument," he said.

"It's good enough for me to practice on. Until I get better, I don't deserve a nicer one."

"Honey, even humble instruments can produce beautiful music." Jackson stood, telling me to stay seated. "If you ever want to moonlight as a decorating consultant, give me a ring. Your taste fits our clientele dead on." I had no idea where he worked and asked.

"DeLuca's."

"It's not listed," offered Ronnie, as though he was sharing a secret. "It's by invitation only." Jackson kept his eyes on mine, ignoring the jibe.

"What he means is that we cater to a unique group of interior designers and buyers who have someone represent them, as opposed to coming in themselves."

I thought about the calls I'd made to the pawnbrokers, the rejections from the antiques dealers. DeLucas was high net worth people. The two were going out to dinner and a late movie, leaving not long after.

After the two left, I laid down on the couch, stretching my legs to alleviate the pains in my abdomen. I'd call first thing tomorrow morning to call him about selling some artwork for me.

Thank you. Again.

My personal life was falling apart, and tomorrow I'd be selling most of my possessions. What more could happen?

CHAPTER 15

The next morning, Jackson answered on the second ring. "Well, that was fast."

"Not for me," I replied, imitating his jovial attitude but failing. I'd woken up at 6 with nervous tension.

"You ready to moonlight already?"

"I may have to if you can't help me."

"What's up?" his voice was now serious.

I got to the point. "I need a substantial amount of money fast and want to sell the artwork you admired yesterday, along with anything else that will help me out financially."

Silence. I wanted to defend myself, to tell him I had been making it on my own, that I was self-sufficient and responsible, not dependent on an irresponsible, unfaithful former husband. But justifying myself would consume valuable time and not change the situation one bit. I was past being mortified. I was in survival mode.

"I'll tell you what went down with Patrick when we have the luxury. Suffice it to say that his dishonest actions have put me in financial jeopardy and my accounts are on hold. To keep my business afloat, I need a lot of cash in twenty-four hours."

"Whew, okay, I'm sure I can help. What I'll need to do is come over again and take an inventory of everything you want to sell. When can I do it?"

"Are you free now?"

Jackson looked dapper in brown silk-and-linen pants paired with a deep-blue oxford shirt. His cufflinks sparkled in the morning light.

"This will take a little while," he told me.

I sat down on the couch and watched him catalog the items in my house as I answered questions. First, the oil paintings and then the three chalk drawings, and a black-and-white charcoal original. He keenly gauged not just the art itself, but the inlaid frames that I'd had made by a custom shop in Sonoma.

"What about this one?" He pointed to the 2-by-3 woodcut print of a jazz player. I'd bought it in New Orleans as a gift for my first piano teacher. When she died eight years ago, her will specified that it should be returned to me, and it had been above my piano ever since.

"I can probably quadruple whatever you paid. Do you remember?" The piece was my first major acquisition, and the biggest single amount I'd spent on a nonessential item in my life.

"Four thousand —six years ago." Twelve months before Patrick.

"It was worth every penny. Few contemporary U.S.-based artists work with wood. I bet this will be the first to go. Then again, I like it so much I might need to find a place for it on my own wall." When he'd finished tallying the items in the living room, I brought out my jewelry box.

"The case alone will get a few thousand." A fleeting tug of pride made me want to say no. But I knew I couldn't afford that luxury.

"It's all yours."

He separated the pieces by category, rings first and then watches and then matching sets, earrings, bracelets and necklaces. He set aside non-name brand sets, preferring the Tiffany pieces and several heirloom ring sets. He held a loupe to his eye, reflecting light through each stone he examined, spending quite a bit of time on an inlaid ivory profile ring with matching drop earrings.

"These are exquisite. Illegal now to create new pieces of ivory. But even if it was still legal, these would be rare." He tabulated the items on his calculator. "Adding in the jewelry, assuming you put in your grandmother's pieces, I can give you $53,500."

"But you said the one piece in the living room was worth $16,000 alone."

"I'm subtracting what my firm needs to make on the transactions, which ranges from 15 to 25 percent. We basically cut what you give us in half and then we add our mark-up back in." He grimaced a bit apologetically. "I am giving you a bit more than we would normally." Even with his generosity, he could sense that the numbers disappointed me.

"I appreciate that, really." It could have been a lot worse.

"Oh, wait. What about the chair you're sitting on?" Jackson looked down, stood up and inspected it from every angle. He told me it was worth $1,500, about a quarter of what I paid for it.

"I'll take it."

"There is one last thing," he said, hesitating. "What about your wedding ring, Lindy? That's not included in the total." How ironic that I'd completely forgotten about it. I'd not worn it since leaving the hospital. The band had been cut off my finger and getting it fixed had fallen to the bottom of my priority list, then off entirely.

I nodded my approval and Jackson lifted it up. The ring had a 3-karat princess-cut diamond as the center stone and two 2-karat trillion-cut diamonds on either side of delicate hearts. Patrick and I had agreed he'd buy the stones and I'd buy the setting. The setting was platinum and gold, an intricate design I'd found in a magazine I'd paid $9,000. But I figured it was a bargain since Patrick told me the stones were $75,000, a good deal because he got them through a friend in the wholesale business.

Jackson asked me what I paid for the setting. I told him. He set the ring back down in the case. "Keep the setting. It's a classic design. But the stones aren't worth much."

"Are they poor quality?" Perhaps Patrick scrimped on the color. It couldn't have been the clarity. He was such a snob about those things.

Jackson grimaced. "Lindy, they're fake. Cubic zirconium, all three." My mortification left no easy segue to another topic. I told myself to stay calm.

"I'll have everything inventoried this afternoon and have a check cut late tonight or first thing tomorrow morning," he said, politely avoiding my expression.

I was stunned. Patrick had lied to me from before we were married, about the very symbol of our marriage. It was a fake. All of it.

"Lindy?"

"Right," I said, doing my best to recover. My mouth was sticky and dry. "The sooner the better," I said in a monotone. "He left me in a bit of a catastrophic situation. You don't want the watches?"

He shook his head. "My clientele won't buy used watches unless they are antique. Keep them or worst case, pawn them."

With this money, I was still $12,000 short according to Alan's calculations, but it might be enough to keep the company afloat.

Thank you, Bondo, for escaping from your yard so I could save you.

"Will I be able to buy any of my things back?"

"Not at the price I'm buying it from you. I'd have to sell at list." Another punch to my gut. I'd be left with the clothes on my back and a few watches to show for all my efforts of the past nine years.

They are only possessions, I repeated to myself. I had my grandmother's memory, I didn't need her earrings and ring. If she were watching now, she'd agree.

"Just tell me when your van is coming for the stuff, Jackson. I'll be here to open the door."

I spent the night crying with no warm arms around me, nor dreams of deceased relatives to ease the pain.

As I drove to the office Friday morning, all I wanted to do was talk to someone I loved.

I hit the speed dial. When the line picked up, I nearly dropped it on the floor. "Charlie, where've you been my whole life?" I cried, relieved that my brother had answered his phone. "Is it really you?"

"It's me. And you probably hear my backup singer." I heard his young son Max singing above the loud rock music playing on the car's CD. I apologized for calling him during his daddy-son time, though he immediately dismissed it.

"It's me who should be apologizing. After I left you that message a few weeks ago, I've been knee-deep in legal proceedings with my former wife, finding reliable daycare — you know. Or you don't. Then I figured the reason you weren't returning my messages was because you were pissed at me. I'm sorry."

"Don't be sorry!" I struggled to keep my voice even. "And what voice messages? I've not received a single one!" I thought of the messages Ann' said she left as well. "The one and only voice message I got was the day of the accident."

"What accident?" The jolt of anger held my tears in check. Was there anything Patrick had not lied about? First I told Charlie about the accident and then the entire sequence of events, up to and including the fake diamond ring. "You can say 'I told you so' now."

"Lindy. I married a woman I met in rehab, remember? The day I left you the message I realized she'd taken my son and we were running around with the police trying to find her. So as much of a jerk as Patrick is, consider yourself lucky you didn't find all this out after you had your kids."

I had to blink back tears as he spoke. In the middle of his crisis, he'd remembered me. "Have you heard from Dad?"

"With the money you sent him, he paid the taxes on the cabin, so thank you, for mom and dad and me. He used the rest to buy some patents from a guy in San Diego."

I was so glad I acted on the prompting to send the money. If I hadn't, it would have been frozen up with everything else. But how many more difficult situations was I going to face where it was too late?

That question lingered as I exited the elevator and into the entryway.

"Is that really you?" I asked Sam. She giggled, sitting tall in her chair.

Gone was the raccoon eye-liner that used to rim her lashes. Her clean, smooth ivory skin had a thin layer of foundation, a hint of blush and mascara only at the tips of her lashes. Sam's hair was parted on the side, straightened as smooth as corn silk, framing her oval face. She wore a lavender sweater over a black lace top, her neckline concealed with a black scarf accented with bursts of fuchsia, blue and green. The look was transformative.

"All of this because you have found yourself a nice man, and together you are going to heal the sick and convert the weary?"

She stopped her laugh short and stood. "Can I carry your purse? You look rather grey today." My face felt hot, dots of sweat lined the back of my neck.

"I should have gone slower." What else was I going to say? I'm running out of time to keep my company afloat.

She brought me a glass of water and under the desk, I slipped off my tight shoes, groaning with relief.

"I found a person who might be perfect for Kay and the work she needs done at her home," I told Sam as she sat down across from me. I told her about Oliver, and she practically pranced out of the office, excited by another area where we were helping the center.

"You ready for another piece of news?" Alan asked, knocking on my door as he walked in the room.

"Don't tell me anything bad right now," I said, only half-kidding, the fragility of my emotions bubbling to the surface.

"Nope. This is excellent." His voice sounded uncommonly giddy. "I spoke to Stacy today. Guess who came in to Fog City last night."

"No."

"With his girlfriend." He paused. "Sorry, Lindy."

"Don't be. My life — though slightly unbalanced right now — is so much better than his will ever be."

"It gets better. Stacy told the staff about the twins. They encouraged him to drink up, treated him like a king. He went on for two hours, wining and dining like a celebration. Orders champagne, the works. The bill comes, and it's over $500. He tells Stacy to put in on his tab, 'as usual.'" Alan paused for effect. "So Stacy says, 'Gee, Patrick, So Stacy says, 'Gee, Patrick, we learned that you aren't an officer at your former wife's company and weren't authorized on the account. So for this, and all future bills, we accept cash or a credit card with your name and one other form of identification."

I brought my hand to my mouth, grinning. "What'd he do?"

"Turned red-faced as his girlfriend looked away. But it gets better. His credit cards were frozen as well, and he only had a hundred and change on him. She actually had to pay the bill! Can you believe his nerve? Thinking he could put it on your tab in the midst of his financial nuclear meltdown?"

It was unbelievable—for a normal person, but I guess not for Patrick. And paybacks were nice, but they don't erase pain or create happiness.

In turn, I told Alan about the fire sale at my apartment. "So here we are, keeping up the front to the employees and running on fumes, figuratively and literally."

He shook his head with admiration. "You do that really well."

The next stop was going to be the pawn shop. I had to cover meals and gas, plus I had Marina to take care of. I was now going to experience exactly what my father had when he was forced to sell his collection to pay his debts—the very ones I could have taken care of had I not been so hell-bent on getting him back for how he treated Patrick.

Funny how life is. We mock what we don't understand, and then get to experience it ourselves.

CHAPTER 16

Jackson worked fast on his end and at four p.m. I had a cashier's check in hand. Combined with ten grand from Alan and the $3,500 I'd gotten from pawning my two Cartier's and Rolex, it was almost enough to cover our bills. It also represented all the possessions of my former life.

Alan left to make the deposit as I reviewed my assets yet again. I couldn't turn in the car. It was leased. It would cost me more money to break the lease than to keep it.

Monson. The money. He might have gotten the letter today, though it was a long shot — a shot I needed to take.

"Monson here," he answered gruffly.

"Hi, Monson, it's Lindy Gordon. How are you?"

"Fine thank you, Miss Lindy. And yourself?" he said as politely as if we'd been talking daily.

"Monson," I began, searching for the words then opting for blunt honesty. "You haven't returned my calls for a month and a half and your company hasn't paid us. This isn't usual behavior for you. I have to ask, is everything okay?"

Monson's silence was so long that I heard the traffic in the background.

"The business has been a struggle, Lindy," he said finally. "We couldn't get our product to our retailers, and then revenue plummeted. I got just a bit of funding in but it wasn't enough to pay your full bill. So, I wasn't even going to bother. Then, on a personal note, my daughter— she committed suicide. She was thirteen. A beautiful girl."

Bereft of words, I sought to express my condolences as best I could. "Why didn't tell me before now?"

Monson sighed, the sound of a man who'd aged years in a matter of weeks. "Pride," he said simply. "It's been all I could do to keep my wife from going into a severe depression and help the kids with their homework while I build the business back up. I do have a little money, Lindy, if it will help."

Pride, I thought. I still had a lot but I was learning. "How much can you part with?" I asked humbly. He offered $5,000 out of the $40,000 he owed. He told me I'd get the wire the following day.

"Lindy, before you go, I want to say thank you. You were the only person who didn't threaten to sue me or assume the worst. Your letter…it was personal. It helped." While I couldn't image the lines I wrote were that extraordinary, his words touched me.

The good will I had towards Monson stayed with me through the afternoon. Now, if only one of the phone calls was from John. The notion that he was out there, thinking badly of me for completely unjustifiable reasons gnawed at me.

Not unlike the way I'm chewing my finger, I thought absently. The cuticles of my left hand were practically nonexistent, all due to my officially former husband.

With purpose, I removed a tube of hand cream from my bag and slathered it on my fingers. The indent on the fourth finger of my left hand wasn't as pronounced now, although the white circle was still a stark contrast to the rest of my fingers.

Never. Again. It would be a long, lonely future for me. Finding a man who had the backbone to handle two children that weren't his own was a tall order.

#

Monson was still on my mind later than night when I fell asleep so I shouldn't have been surprised when it was he we saw next, but I was.

Grandfather and I stood on the sidewalk of a two-lane street, the uncut branches of the maple trees poking the 19th-century wrought-iron streetlamps that dotted the sidewalk. Expensive sports cars with out-of-state license plates eased through the 25 mile per hour zone, following worn out pickups loaded with bales of hay. A lone cop watched from his patrol car outside the Pony Express, the single coffee shop in the North Carolina town of Maltby.

A gleaming black Escalade pulled in front of the four story, red-brick building across from the Pony, into a spot marked "Reserved." A black, wrought-iron sign that read "Langton Lodge, Est. 1812." Monson emerged, the afternoon sun absorbed by his black shirt and pants. Light danced from the small diamonds at the corners of his narrow sunglasses. As he made his way up the old stone steps, his shoulders stretched the back of the shirt. His walk to the door was a strut softened by the weight of a man past his prime.

When he stepped inside the front door, Grandfather and I were waiting at the bottom of the stairs. The dark boards groaned with age as he crossed the foyer. Monson held the banister for balance, pausing at each floor level to catch his breath.

"I can do this," he rasped to himself over and over. He avoided looking into the offices, though the doors were open. The antique desks were covered with computers, scattered files, even coffee cups, as if the occupants had just gone out for a stroll, intending to come back. When he reached the fourth floor, he headed directly to a set of 8-foot-high double doors and looked up at the ceiling, committing himself again.

"This is my day. I'm going to make this happen."

Monson's office was as big as my living room. A two-story, brick fireplace centered on the far wall had a line of black soot up the front, evidence of decades of use. A painting of a duck hunt rested on top of the molded mantel. The walls were covered in hand-painted murals, rich, warm greens depicting the gentle landscapes of the famous Eastern Seaboard. An enormous Oriental rug covered the distressed, dark-wood floors. Unlike the other ancient artifacts in the room, the computer on the desk was the latest and a pair of side-by-side 20-inch, flat-panel LCD monitors.

Monson placed his cellphone in a black cradle, touched his computer and sat down in his high-backed, triangle-stitched leather chair. He opened a drawer, retrieving a worn ledger. He turned to accounts payable, the page already three-quarters full. From another drawer he took a stack of unopened bills and a silver Tiffany envelope opener. One by one, he sliced the top of each envelope before reviewing each bill carefully. When he was satisfied, he initialed the bottom right corner, near the total due, and finished by adding a new number to the ledger. I saw my company's name and invoice amount. My bill wasn't as much as some, but it was a lot more than others.

A tap at the door was followed by the entrance of a tall, elegant man wearing an olive green button down shirt that hung over his linen pants, his leather loafers making barely a sound as he crossed the floor.

"You got my message? I had to remind you of this, but you need to call her," the man said. Monson set the bills aside. He opened a drawer and pulled out a stack of unopened greeting cards. I saw that his hands were shaking. "Monson," the man said again, sitting directly across from him. "She could kill the article with a single phone call, one that we desperately need to run. It's our only chance to keep awareness up. We've run out of money for marketing."

Monson pretended not to hear. He opened one of the cards. Over his shoulder, I read with him: "We are sorry for your loss." On the inside of the card was a bright pink flower. Underneath was a handwritten note:

We'll miss Jolene. She was a beautiful girl. We love you and your family. Anything we can do to help, Love, Benny and Gillian

"Monson!" the man nearly shouted. This time, Monson looked up.

"I heard you, Miles" he said quietly. "That's why I won't call her. It will guarantee she does it. This way, it might slip by her."

"Nothing slips by Lindy Gordon, Monson. My staff and I have a log of calls, emails and texts from her staff and herself. It's been a month now. It's going to get ugly."

Monson picked up another letter. By the slowness with which he opened each subsequent card, I could tell it was getting harder and harder. Each one expressed condolences for Jolene. I realized then I didn't know the names of his four children. I guess I'd never asked.

"You're not even giving her a chance," Miles said fiercely. "I think she'd listen to your situation and be fair, maybe even give you an extension. You have no idea if she's been through something like this herself."

Monson pulled a picture from the left drawer, a family photo in an ornate silver frame. A small black-and-white photo was taped in the bottom right corner. It was the type of photo you'd take in an arcade booth, four for a dollar. His daughter's teeth were covered with braces, her smile wide, full of life. Monson fiddled with the tape and removed the photo, first holding it at eye level, then turned it around for Miles to see.

"You think she's been through death? Anything near to what I'm going through?"

Miles drew a deep breath. "What I meant was experiencing financial stress. I'm sure she has. All small businesses do at one time or another." His look was pleading. "Give her a chance."

Monson held the small picture in both hands, finally looking up. "No. I won't beg for her to give me time. I can't do it Miles. I've lost a daughter and am on the brink of losing my company. I won't lose my self-respect too."

Miles said nothing, but left, shutting the door behind him.

For a few seconds, Monson sat still. Then he put his elbows on the surface of the grand desk and placed his head in his hands. His shoulders caved in and he sobbed.

One moment we were the room with the weeping man and the next, we were out on the street. The crisp air of fall was around us, leaves of bright yellows and oranges rustling, making the only sounds I heard.

"You did good," Grandfather said.

"Sending him the letter?"

"More than that. You also gave him the benefit of the doubt."

I held down a ball of regret that had lodged itself in my throat. "I guess I've never been too good at giving people credit or questioning circumstances when someone acted out of the ordinary. Having perspective can be pretty hard."

"You didn't have a lot of examples growing up."

Suddenly the cool East coast weather was replaced by warm, Southern California. Grandfather and I sat to one side of an empty baby seat in the back of a sedan.

"Where are we going?" demanded a man in the front passenger seat. My brother Charlie slowed the vehicle as we approached a corner before he revved the powerful engine on the straightaway. Another turn and we were on the ramp to the freeway.

"We're going to find my ex-wife and child," stated my brother, his jaw clenched, the muscles rippling under his cheeks. Day old stubble skipped over the skin on either side of his chin. The Spanish ancestry came through in him as it did on my dad: neither of them could grow a complete beard. A goatee was impossible, the effort ending up as a wispy splotch of hair. "And if you're going to report me for missing the AA meeting, I'll slow the car down enough so you can roll out on the grass."

The man lit a cigarette, prompting my brother to roll down the window. Charlie gunned it to 80, the air tunneling the smoke out of the car before it had a chance to make its way to the back seat.

"Getting a ticket isn't going to help us get there faster, Charlie." The car slid in and out of the lanes on the six-lane freeway with ease.

"This is L.A. The cops ticket you if you're not going 80 in the fast lane." He pulled off, turning into the parking lot of the International House of Pancakes. "Look for Lana's purple Volkswagen with a baby seat in the back."

Lana and Charlie had met at an AA meeting at the local YMCA. Both were recovering addicts: he for alcohol, she for drugs. After she got pregnant and they married, Lana started disappearing from the accounting office where she worked for an hour or two here and there. At first Charlie thought she was using again, but she tested clean. Her erratic behavior affected her work until she was let go from her bookkeeping job. But as an accountant, she was able to work from home, keeping the books for a couple of clients. It worked until she got pregnant.

That's when her mood swings started. A few times, Charlie came home at lunch to find an empty house. Lana couldn't recall what she'd done or where she'd been, accusing him of being a jealous husband. By month five, she would leave for days at a time without explanation. During the end of her pregnancy, Lana's doctor took another blood sample, which showed drugs in her system. When the doctor called Charlie, Lana lost control, actually hitting the doctor with two nurses barely able to restrain the 5-foot-4 tornado. At the advice of his attorney, and with the support of her parents, Lana was put on house probation to ensure she didn't harm herself or the life of their unborn child.

Only then did Lana's parents gave Charlie the medical history of their daughter and he understood the full extent of her problems. She had a 20-year history of bipolar schizophrenia. When she stopped taking her medications, the imbalance in her system made her paranoid, so fearful that those around her were trying to take her life that she stopped taking her pills entirely. The bright side, Charlie later told us, was that her refusing to take her prescriptions was probably the only reason Max was strong, healthy, as far as anyone could tell, a developmentally normal child.

Through it all, Charlie's performance on the job hadn't suffered. In fact, his ability to make his sales quota had improved. He skipped lunch meetings and avoided traveling out of town if he could help it. His boss rewarded him with a pay increase and a new title. Instead of buying a car or taking a vacation, Charlie sought marriage counseling. We all expected his marriage to get better. Instead, it got worse.

"When did she disappear?" the passenger asked. "And is this going to trigger a relapse?"

"Don't know. The daycare said she picked up Max at 10:30, and no, don't worry. Stressful situations tend to make me more lucid not desperate for a drink." The man eyed my brother carefully, then looked at the time. It was now quarter past 3. I guessed the man must be my brother's AA sponsor from his look and watchful eyes. "My ex, on the other hand, goes the opposite direction, as you know. She called a couple of times today, less coherent in each message."

Charlie paused to press a button on his cell phone.

"Dr. Watts, it's Charlie. She's gone again. This time she's taken Max. I've been chasing her around Los Angeles for the past five hours… Kidnapping? Is that really necessary? Okay. Can you do it, then? You're her doctor...Yeah. Thanks. I'll just keep driving around."

"Police?" the passenger asked.

"Watts is calling them. If I do it, they won't respond as fast. He has no choice but to call it kidnapping."

"Won't matter," said his sponsor, flicking his cigarette butt out the window. "If she's not on her meds, she won't care. Speaking of which, how'd she get Max in the first place?"

"Every other Thursday is half-days at the daycare. She picked him up and they gave him to her because she is his mother."

My brother had refused to have his wife institutionalized, even when her parents begged him to commit her. Instead, he enlisted her doctors to test and retest her and explore alternative therapies. But Charlie gave up when Lana told him she didn't want to take care of Max anymore and that she'd relinquish custody. That's when Charlie reluctantly filed for divorce.

Charlie took a call on his cell. "Yes, I know where it is. I'm on my way." Turning to his companion, he said the police had tracked her cell phone. "She's at the zoo." He flipped the car around, gunned it and headed back onto the freeway. "Dial Lindy, will you? She's in the address book." When the phone rang, Charlie took it back.

"Hi Lindy, it's Charlie. How are you? Just wanted to call again. Hadn't heard back from you this week." His voice was friendly, even a bit lively. Had I not been sitting in the back seat, witnessing these events firsthand, I would have thought he was out walking in the sunshine. "You usually get back to me fast. Anyway, hope all is well. Call me."

"Who's that?"

"My sister." My throat tightened. Although Charlie had his demons, caring for those he loved wasn't one of them.

"I don't recall meeting her at the wedding."

"She wasn't there, but it wasn't because I didn't invite her. I think it was because she wouldn't leave that prick of a husband at home and come by herself."

His friend took a drag on his cigarette. "Bad options."

"Let me tell you something. Lana was crazy — is crazy. But I know she loves me. And when she's taking her meds, she's the sweetest person in the world. That's why I fell in love with her in the first place. But Patrick…"

"You worry she's being abused?"

Charlie rolled down the windows again. "Not physically, no, but I wonder if ignoring someone is a form of emotional abuse. I can't say I really know what's going on. I've been a pretty pathetic brother. Didn't call her for the better half of a decade, and all the while she remembered every holiday in the book. I've got enough macramé Easter eggs and Halloween plates to start a gift shop. But no matter what, she always calls me back. That's how I know something's wrong."

"Why's she still with him?"

Charlie shook his head. "Probably doesn't want to be seen as a failure."

His sponsor lit another cigarette. "You should tell her we're all failures.

The only difference is that some failures are more public than others."

My brother sped up and around a slow moving car in the fast lane. "When I was getting in deeper with the alcohol, closing the family out, she kept calling, writing, stopping by when she was in town. At the time it made me mad. I had to hit rock bottom on my own time, my own terms, and I had to be the one to change. No one else could do it for me. And when I started to come back up, she was still there, like always. So, I call, leave her a message, tell her I love her. And I'll keep doing it for a decade if I have to."

"There they are," said his friend, pointing to the blue-and-red flashing lights from three patrol cars surrounding the purple Volkswagen outside the zoo.

Charlie pulled off the freeway. "Let's go get my son."

CHAPTER 17

The following morning the doorbell rang with such consistency I knew it wasn't going to stop until I got up. It was Marina, her hands full of food.

"I brought this for you," she said, politely ignoring my hair in a ponytail and pajamas. "Not too much sugar. My favorite Brazilian dessert."

"Please, come in," I said, inviting her inside. With the wire from Monson I'd have 5,500 in the bank, more than enough to cover the bills for two weeks. Alan had wholeheartedly agreed that paying Marina what she was owed was the right thing to do. I gave her an envelope filled with $100 dollar bills. "I also have something else." I gave her a card with Kay's information and told her what it meant, she nearly broke down crying. "She's expecting Oliver's call for a job and can meet with him today. You can call him with my phone if you want."

I went out on the deck to give her privacy. The sailboats were out in force. It was a warm morning, the sun shining brightly on the bay. It had not been all that long ago that I'd been the one down on the Embarcadero, taking morning walks with my cousin Ann, smiling at those rollerblading on the flat pavement, grabbing a croissant at the San Francisco sourdough bakery. When Patrick had entered my life, those walks with Ann had stopped and my strolls with him had begun, peppered with stops in bookstores and galleries. It had been a life of material things. The cars, the clothes, the apartment. The art on the walls was bright and shiny, expensive and worthless, just like Patrick.

In regretful hindsight, I'm sure I didn't recognize it as a negative, if I had seen it at all, because it had become the norm.

Marina excitedly told me her husband would be calling Kay directly and we embraced, the feeling of renewal strong and sincere.

The weekend was free of appointments and dreams. Perhaps Grandfather knew that I was going to experience overload at some point. Another possibility was that I was more receptive when I had less sleep. My barriers were down, my sensitivity higher.

I checked in with Ann, asking if she was free.

"If you can believe it, Jared got a new job. Tonight is an informal couples dinner." She sounded so enthusiastic, I didn't want to bring her down with my news. Congratulating her, I suggested getting together later in the week if she was free.

"Yes, and I'll bring lasagna."

Vanessa returned my call, the line crackling because she was calling from a plane. She had a fashion show to attend in London and would be back the following Friday.

Alone and lonely, I held Remus. It had been three weeks since the date of my accident, and I wondered how Dr. Redding would respond to all that had happened.

On Monday morning at eight a.m., I had my appointment with my OB doctor. As Dr. Kustin waved the wand, the creases in the center of his eyes deepened and his jowls turned down.

"This is worse than the last time you were here," he said, pointing to a large black mass on the screen. "If this grows a few more millimeters, you will lose both. Was I not clear?"

"But I've been off my feet entirely," I stammered. "Only driving to and from work."

"But you are walking, are up and about. The progesterone doesn't work if the host isn't cooperating. You want these babies? You are now on bed rest. You get up only to use the bathroom, that's it. Keep food by your bedside or have it brought to you." His adamant look of concern hit me hard.

I drove directly home, calling Alan from the car. After we discussed the mechanics of me continuing to work from home, I affirmed he was handling the operations of the company, just as he'd done while I was recovering. "At least you're prepared this time around."

"We are still a few grand shy for our end of the month bills," Alan said, his voice sober. "I'm going to call a few of the outstanding prospects that are waiting to make decision about whether to move forward with our company and sweeten the deal if that's okay."

"It will all work out, Alan. Have a little faith."

Ann brought by take-out before she picked up her kids from school and threw in a batch of laundry before hustling to get her kids. When I apprised Charlie of my situation, he told me he'd locate my favorite chocolate and send me a care package. Vanessa sent a text in response to my update, telling me she'd found the best lingerie for pregnant women in her present location of London, and that all the Victoria Secret's models who were pregnant swore by them.

"As if that's going to do me any good," I said out loud to myself, already changing into my lounge wear which were glorified pajamas. I put my hair back in a ponytail and started working on the items waiting in my email.

At noon, Sam called.

"You have had several calls from John, who is getting rather insistent about talking to you. First I told him you were out, then I told him you wouldn't be coming in for the foreseeable future."

"Did you pass him to Alan?"

"John said he needed to speak with you. That it was personal."

The phrase hung in the air.

"What did you say?"

"That I needed your permission to give him your cell phone."

"Sure, why not?" I said without enthusiasm.

"Lindy, I don't think he's going to be rude. He sounded rather…contrite."

"Yeah, and he might, but it's not that. I just hate phone calls like this. At least in person you can see the facial expressions and get the full read behind the words."

"You do have a point," Sam empathized. "By the way, I found a notary that is able to make a home visit. That okay with you?" I told him it was, unconcerned with my appearance and state of attire. The individual would be in, notarize the stock certificate transfers for the GeorgiaLiman stock and be out the door in five minutes.

With the lessened volume of emails I found myself surfing Pregnancy.com. Time went quickly as I waited for the notary, who rang the doorbell at two p.m.

"Coming," I called in what I hoped was a voice loud enough for the notary to hear me through the front walls. I slowly made my way to the door, straightened my top and opened the door.

I stared in shock.

"Hi Lindy." It was John Abrahms. My outfit. My hair. "I guess you weren't expecting me," he said, the sound of his voice like his feet, on the precipice of staying or leaving. I noticed the canvas and leather messenger bag over his shoulder.

"You're the notary?" His eyes held mine.

"You still need one, don't you?" Damn Sam! *Damn her*! My mind was telling me to speak, and do it fast.

"Yes, very much so. Please, come in." I stepped back from the entry way, gesturing him through the door as I shut it after him. I led the way, slowly, past the piano and around to the other side of the coffee table. My discomfort multiplied, knowing he was behind me, perhaps looking at the barren walls or my expanding derriere.

"I promise this isn't my usual way of greeting people who come to my house," I said, glancing over my shoulder.

"Sam indicated you would be alone and I should help with any walking you need to do."

I was already lowering myself down when I stopped, thinking of my briefcase back in my bedroom. The uncoordinated act caught me in a bend, and I gasped as a cramp hit my side. He dropped his shoulder bag and was immediately at my elbow, one hand on my lower back, the other holding me steady.

"Easy. There you go." I bit my lip, nodding. "Ok, lower down slowly. I'll take the pressure off your back and legs."

Warmth had replaced the distant professionalism, the tone of comfort a parent gives to a child starting to fall over on a bike.

"You need a minute? Some water?" he asked me, glancing at the kitchen but not before I caught the dark speckles in his hazel eyes. Unexpected emotion welled up within my chest and I forced it back down again. I shook my head.

"Just a sec," I said. The movement had sent spikes of pain up through my chest; his unwarranted kindness sending pangs of loss and grief to my heart. "Thank you…for helping me." I looked up, hesitant.

"The look on your face," he began, sounding equally uncertain.

"It's not the pain. It's actually you, here in my apartment. It's all a bit odd," I said honestly, the absurdity of the situation lifting my mood ever so slightly. "Well, that and your facial hair. It's changed."

"That must mean you don't totally hate me for what I said when we spoke on the phone. I'm sorry about that. Very much so. It's why I kept pestering Sam. I wanted to apologize."

"Sorry to tell you this, but with all that's happened in my life recently, a well connected, slightly famous executive being mad at me didn't even rate in my top five."

John's tense look eased, but he still leaned forward, as though to be prepared in case I needed his assistance. "You can relax, but don't expect me to. I'm pregnant and in my pajamas while you are—well, perfectly normal, looking like you are straight out of an urban catalog. Well, except for the hair thing again. Is that called a Go or a T, because I don't think it's quite filled in enough to be a full goatee."

My comment broke the tension and he laughed. "I am a hodgepodge of European ancestry, which is evident by my seeming inability to grow facial hair. And you are right there with my daughter, who says to do one or the other since the lines aren't connecting. But back to my apology," he said, leaning forward again. "I truly am sorry for misjudging you. I had no idea you were in the middle of a personal hailstorm."

"Forgiven, as long as you don't charge me a notary fee. Fair?" At that, he smiled and nodded, sitting back. He was right next me, having not moved after he helped me down. "Actually, to be fair," I said, emphasizing the word, now that I was becoming more comfortable in his presence, "I don't think you need to apologize for getting angry at a man who is now my former husband." Whatever John was going to say was halted by my comment.

"Did I…did my coming to your offices cause that?"

"That would be hilariously tragic, wouldn't it?" Consciously or not, John looked at my left hand then caught my eye.

"If it wasn't me…was it because of your work with the center?"

"No, I believe the ultimate trigger was getting pregnant." I emitted a laugh but it came out broken, just like the relationship had been. But that was then and this is now, I told myself, brightening. "And I can't believe I'm telling you all this. I should be so embarrassed!"

He watched me, his humor tempered with concern. "But you're not."

"The last three weeks have revealed I wasn't quite as smart or insightful as I thought I was. So," I said, changing the subject. "Shall we do the paperwork? I'm sure you have actual work to do today that doesn't include sitting here with a homebound pregnant woman."

John cracked a smile. "I like your attitude."

"It's about all I have left." He continued to look at me and I felt a flush spread across my chest, and up to my neck. "Oh, you're waiting for me. What do you need?"

"The documents that need to be notarized and your driver's license." John had a look of disbelief as I put my hand behind my rear and pushed to the edge of the couch. "You're a stubborn one," he observed, placing his hand on my leg, the unspoken command non-negotiable. "I'll get it for you."

"No. No way," I argued. "You are not going into my den of despair for my purse." John's laughter was louder than I expected and playful, like a rock skipping across the water. He stood, ignoring me.

"I've got a pre-teen daughter. You cannot conceive what that place looks like after a sleepover."

"Of course I can!" I countered. "I was a teenage daughter once and I know exactly what the rooms look like." I didn't care about his daughter's underwear on the floor, I cared about mine. As if he were reading my mind, his lips formed a wicked smile.

"This is going to kill you isn't it?"

"It might," I admitted, my voice croaking. He shook his head, walking away.

"On the dresser, the far side of room," I called after him. I counted the seconds until he returned.

John handed me my purse, preparing to sit down when he scrutinized my face. "You look pale. I'm going to get you something to drink," he announced, leaving before I could say a word.

"Juice? Milk?" John asked, poking his head around the corner, pausing at the open doorway to the kitchen. He'd been in my room and didn't seem the worse for it. Now he was in my kitchen.

"Orange juice would be great." I heard him opening doors.

"No OJ. You're out. Water will have to do." The ice machine cranked on, followed by the sound of running water. My emotions collided, discomfort with gratitude, interest and caution. Had my self-esteem bottomed out so bad I felt awkward being on the receiving end of common respect?

"Fluids," he said, his voice coming from my right. I nodded silently, blinking back the tears before I turned to him. He handed me the water, taking in my facial expression.

"I should know better than to ask a pregnant woman about her feelings, but I never was very good with ignoring what's right in front of me."

I took a drink, nodding again, getting myself together. "You'd look like this, too, if some stranger went into your bedroom without time to straighten up." John gave me a look of skepticism, but he didn't press me to elaborate.

"And can you get the paperwork?" I pointed to my dining room table. When he returned, he set my briefcase by me and I removed the pages for him. We were interrupted by my phone ringing. He handed it to me before I could ask and when I saw the caller, I asked John if he minded.

"And I won't hear a thing, like any good man."

It was Vanessa, informing me she'd picked up more clothes for my to-be-born children. "It's Hermes," she said, her voice lacking any smugness. Only Vanessa could say the word Hermes using the same inflection as Target. "I'll make a drop off sometime this week."

John spoke after I set down the phone. "I didn't know the RAC remix was on a ringtone," John said, referring to the Lana Del Ray that had played.

"It isn't," I answered coyly.

"Then how'd you get it?"

"I have friends in low places."

He blinked. "Is that legal?"

"Probably not, but then, we do live in the middle of dance club central. Smart engineers. Lots of Red Bull. Ringtones will happen. But lest you think I'm a complete thief given to copyright infringement, I'm not reselling or distributing unlicensed music. It is for my own personal use."

I'd said the words with the monotone inflection of a voice-over recording of a legal definition. He laughed again. "I need to get in with your crowd."

"You can take me to the Museum of Modern Art next spring and I'll get you a ringtone for free."

The words were out of my mouth before I had time to think. A quick, sassy comment that erupted so naturally I didn't have time to put a muzzle on.

"You're on." And that was that. I'd just made him a trade for a date and he accepted. My heart rate dropped, and then shot up like a rock out of a slingshot.

John, on the other hand, acted as though nothing out of the ordinary had just occurred. He proceeded to lay out the paperwork, separating the pages by the tags noted for the signature. He retrieved his seal from his bag, placing it to the right of his ledger and insisted on holding the pad in front of me while I signed. Each time he leaned close, I felt his warm breath and inhaled the smell of his cologne. He gave no indication of the content on the pages, a relief and disappointment at the same time. I was doing a whole lot of good for my employees, and a fragile, but prideful part of me wanted him to know it.

"Are you going to be staying here until the baby is born? It's got great views and a perfect floor plan."

"Spoken like the real estate professional you are," I commented, adding that I hadn't really thought about it. "My lease isn't up for another six months, but then…" I stopped. My name was on the lease alone. Not Patrick's. Why hadn't that ever occurred to me before?

I glanced out the veranda window. "Don't most people move across the bay when they have kids?"

"I'm still living here, so not all of us do."

"Fair point. Still, I want my kids to have a yard like I had growing up and lots of parks, not a concrete playground. "

"Kids?"

"Twins."

His jaw went slack for a second before he spoke again. "You may want to consider staying in the neighborhood. You'd be surprised at what's here for you to do with children."

As John put away his stamp, I scooted my butt to the edge of the couch, pushing my fists down on the corners, preparing to stand.

"No, you are going to stay right here," he said firmly, his deep, hazel eyes holding my own. There was no denying it. I didn't want him to go.

"I'm only trying to be polite," I claimed, hoping he couldn't hear the lie in my voice. He picked up his bag and I thanked him again for coming.

He walked to the piano, hesitating. "Do I need to worry about locking the door?" That was a dilemma. Seeing I was preparing to rise, he came to my side, his hand under my elbow, the other on my lower back.

"I know this is rather intimate for a first notary visit," he said slyly. "But we'll be over the hump for the next one." His remark caused me to giggle, easing the discomfort I felt. His firm grip did help, and I was grateful. "But what do you do when you have to sit down again?"

"You won't be here to give me a cramp," I said archly, "so I should be just fine."

He laughed as he let go of me, walking beside me to the door. "Sorry about that." He reached for the handle.

"It was…really nice that you came. I'm glad we cleared the air, so to speak."

"Anytime you need a notary, just call." I assured him he would be first on the list. He gave me a closed-mouth smile, his eyes giving me the pleasure I felt with the morning sun—a little bit of hope that the day was going to be brighter.

CHAPTER 18

"You are lucky Alan's in charge because I would definitely put you on probation." Sam merely laughed at my scolding, happy at my words, but more importantly, my tone. John's visit had given me a spirit of optimism.

"Now that the transfer paperwork is signed---which you will be getting shortly—grad school, a new home, vacation, whatever, will be yours shortly."

"I can't even believe it," she said in a low voice, giggling.

"Go out and have a nice dinner with Greyson," I encouraged.

"He surfs, did you know that? Oh, and I was going to tell you, so does that guy, the doctor who treated you."

"Dr. Redding?"

"Jake, yeah." Small world.

"Thanks for reminding me. I need to schedule a follow-up appointment." After we hung up, that's what I did.

Keeping to my promise, I stopped in the kitchen, loaded up a plate and went back to the bedroom. Mid-way through reviewing a product launch plan, the phone rang and I saw it was Darcy.

"I understand I'm not going to be seeing you for the foreseeable future," Darcy began.

"Would you rather be on bed rest, pregnant with twins, or there, working with highly strung business owners and executives?" I grinned as she gasped. "I guessed Alan hadn't told you everything."

"He most certainly did not. I knew you were in a financial crunch, but after a few days it was taken care of with cash."

I looked at the time and asked her if she wanted me to pull back the proverbial kimono on my life.

"Absolutely," she immediately replied. "All I know is you are married to a gorgeous sales executive and live the life most women dream of."

"Then I had you fooled too. Actually, Darcy," I continued, pausing for effect. "I was fooled as well. Where to begin. How about with my accident?"

Darcy listened with all the diplomacy of a trained financial executive, issuing few comments and passing no judgments even when I ended.

"No wonder you always turned me down for the events I asked you to attend."

"The only consolation I can give you is that it's become mightily clear that you weren't the only one. My marriage affected every woman or relationship I had."

"He'd been cutting you off bit by bit."

"And I was too busy and in love to notice."

"Don't crucify yourself. Been there. Done that."

"What? You were married?"

"Long ago and far away, like Star Wars, but we'll talk about that another time. Right now, I want you to know that you and your employees will be able to do whatever you want on Monday. No holds."

Thrilled, I typed out an email to Alan. He could inform the rest of the staff since he was leading the company now, not me. He responded by telling me he was in a meeting, and could I please call Darcy back and schedule a meeting with the staff. They needed to be educated of their choices about whether to start an account, sell or a mix.

I called Darcy right back at her office but it went to a recording. It was past five, but she might be able to get it on her schedule if I could reach her. Dialing her cell phone, a man answered.

"Darcy's phone." His gruff tone and statement caught me off guard.

"Is Darcy available?"

"No, not at this time. May I help you?" His voice was low and scratchy from age.

"You're not a kidnapper holding my banker-friend hostage?"

"That's sharp," he said, his gruffness easing.

"And you are?" I inquired.

"Her former father-in-law."

"Oh, well," I said, searching for the right words. "That means you and Darcy are the modern day example of what we should all aspire to but don't have, civility with your former in-laws." The comment must have passed his test, for he fessed up his name.

"Joseph Adler."

"Lindy," I said.

"No last name? Like Madonna." I laughed.

"Maybe I should consider that. Do you happen to have another cell phone number for Darcy? I'm a client from the bank, and I have a late request to make."

"That bad?"

"No, not this time," I joked. "Just a meeting. Nothing too terribly urgent."

"True, but you are calling on a Friday night, so it can't be good."

"What I have been through has been bad," I admitted.

"Most certainly."

"Well, if you wouldn't mind telling her I called, that would be great." I expected him to get off, but he held on, as if he wanted to know more.

"Hold up now, young woman. Tell me about your business. I like to keep up on the current trends."

It was Friday and I was going nowhere fast and had no one to talk to, so I humored him, giving him the Reader's Digest version of my recent business challenges. He stopped me periodically, asking about margins, employee retention issues, and prospects for acquisition.

"In other words, you're sharpshooters, and the internal groups love to bring you in for short-term projects but don't want you hanging around.

Like dating versus marriage." It had taken Joseph all of five minutes to figure out my industry.

"Indeed. Well, thanks for---"

"But you know who'd love to buy you out?" he interrupted. "A hedge fund. Those guys are always scouting for good investments."

Hmm…if Joseph's crowd included hedge-fund billionaires, perhaps they had philanthropic tendencies toward helping the community.

"Since you asked about my work, I do have an interesting, but challenging project…" I told him about Kay's situation, the need for capital, a partner or both. "We need someone with enough strength of character or sheer determination to deal with obstinate, arrogant people used to getting their own way, people who have a checkbook in the place of a soul."

He whistled. "Passion is good. Realism is necessary." I agreed that it was, but the looming deadline was going to come whether I liked it or not. "I tell you what. I have a few days in the city before I leave. I'll place some calls for the center and see what turns up," he said.

I'd been prompted to talk to him about the center and listened. It was coming, just as Grandfather had said.

Still, as much as I'm learning, it's not enough. I don't trust myself…or those little impressions. Not fully.

I turned on the television, the news in the background lulling me to sleep. The week had been a long one, but thankfully it ended on a high note.

CHAPTER 19

"It's changing," I observed to my Grandfather, who looked at me expecting elaboration. "Rather, what I'm seeing is changing. These events are coming closer, more in the present." What I'd seen with Ann and Arlene had happened the day of my accident. The same with Charlie. But Monson's scene was after I'd returned to work, and my parents after that, because I'd received the watch not long after being released from the hospital. "Marina was in her apartment right before she came to me. We're nearing the end of our time together, aren't we?"

"It's been a month today since the accident." Dr. Redding's words now seemed prophetic. A sense of trepidation filled me.

"The elite athlete pushes the hardest the last ten feet. We are there now. What you will see next is the present."

"Can it wait?" I asked, wanting more time with him and to think about what I'd previously seen.

"No."

I woke to the sound of the doorbell ringing.

"Just a minute," I called out, now used to using my elbow to push myself off from the pillow. Putting my arms beneath my knees, I lifted my legs up and rolled them over, being sure to keep pressure from the points between my hips.

A familiar voice was speaking. My fingers trembled as my hand rested on the handle, my eyes filling with tears. I took a breath then slowly opened the door.

"Hi, Dad," I managed to choke out, a nervous smile on my face. Mom and Dad, standing side by side, looking every bit as fearful, hopeful, relieved, sad, and happy as I felt.

Dad stepped forward and wrapped his arms around me then moved aside for Mom to embrace me.

"Charlie called us about the accident the day you spoke with him or we would have come much sooner," Mom said, apologetic. I pulled back, scouring her face.

"Patrick never called you?" They both shook their heads. "I hope you didn't spend a fortune on the tickets."

"Your father didn't want to call and ask for permission," Mom said, glancing at Dad.

"Come in, and sit down with me. I can't stand for long." Walking directly to the couch, I asked Dad to shut the door. Remus walked around and through my parent's legs as they joined me.

A few awkward moments followed as Mom and Dad looked at one another. He spoke first. "I have something to say. I should have kept my comments about Patrick to myself, but I didn't. Then I should have given you my blessing, but I didn't. I'm sorry. I hope you can forgive me and we can move on."

"No. You were right Dad. The entire time, about everything." My shoulders rose and fell, and I wondered whether or not to divulge the entire saga now. First things first.

"It was me, Dad. Not Patrick. I'm responsible for not taking control of my own life and being obstinate; for not at least giving you the respect you deserved as my parent to at least listen without lashing out. My decision to marry him might have remained the same, but I didn't need to be so juvenile about it. What you were expressing was an opinion and I should have treated it as such. I'm so sorry for that." I paused, feeling the tears welling up now. "And I'm even more sorry that I haven't done more for you both during your financial hardships."

"But you sent us the money."

"Late," I whispered. "So late. Can you forgive me for how I've treated you?"

Mom sat beside me, putting her hand around my shoulders. "You left my side but you never left my heart," she said softly. All I could do was nod my head as I cried harder.

When she moved back, I eased back into the pillow. Mom watched with concern, but it wasn't yet time.

Listen. Grandfather's words were now a constant companion.

I put my hand on my stomach, but my parents didn't notice. "You must have been listening to that little whisper to visit me, because I'm going to need your help."

Dad's eyebrows raised. "You never need help."

"Funny how things change, huh? The reason I'm home early is because Patrick gave me one final gift before he took off. I'm pregnant. With twins."

My dad's mouth dropped open slightly. "You and he… He left?" I nodded.

First, his taught jaw line flexed as he fought against the rage he felt inside. After a few seconds, he relaxed, the jowls returning to normal as he absorbed the reality he'd been right.

My mother, on the other hand, did what every grandmother-to-be does; she started crying.

"I told you," my mother said to my father under her breath. I gave Dad a questioning look.

"For two weeks, your mother has been advocating the case for a visit. Isn't that right?" he asked as she nodded. "But I said no, it wasn't time. But she knew, all right. Mothers always know." I thought of both my grandparents, Aunt Mamie and who knows who else giving inspiration to those of us still in this temporal world.

"You can't be a mother and not think about your children every day," said my father. "How long will it be before you are in the clear?"

"I have to go in every week for a checkup and am on total bedrest. Since I can no longer drive myself, it was going to be taxis."

"You're looking at your taxi driver right here," Dad said.

The rest of the afternoon was filled with catching up until Mom insisted on making dinner, unthawing the chicken and making potatoes and salad. They were here, with me, when I expected to endure the weekend alone.

Tender mercies, I thought to myself.

Over dinner, we talked of Charlie, Ann, and I touched on Vanessa's situation, focusing on the fact she was leaving the city and not why. "I simply can't understand why I didn't get messages from any of you." I showed my father the phone and he was mystified. No incoming phone calls showed on the call log, and certainly no saved messages. He shrugged, handing it back.

"We are here now, that's all that matters."

Dinner was over and at seven they were relaxing, mom in the bathtub and my father reading. I went to the bedroom, unwilling to go to sleep. I feared my Grandfather would come and my time with him would be over.

The hours went by, first with the television, then a favorite book and finally, to the Internet. I searched "Book of Life" and up came references to the book of Revelations in the Bible, the Quran and the Torah, as well as similar phrases in other cultures. The living and dead, works and actions, deeds and recording, were interchangable but similar, all conveying a simple message. What we did here mattered. It was catalogued and would be with us when we left.

My breathing became heavy and I tried to answer my own question, the one I'd posed to Grandfather. Was I ready to see it? No. But I had to agree with Grandfather. I'd never be ready. I simply had to do it.

As though staring at the blackness within my eyes, I encouraged myself to fall asleep. It was time to face my present life.

Shouts from volleyball players drifted over the rectangular sand court, wafting up and through the open window of Vanessa's bay-shore home. From Vanessa's room, I saw the young, attractive professionals on the large playing field that seemed to stretch from the Golden Gate Bridge on the left to the well-traversed tourist destination of Fisherman's Wharf. On the other side of the water, lights flickered inside the upscale restaurants dotting the hills of Sausalito.

A persistent ringing in the background disrupted the silence, stopping and then starting again, its musical theme muffled from within Vanessa's purse on the floor. My friend was in the center of her four-poster bed. She wore black leggings under a grey cashmere top, her legs curled so tight against her chest she resembled a snail in her shell. Her hands were clasped around her knees, gripping the wrists in a death lock. Her body moved from a tremor, strong enough to jiggle the pink canopy stretching from post to beam. Feelings of pain and loneliness permeated the room.

The downstairs phone rang again and then the cell. Someone wasn't giving up. Vanessa stirred, rising to enter the bathroom. A rattle of pills followed the sound of a cabinet door opening and shutting. When she emerged, her left hand was full of containers, prescription and non-prescription alike. In her right hand she held a glass full of water.

I suddenly felt sick, the acid moving throughout my bowels, the physical sensations as alive and as painful as if I were awake, not dreaming.

Vanessa placed the water on the nightstand and dumped the contents of the bottles in the middle of the bed. The pile grew, a compost of red caplets, white tablets, light blue pills and an unknown mix of two-toned caplets. Vanessa separated the mass of pills into four separate piles, then started to count each pile, pill by pill. My heart ached with a sense of impending tragedy as I watched her go through the process.

Was there something we could do? I looked at Grandfather. He placed his hand on mine without saying a word. This was not my choice. The phone rang again. Then again. Vanessa lost track of her count. She started over, only to be interrupted by the phone one more time. I heard the buzz of a voice message. Vanessa slowly dropped one leg to the ground, leaned over the bed and retrieved the cellphone from her purse. Flipping the top up, she peered at the screen for many seconds, debating.

She closed her eyes, pressed the button for speaker.

"Vanessa, if you're there, it's Arlene. I missed you at the center this afternoon. Don't despair, honey. This is the hardest time, I know. But I'm with you. So is your friend, Lindy. We're all with you. You can make it. You can survive. Don't give up now. Fight like hell. We need people like you in this world. I'm here, so you can call me anytime. You have my number. I'll try you back in a little while."

Vanessa sat still for a long time before she dropped the phone on the floor. Returning to her pills, she took a handful, shoved them into her mouth and gulped her water. Another handful, then she drained the glass. Shaking, she went to the window where she could hear voices and laughter carried clearly across the park.

Outside, a man Rollerbladed down the walkway, moving around a girl whose arm was looped through her companion's. She laughed at his joke, throwing her head back and playfully punching him in the shoulder. The cry of a baby, the exuberant shout of a toddler and the kind scolding of parents blended into the park scene, evocative of any park in any city in any country.

Vanessa turned from the window. Her breathing was heavy, her own inner struggle separate from the pills that hadn't yet made their way down to her stomach. She wavered slightly, then moved her hand across the bedspread, scattering the pills across the floor. With a lunge, she moved into the bathroom. I heard the toilet seat crash, but up or down I didn't know until I heard the welcoming sound of Vanessa throwing up.

Continuous flushing overshadowed her choking.

I'd never heard a sound so lovely in my entire life.

When Vanessa reappeared, she was on all fours, crawling to her bed. She barely had the strength to pull herself up, making it halfway before she stopped. Her arms were laid out on the bed and she rolled her head to one side, weeping uncontrollably, giving herself up to the pain and anguish that had made her attempt to take her own life.

Slowly, a brightness entered the room, a glowing that had nothing to do with the reflection of the bay or the afternoon sun. Its intensity grew, expanding, moving down and around Vanessa's body. With the light was love and a peace so kind and full of grace that my eyes welled, my heart about to explode. The intense pain that I'd felt for her was now mine, and as quick as it came, it left me. My comfort turned into a joy that I'd never known before, one that I wanted to remember and hold and cherish. When the light around Vanessa faded, she was curled into a ball, her eyes closed but fluttering open, each time growing brighter with the light that had been with us both.

Tears were running down my face, the beauty and love of the experience both wonderful and crushing. Grandfather and I faded while the light was still bright.

"Why didn't I have that kind of experience?" I asked, thinking about my anguish and heartache in the hospital room, scared and alone after Patrick had first said we had to think about the pregnancy and what to do. I'd been sobbing. In that moment of my crisis, even a mist would have been welcome.

"You weren't ready," Grandfather said simply. Anger cut through my emotions. Not ready for what, unconditional love? An embrace and comfort? "You weren't in a place to acknowledge all that could be given," he added. In other words, I was too full of noise. Too full of myself.

"Would you really endure what's necessary to experience something like what you just saw?" His question was unexpected and it halted my resentment. Would I want to be assaulted, then rejected by my parents, taken in and counseled by a stranger, then still feel so alone I wanted to die?

But then, if that was what was required to feel the unequivocal love, so complete and fulfilling I never wanted to leave….

"Yes," I answered quiet and firm.

I woke, shaking. It was midnight. I couldn't…shouldn't, but I did. Sweat went down my arms and my heart beat erratically until Vanessa answered.

"What are you doing calling me?" she asked, groggy. I was so relieved, my voice cracked even as my eyes watered.

"I just—wanted to hear your voice," I got out. My sniffle was audible, and she sounded more alert when she spoke.

"Why would you be upset? Has something happened?"

"All I can say is you have been on my mind. Are…you okay?" The pause felt eternal.

"I'm great."

"Really?"

"Yeah," she said quietly, but with an assurance that would have mystified me had I not seen recent events. "It's been brutal, but I feel good."

"Can we get together? Do you want to come over this weekend? My parents showed up unexpectedly and they'd love to see you."

"Tomorrow I'm going down to the center to see Arlene and then spending time with my parents, but maybe Sunday? Or Monday?" More time to be alone, I thought, but she sounded more at peace than I did.

Have some faith. The words I'd used with Alan came back to me. I told her to call me when she was free. I felt better now. Vanessa was alive. She'd been encircled in the arms of His love. She'd experienced the greatest gift of all.

After a few sips of water, I laid back down and fell asleep.

CHAPTER 20

My Grandfather and I were in the loud, bustling restaurant, Fog City Diner, off the Embarcadero. It was late, but crowded as it always was on a Friday night.

I took in the silver metal of the molding, black leather bucket seats, and the distinctive checkered menus. Doug worked behind the bar, pouring drinks as he chatted with several patrons seated on the silver-and-black swivel bar stools. A line of people two deep stood behind them, waiting for a stool to be vacated. Every so often, Doug smiled at the hostess, Stacy, his wife of seven months. I'd attended their wedding in the Presidio, a beautiful ending to a love story that had evolved about the time I'd discovered the diner, nine years before.

Stacy deftly managed the crowd hovering around her hostess station. I recognized several faces: a prominent attorney, his one-liners often quoted in the San Francisco Business Journal; a City Council member whose comb-over was forgotten when he stood up for the city's homeless population; an ad executive, her short, pencil-straight blond hair skimming her high cheekbones. Although I'd seen each one many times at the restaurant, today they looked different.

The attorney kept his companions laughing with hand gestures and funny remarks. Yet a sadness lurked beneath his words and actions. Dining alone, the City Council member whispered into his cell phone, his harsh, venomous words berating the person on the other end. His eyes, red with rage, stood against a grey shadow that hovered about him as he inflicted more damage with each word. His eyebrows raised and lowered in a dance of recognition of constituents who passed him, keeping a respectful distance so as not to disturb his phone call. The female executive's glacial expression broke the instant a friend arrived. With lightning speed, she inquired about the health of her friend's newly adopted infant and gave her friend a hug. The protective coating of fear she'd worn lifted; her eyes shone bright with love.

My looking glass was no longer dirty.

Paul, one of the senior waiters moved by us carrying plates filled with food. The room buzzed with conversation and background jazz music, a soothing ambience for the tourists and locals enjoying crab cakes and other small dishes. When I started my business, Fog City was the restaurant where I took clients, business partners, and even recruits. It was where I told my employees we were going to Mexico on a 5-day vacation after we hit our revenue milestones six months ahead of schedule. After Patrick and I got married, it was our destination for lunch on Saturdays, our presence so predictable that a table was held for us with or without a reservation—a booth in the front, oversized for six, yet graciously given to a party of two.

My eyes drifted to the table Patrick and I usually occupied. A small brass plaque on the wall was engraved with the name of Hal Riney, the famous ad man who'd been coming to Fog City since it opened. Regular patrons were rewarded with such plaques. Most had the names of two or three people. Hal had his own. A month ago, I'd been told that management was reviewing whether three years of patronage was enough to warrant a plaque for Patrick and me.

Then it dawned on me we weren't here for nostalgic reasons.

Stacy passed in front of me, her eyebrows creased into a frown. She motioned to Doug with her fingers. He leaned over the counter.

"Can you believe this? Even with him paying his own bill! What am I supposed to do with those two?" She perked her head to the side to direct his eyes over her shoulder.

Doug took in the scene, then turned, grabbing a bottle from a shelf on the bar. "You seat them. Same as anyone else."

"What if she shows up?" Doug glanced up and down the bar to see if anyone was listening before he leaned his burly bulk forward, speaking in a low tone.

"She's at home on bedrest and he knows it." His wife shook her head in disgust.

"It's one thing to carry on. But at the very place you came to with your wife…" She let the rest of the comment drop as she returned to her station by the door. She wore a painted-on smile as she motioned for Patrick to follow her to a table at the far back of the restaurant. His chin flipped up, awarding her the slightest recognition as he called to his companion.

A woman who I didn't recognize tilted her head coyly, dangling a light brown Prada purse with yellow piping from the arm that was not linked with Patrick's. She also wore a mocha colored shearling jacket identical to the one I was missing.

It registered that the noise level of the restaurant hadn't dissipated one decibel, but it was as though the room went silent.

I watched the two of them, sitting in the far corner, their eyes focused on each other, intense and passionate. Patrick reached his hand over the table and she immediately extended hers. Through the veil, I'd felt peace and love in death, as well as shame and regret. Why should I be protected from heartbreaking pain?

As I watched in anguish, I heard my father voicing his reservations about my choice several days before my wedding to Patrick. Then there was my assistant's tendency to avoid my eyes when hearing his name. My cousin Ann had invited us for dinner after Patrick and I were married then the invitations waned, finally stopping altogether. Even then, I'd smoothed over both incidences for him, taking responsibility for not telling Ann about Patrick's food preferences. But now in this dream, my memory became sharp, its precision edge cutting through my earthly denial.

The longer Grandfather and I stood watching the couple in front of us, the more quickly I recalled other scenes involving Patrick. Always I was on the outside, defending or justifying his actions and in the process losing friendships. The transition had happened so gradually I hadn't noticed. Work had stepped in to fill the void. No wonder my last day was spent consumed with it; there was nothing else to occupy my time. Not even Patrick.

He leaned over, giving his date a kiss. I felt the air go out of my lungs as if I'd been punched. This physical pain was different from what I'd felt with Vanessa, when I'd empathized with her anguish. The recognition of betrayal hurt even in this dream.

But this wasn't a dream. This was real life.

Finally, Patrick guided the woman out the front doors. The car drove off in a direction opposite to the route we took to go home. Grandfather and I stood on the sidewalk.

I was enveloped by an overwhelming sense of loss. Patrick had been giving the good parts of our marriage to someone else and leaving me with the entrails.

Grandfather took my hand. His palms felt rough, the calluses I remembered as a child were still at the base of his fingers. The archive room bustled with quiet activity.

"When Dr. Redding was trying to save me, I had these flashes of images. Some I've seen, like Ann on the gurney but others I haven't."

"Those are the future." I looked down at my book. The writing on the page had paused. I was sleeping.

"The twins," I said, thinking of the two girls who'd been in the archive room the first time I'd entered. "Are they certain?"

"Yes, but not necessarily in the way you may think of them." He held my hand, the tug unnecessary. It was time to leave. "You have grown already Lindy. Don't lose sight of how far you've come."

"Right." His eyes were filled with the knowledge I would make him proud. I intended to do that, and more.

CHAPTER 21

The following day, I overslept, grateful my mother didn't come into the room until after ten. I was exhausted; mentally fatigued and physically incapable of more than lifting my right arm to get a glass of water.

I did want to make my Grandfather proud and intended to do so…later. Right now, it was too much to bear; the weight of my mistakes encouraged me to go back to sleep. At least this time I didn't fear it. No more experiences to relive or revelations to absorb. What would happen in my life from this point forward was my own doing.

Sleep, food, the bathroom and more sleep was punctuated only by my mother asking if they could take my car for a drive around town and to the Flowermart.

"The car is yours from here on out." Before they left, Mom brought in another tray of food, full of snacks, veggies and a sandwich and a full jug of water.

"Only the bathroom," she intoned, wagging a finger. Very little changed in my schedule for the weekend. Monday I was offered a reprieve when Sam called.

"We've erected a shrine to you on my desk," she said, getting a laugh from me.

"And my stomach is soon going to be its own Buddha belly. What's up?"

"I got a call from Erwin Brewer. Have you ever heard of him?"

"A prospect?"

"Nope. He was calling because of an introduction by a man called Joseph. He wants to see the building and meet Kay. He's a potential financier. Seriously, Lindy. You did this while on bed rest?" She had awe in her voice, and my face flushed as I sat alone in my room. It wasn't me at all. "I know you aren't supposed to be doing much, but I can still call you can't I?"

My heart melted. Sweet, crazy, previously-raccoon-makeup-eyes Sam, now responsible, beautiful young professional. Even though I'd handed the baton to her, she wanted me to see her crossing the finish line.

"I'm not going to leave you hanging, Sam," I replied.

"Oh! I got a new outfit yesterday so I won't embarrass the team, and if it's OK with you, I'm going to meet up with Kay and go through the presentation."

"And I bet you know just the right computer guy to help you when you get stuck." Sam emitted one final laugh before we said goodbye to one another and hung up.

She sent me an email confirming the meeting would be Wednesday, noting that John would be attending, along with Joseph, Kay and Erwin. Sam would be taking the lead, without Lindy or Alan present.

I'm being replaced.

The thought was emphasized several times over that day as other managers gave the final sign-off on press releases, only sending the highest profile ones to me for review.

I was on the couch and mom brought me food, sitting with me while I ate. I asked her about each of her two pregnancies, hoping to glean something from her insight and wisdom.

"Nothing I can say is going to be relevant," Mom told me. "Twins will only compound what I encountered."

I told her about the shopping trip with Vanessa and she asked to see the clothes. Once I told her where I'd placed all the items, she merrily walked down the hall, humming to herself as I heard the opening and shutting of drawers and rattling of the hangers in the closet. When she returned, she took her time, lifting up each item, turning a dress this way and that, examining the stitching and commenting on the tops, the tuck and hemline of the skirts. By the time she was done, I had determined she missed her calling as a stylist.

Mom placed her hands on the soles of my feet. She rubbed; I moaned. It had been many months since hands other than mine had touched my feet.

"Your father spoiled me so much when I was pregnant. It seemed like he'd come home with a new outfit every day from Bergdorf Goodman or Saks in his arms."

"And jewelry," I interjected.

"Rings were his favorite, though I had to stop wearing most of the rings by the time I was seven months along. My hands were too puffy."

Her fingers were bare of rings now and I thought of the dream with my father. It too, had been real. Small, white pearls were in her ears instead of the massive diamond studs she normally wore. My fingers were touching my ears before I realized it. We were living our lives like two cars on the same road, the older model and the younger model, experiencing the same ups and downs, meeting at the same point.

"Do you miss all the…things?"

"Not much, but some of the items had such meaning because they were milestones in my life," she admitted, her long eyelashes fluttering.

I asked Mom to forgive me for selling Grandmother's items and she touched my leg again.

"We don't take it with us, do we?" she asked. She'd learned the lesson long before I had. If she was OK with it, then I was, too.

"Had I known how much losing everything would affect him, I'd have given it all up in a heartbeat years ago," she said.

"Given what up?" came Dad's voice, rounding the corner.

I answered for her. "All of your stuff so she could have a kinder, gentler you." I was expecting a smart comeback from him, but he said nothing, just kept grinning like a Cheshire cat. "You should be unhappy at my comment, not smirking. What's up?"

He sat on the side chair. "Nothing much, other than connecting Darcy and Charlie."

"Darcy?" I questioned. "How do you even know who she is?"

"Your phone was ringing so I answered and got her talking. Charlie just happened to come up." Joseph and my Dad, I thought. They were so alike.

I gave Mom a look, shaking my head.

"Darcy couldn't stop talking about you. Her only bone of contention is that she wanted to know why you hadn't been the one to suggest Charlie. Oh, and she said she wants to throw you a baby shower."

We had so much more to say to one another, and I wanted to continue, but my eyes were already drooping.

The following day, I heard a commotion at the front door, some hushed shrieking and then Vanessa and Ann were sitting on the edge of the bed, looking more like they were ready for a sleepover than a single, working professional and mom of three. They insisted I give them the gory details of Patrick and the IRS, getting up to stalk the house for items that he might have taken that I'd not yet discovered missing.

"I know the purse you are talking about," Vanessa said. "I swear to you if I see him and her with it, I'm going to rip it right off her arm."

"You do that," I encouraged. "In fact, every blond woman in this city that has a brown Prada purse with yellow piping, rip away."

Ann had brought food and she left the room several times to talk with mom. More than once, Vanessa's phone rang and the last time, she excused herself to answer it.

"It's a new job opportunity," she said with a whisper, as she left the room.

"So, what's the latest with Jared?" I asked Ann. Her cheeks weren't as sallow as they had been, her voice was bright and healthy. "You look downright…" I hesitated to say what was so clear to me for fear of offending her.

"Happy?" my cousin finished for me, as if she could hardly believe it. "Jared's full-time position has blossomed. The start-up just moved from the South Bay to the Mission district. Friday he took a language test for the German support team and he got such a high score, they upped his pay another twenty percent."

"Wow," was all I could think of. For so long, Jared had been unhappy about his employment but lacked the motivation to act. Maybe the harsh tragedy of their baby's death was what Jared required to get his butt in gear and look for something better.

"This is the biggest part, you ready?" Ann questioned, looking past me to the other room. "You know the back problems I've had for years. The therapist said that my L3, L4 and L5 were displaced and ruptured from the other births. He believes that if I had carried the baby to term, and any one of those bones would have ruptured, I could have been paralyzed — for life," she emphasized. We stared at one another in shock. "When I talked with Dr. Redding, I told him what the therapist said. He agreed it was absolutely possible."

She shook her head, the relief transparent on her face. "I don't think I could have lived without the use of both my legs, confined to a wheelchair, trying to care for my family and raising three kids."

"You would have found a way," I said fervently, convinced of the unknown depths of the human spirit.

"Yes, I would have found a way to drive myself off a bridge and not come back." Paralysis was a scary thought. It took a special kind of individual to deal with a physical disability and carry on with life, let alone be happy. "I've come to the conclusion that we dodged a bullet by losing this child. And if you ever repeat that to anyone, including Vanessa, I will disown you first, and then I'll kill you."

In the hours that followed the departure of my friends, I reflected on Ann's experience. Talk about a divine master plan. I used to believe people were disconnected, the universe and the people within moving independently from one another, intersecting and overlapping when desired. I wasn't so sure of that anymore.

CHAPTER 22

"It's the big day," Sam said excitedly. The meeting with Kay was at eleven. I expressed confidence in her ability to wow the group and encouraged her to hold her own with Joseph.

"That's what Alan said."

It took a little while, but I finally came to terms with feeling obsolete. Here is where I'm supposed to be, in or on my bed, and the world beyond was continuing, as it should.

I was just dozing off when my phone rang and I saw the caller ID.

"Aren't you supposed to be in a meeting right about now?"

"I am outside," replied Joseph. "I just learned you weren't going to make it. Bedrest I understand." I said it was true. The older man grumbled that he might have to come over and verify himself, making me laugh.

"I will share with you that Erwin has already begun his due-diligence. The old codger knows the area well and doesn't have a high tolerance for the condos going in." I sincerely thanked him for his help. I was nothing more than a conduit for putting two people together, and it would not have happened had I not indulged his curiosity long enough to bring up the center during our conversation.

"On another topic, I had some time to kill read about your clients and what you've accomplished. Then I just happened to be speaking with one of my hedge fund buddies who expressed interest in buying your firm. He thinks it's a no-brainer for his business. Much cheaper than the millions they spend on agencies every year between his portfolio of companies."

Set aside the fact that I'm on bed rest and I'd just turned the company over to someone else.

"Joseph, did you mention I'm pregnant?"

"It was a non-issue. Women do get pregnant, Lindy, even executives." His voice chided me. "The CEO said he would likely want you to remain on as a consultant part time, during your pregnancy and maybe for a period thereafter. But no more now," he said, stopping the conversation. "The meeting is going to start momentarily."

The hours dragged by until I gave up waiting for a call from Sam or Joseph and took a nap. At 3:30, I woke and checked my email and phone to see if Sam had at least sent me a text. She had.

"Success!" she wrote. One word. I wanted to both shout with joy and explode in frustration.

An hour later, I was mentally pacing, still confined to my prison of a couch, having gotten more concerned, feeling insecure and then angrier by the moment. Who am I kidding? I'm not reconciled to my nonexistent role in the company.

My uncomfortable emptiness was still lingering when I received call from a phone number I didn't recognize. I answered, using my stiff voice reserved for solicitations.

"Lindy? It's John."

"Hey John, what's up?"

"I thought you'd like to hear how the meeting went, the parts that Sam didn't already tell you." I refrained from a sarcastic retort, inviting him to share his perspective.

"The meeting began a bit bumpy when Erwin treated Sam like she was a kid, but she handled it like a pro. She was respectful, but make no mistake, she gave it right back to him." I chuckled, grateful Sam's background and sense of self was strong enough not to be intimidated by an old warhorse. "Then it was Mom's turn. The entire discussion lasted nearly two hours and then we took a break for lunch. Erwin insisted on paying for the group to go to the Boulevard. By the time dessert had come around, Sam was bantering with Joseph and Erwin about her medical student-surfer friend."

John described how Erwin would be a silent financial partner for the center, the money put in a trust with Kay, himself and a group of trustees for oversight. "With good management, the money will multiply and the interest alone should carry the expenses. The best part is that Erwin asked Sam to be the liaison between his group and the key people in the city."

I had a flash-forward moment, visualizing Sam in five years. She'd be running her own business and making a ton of money. What a day for her. No wonder she didn't text more information. She was likely floating on cloud nine, her fingers probably too shaky with adrenaline to type.

My emotions took a dip as I regretted my internal impatience at not receiving a response. About the time I was wondering if I'd ever learn not to judge or presume about others, John called.

"How are you doing? Any better at lying around with nothing to do?" His tease had a warm, caring tone.

"No, not at all," I admitted. He chuckled and asked if I'd like company. "Sure. You can come over, do my laundry and feed me. Sounds super exciting doesn't it?"

"I'm a single dad with an eleven year-old. My whole world is exciting. That said, I'll work on a time when I can get out of the office for a clandestine meeting, salad style." I was still laughing when we hung up.

On Thursday, I had my weekly checkup with Dr. Kustin, who informed me the blood in my uterus hadn't increased, but it hadn't diminished.

"This is progress, so whatever you are not doing, keep it up." On the drive home, Dad updated me about his patent acquisition.

"The first check is going to arrive next week," he said, his voice full of hope and excitement. "Mid-five-figures," he clarified.

"Impressive. Can you hold onto it?"

"Not the first twelve grand, which I'll be giving right back to you."

"No you won't," I retorted.

"I'm the dad, and you're still my daughter. End of discussion." I smiled, knowing his tone of finality and giving in. "I will be spending money on two cribs."

"Oh no, you won't!" We joyfully bickered about who was going to make the purchase the rest of the drive home.

We were just sitting down to a table covered with food when the doorbell rang. Dad rose while I told them both I had no idea who it could be.

The door opened and I yelled. "Jackson!" startling my father, who looked at me then back to the two men at my door. "Come on in!"

My father took the lead, introducing himself with handshakes to both and gestured they do as I asked.

"Don't upset the pregnant woman," he muttered loud enough for us all to hear.

"Ignore my father and join us." Jackson and Ronnie came through the door, and seeing me and mom at the table, Jackson balked, apologizing.

"Meet my parents, Sophia and Mark. I know you two probably haven't eaten so join us. You won't get a better meal, at least not tonight."

Ronnie leaned down to give me a diagonal hug, congratulating me on "being a good girl" and not standing, followed by Jackson.

"Here Jackson," my Dad invited. "Why don't you take the end seat, and Ronnie you sit here by Lindy," he suggested. Mom was already up, retrieving plates and silverware. The two men looked at each other, admitted they had no dinner plans and joined the party.

"So, what's the occasion?" I asked.

Jackson answered. "We just wanted to see how our favorite pregnant gal was doing." I laughed, teasing them that the city was absolutely teaming with single, pregnant women running amok.

Ronnie took the opening to give my parents his account of my rescue of their beloved pug, how I'd taken the dog to work and spoiled him silly. "I swear he now has a taste for pastrami sandwiches," he said. Mom accused me of not telling her about all the fun things that had been going on.

"I was slightly more preoccupied with saving my financial butt. This is the Jackson of the antique store I've told you about," I said to Dad.

"Thank you for helping Lindy out," Dad said. "She could use some good friends." I slipped my hand on my Dad's knee and gave him a squeeze. He placed his hand on mine, the quiet and invisible thank you received and acknowledged. I was so proud of him for being kind.

"Don't go thinking he's a philanthropist," broke in Ronnie. "He made out good enough." We all laughed, and listened as Dad told stories about his old collection of antiques from Spain.

"We had a lot of amazing furniture, but like a lot of people our age, we downsized."

"Estate sales are where some of our best stuff comes from," Jackson said.

Dad agreed. "Dead people make for great deals." Mom and I protested at the harshness of the statement, but the men kept talking about items and deals to be had in the market as though we hadn't said a word.

When dinner was over, I told Mom about Ronnie's musical background. "I'd love to hear you play," she said, inviting him to sit down. Ronnie started with a Beethoven medley that he somehow switched to Dave Brubeck and then into a jazzy piece I didn't recognize. Mom hovered above him, watching his fingers, nodding her head in appreciation.

"Try as I might, I never did have the natural 'touch,' as my teacher used to tell me," she said. "I have the technicality down, but I never possessed the natural talent like you have, or Lindy."

Ronnie stood, motioning her to take his place. Mom did so and pulled out some of my sheet music. After playing several pages, she stopped. Ronnie shook his head.

"I'm not sure what you're talking about. That was superb." Mom demurred, and I rolled my eyes.

"That's Mom, ever the modest one, always forgetting she's been a concert pianist."

"My biggest disappointment was that I've never been able to improvise," she admitted. "Now I'm too old to learn."

At this, Ronnie scoffed. "Scoot on over lady. I'm going to show you something." Ronnie proceeded to take her through the fifths, and within a few minutes, Mom was stringing together like-chords. Her eyes grew wide with amazement, as though she knew the principle, but had never taken the walk over the invisible bridge that joined written music on a page with the freedom of free-form improvisation. The expression on her face was one of delight in the newfound wonder of the technique.

"You're hired, Ronnie," announced Dad.

"If you are interested, I could get you hooked up with a quartet that needs an accompanist," he promised. "The pianists around here are flaky," he continued.

When Ronnie offered to get her opening night tickets to the opera, she politely said late-season tickets are better. "They're more in tune," she said, her eyes steady.

Ronnie softly punched Jackson in the arm. "See, aren't I always telling you that? The show-stopping posers want to hit opening night, but the real musicians go later in the season." He nodded his head approvingly, as though Mom had passed some sort of test. She had. In fact, both my parents had passed, with flying colors.

CHAPTER 23

That Friday evening was one of the most relaxing I'd had in five weeks. How my life had changed.

As Mom played the piano, Dad and I watched the light of the setting sun bounce off the bay from the couch.

"Have you heard that the Lord challenges those He loves?" Dad asked me.

"Did you actually use the word Lord?" I asked. He waited, expectant. "Are you suggesting the more He loves me the worse my life is going to be? Haven't I already been through the worst?"

"All these years, your late teens through your twenties, you have been self-reliant, making your money, achieving success according to the world. How else would you know He's there for you unless He gave you some hard circumstances to overcome?"

I sighed. "You always did tell me that nothing worth having came easy."

Dad looked pleased.

A large sailboat sliced across the waves, its destination the Bay Bridge and then out toward the ocean. That was me throughout my twenties. I'd been moving away from all I'd been taught, focused and heading in my own direction, charting my own course, relying on my skills. But my sophisticated, internal navigation system had been ignored. It hadn't take much to get me off course. Then, the storm came. It was what took me praying like a sailor thrown overboard, clinging onto the dinghy for dear life to remember who was in charge.

Later, as we headed off to bed I said to my mother, "You know, San

Francisco has the best performing arts on the West Coast," as though this would be news to her. "The opera house is 10 minutes away. I know you haven't been in a while, but if you guys stayed, the three of us could start going again. Of course, you may have to get used to sitting in the cheap seats with the rest of us peons instead of the box."

"I can enjoy the music from anywhere in the auditorium," she said, playfully pinching my leg in retaliation.

"Would you two consider staying here until I figure out where I, or we, are going to move?"

Mom's eyes opened, excitement and eagerness evident before she glanced at Dad.

"Seriously Dad. You're the only person who can drive a stick, and I have weekly doctor appointments. You need a car, and renting one is ridiculous, so you staying here will make everyone happy."

It wasn't long before I was down for the night, snug in my thoughts of Mom and Dad here with me, exactly where I wanted them.

The following morning, my hunger pangs were severe enough to wake me. I leaned up from the bed, using my arms, not my waist. I carefully slid my arms in to my bathrobe and drew the sash tight. Dad was reading his phone.

"Good morning, baby doll," he greeted me, but then scowled. "Why aren't you in bed?"

"Food," I said. Mom immediately rose from the table, leaving the cookbooks open. From the smell of things, she was already done making breakfast.

While I made my way through the small buffet of steel-cut oatmeal and eggs with tomatoes and bacon, we planned the menu for the rest of the week. I gave her money for the store and they decided to hit the flower market while they were out.

"Take your time. I'll be doing nothing except for eating and sleeping. Stay away. Enjoy yourself."

They said their goodbyes and in seconds I was checking my email account. Nothing required my attention, and my thoughts turned to those people in my small circle. I was glad to have my girlfriends back in my life.

Around ten, I was dosing, a restful sleep impossible because of my consistent hunger pangs when the phone rang.

"Is this my laundry service?"

His laugh told me my comment had been on point. I laughingly told him I was teasing, that my mother was cleaning and cooking.

"That's well and good, but I know you're eating non-stop and I'm between meetings. Honestly, I'd just like to see you, so don't make it so hard on me."

What good manners my mother had taught me went out the window with the divorce. "Sure, as long as you let me pay for it."

He asked me if I had a food preference, and I suggested Dim Sum, the dumplings sounding wonderful.

"I must warn you, I think I look worse than I did the last time."

"Pregnant women get better looking as time goes on, didn't you know that?"

I guess I didn't.

The hour was spent trying not to obsess over my looks, outfit or general state of my complexion. I was not going to get up for any reason and was thankful my parents left the door unlocked. He'd be letting himself in, which is exactly what he did after he knocked and I yelled an invitation.

"You look well," he started.

"And you prepared for a storm." John wore a deep blue trench coat that hit his lean thighs, underneath a grey mock turtleneck and thick corduroy slacks. John took a seat on the couch, pausing to move the books to the end table, making way for the food.

"The microclimates of this city means you always have three coats in the car and at least an extra pair of shoes."

I totally agreed with his comment, commiserating that it was sunny in the Marina, cloudy in the Presidio and windy over on the Embarcadero.

"When my former wife was pregnant with our daughter," John started, "she had a condition of that morning sickness that gets you hospitalized. Not fun."

"I'm lucky on that front, so far. Tired and eating like a horse, but no sickness. You said your daughter is eleven. What's that like?"

He looked at me with a smile on his face. "Like a pre-teen girl who is really twenty-one. Right now, she's hitting up the Stanford Mall down in the valley, spending her Grandfather's money instead of mine." I smiled, thinking of my own shopping excursions with my Dad.

"Is she a tall, female version of you?"

"Yes, though the braces keep only half the boys away."

"It's only going to get worse you know," I said, remembering what I put my parents through. "Think grey hairs. Sleepless nights. The boys might be the least of your problems."

He groaned. "I can see you have a lot of compassion." When John squinted at the sudden burst of sunlight through the window, I made a move to rise. His hand shot out, stopping my progress. I expected him to stand and adjust the shades himself. He didn't. Instead, he moved closer to me on the couch, eliminating the glare from his eyes.

Keep calm. It was a bright light in his eye, not a means to an end of his hand on my leg.

"The worst part of it is that she's so mature for her age, she gets mistaken for my much younger girlfriend," he continued without missing a beat, "until she opens her mouth and the braces shine through. I don't even get the benefit of the doubt."

"And what? You're afraid people are going to think you're the nasty Uncle?"

"Can you imagine?" he asked in horror.

It was so good to share a moment of fun with a parent who could identify at least on some level with me. As the time passed, the excitement of having John stay turned to dread as I thought about the forthcoming scene. My parents would walk in, see me with a handsome, strange man who they'd never heard of, the ink on the divorce papers barely dry. The hair on the back of Dad's neck would rise along with Mom's eyebrows, and we'd all share an awkward.

John must have observed my emotional state changing. "Finished? I don't want to overstay my welcome."

"Actually, I have another man coming in about ten minutes. Schedules to keep, that kind of thing." I'd used such a dry, matter-of-fact tone he stared at me. "Gotcha!" I laughed. "The truth is, if you stay much longer, you can meet the parents. That would be a great shock to them. My husband's gone not one week and I'm having strange men in the house." He continued to gaze at me with the look one gives when told ghosts do exist.

"Seriously, would you rather I not be here when they arrive?"

I instantly decided to do what I'd never done with Patrick. Exercise brutal honesty. I had everything to lose then and lost it anyway. Why not take some chances?

"*Seriously*," I teased, "I think it would be as funny as heck. At the same time, I'm not kidding when I say it's only been a week and here you are, and I'm in my lounge wear."

John had a mischievous twinkle in his eye. "I think I'll stay and we'll see if your dad swallows his tongue. This is excellent," John continued, making himself more comfortable on the sofa. "You're not even officially divorced."

"Correction. I am divorced and have the paperwork to prove it." That subdued his laughter.

"How does that work?" I'd just finished telling John about the marvels of a Costa Rican divorce when my parents walked through the front door. Mom was first, displaying exactly the startled look I expected. Dad followed after, wiping the bottom of his shoes.

John stood up and closed the distance to Mom before she'd put her bags down.

"Hi, I'm John," he said to her, extending his hand. Mom was never one to embrace strangers but was polite. Dad, on the other hand, shook John's hand as though it was perfectly normal I had a male visitor in my house.

"Hi John," he said, gripping his hand. "Nice to meet you."

"John is the notary Sam had come over," I explained. "And he is also Kay's son."

"I kept her laying down," John added, generating a grateful glanced from both parents.

"We were pretty fast through the flower market," mom said, bringing the bags over to me for show and tell. "We skipped lunch because we were worried about you not being fed, but I can see you were taken care of."

"Sorry I didn't call you. It didn't even occur to me."

"Hmm," my dad said, a funny twitch playing on his cheek.

John went to mom's side, inspecting the bags. "You moms. Mine is forever filling every pot we have with flowers for each season."

"Mom, there's a vase in the cupboard." She found it, commenting on the delicacy of the etchings on the outside

Dad turned to John. "When you see Joseph at the next meeting you have regarding the center, put in a word for our son will you?" I rolled my eyes.

"Brother?" John asked me. I gave dad a glare. John responded with a smile that was wide, genuine and beautiful.

"Who gets the good word for your brother?" John asked me.

"The story is simple, but a little…funny," I began. "Charlie, my brother, met a gal in rehab, they got married and had a baby, but not totally in that order. She is mentally ill, they divorced and Charlie has custody of their child. Dad spoke with Darcy, Joseph's former daughter-in-law and my banker. Dad being Dad, he immediately divined that Darcy was ideal for my single brother, no matter that Charlie lives five hours away. Now, Dad is asking you to put in a good word for him when you see Joseph, as if you could possibly find the right moment to pass along such a recommendation about someone you don't know. Got all that?"

"And you're surprised by this how?" John asked me. "The woman who is breaking down the walls of Jericho for the youth center from her couch, when she's supposed to be on bed rest?"

"She takes after her father," chimed Mom from the kitchen, disavowing any part of my nature.

"This is called double-teaming, and it isn't fair," I pouted.

"Who cares?" John asked, good naturedly challenging me. I bristled. Too many times, Patrick had asked the same question with his all-or-nothing attitude, "why not" a euphemism for 'it's my way.' I took a breath. John wasn't Patrick, and I shouldn't immediately project all Patrick's bad habits on him.

"What I meant to say is that I don't want you to be put in an uncomfortable situation. But if you're OK with it," I continued, "go for it."

John looked eager to convince me otherwise. "Here's another way of looking at it. Don't kill the dream, let reality kill the dream. Your dad wants his son to connect with an intelligent woman. Let him have the dream until it's proven impossible," he added, as though my father weren't sitting with us. "If Darcy and Charlie can't make a go of it, it's reality killing the dream, not you."

"I've never heard that motto before but it works." Dad complimented. "I'll be using it, unattributed of course."

His comment elicited a laugh from John.

"Plagiarize at will," John said, throwing me a glance.

Dad took up the conversation then. He asked John where he was from, his background, where he attended school. Finally, Dad asked John how he knew me.

I cringed.

"I tried to hire her company, but she turned me down," he said flatly, causing my Dad to laugh. "Can you believe it?"

"Did you have a good reason?" Dad asked me.

"I thought I did—and actually, still do—from a business front." I turned to John in an explanatory mode. In as few words as possible, I told him the difference between product launches and crisis communications. "At the time, I thought I couldn't handle stressful situations. Clearly, I have risen to the occasion."

He raised his shoulders. "And now they are over and you aren't taking on any new clients."

"Nope. Only babies." As if that was his que, John stood.

"I'll get going."

Out of the corner of my eye, I saw Dad observing me. "I hear the mixer and smell the graham crackers, which means she's making me a key lime pie," my father remarked.

I wondered if Grandfather had known John would come into my life. And had he, or another spirit in heaven, whispered to Sam that she should call John to be the notary?

"Do you want to text Janaye to see when she's due back?" I asked him. "His daughter," I told Dad. The gleam in his eye grew brighter.

I made small talk with Dad while John texted his daughter. Our conversation was interrupted by a ping, and John's hint of laughter.

"She responded?" I asked.

John held out his phone, reading while he showed me the text. "I'm at Lindy's and she's asked me to stay a little longer. That okay with you? And my daughter replies three letters: GWM"

I turned to him inquisitively. "What does GWM mean?"

"You obviously don't speak teen," John responded. "It means, good with me."

He typed for a few seconds and then put his phone away. "I have to tell you both, girls confuse me." He turned to my father. "If you have any tips you want to share on a formerly wonderfully sweet girl turning terse and using an over-abundance of one-word responses, please impart your wisdom."

Dad put his hands up in ignorance. "You think I know?"

"He's not telling you how much grief I started giving him at thirteen. I lost my mind but it came back, eventually."

The conversation meandered from topic to topic, from business and Dad's background, music and the conservatory where Mom studied. John shared his daughter through pictures on his phone, and admitted his musical taste was stuck in the dance music of his college years.

Through it all, he didn't exhibit an ounce of entitlement. No name-dropping of other families or private schools. When Dad got him to identify where he grew up in Seaside, Dad remarked on the scarcity of available coastline real estate. John didn't gloat. He just thanked his grandparents for loving the ocean.

In all the time Patrick and I dated, we never had that kind of dialogue with my parents.

"Personally, I like the East Bay," John offered. "With the miles of hiking trails that are deserted most of the time." John then told us about his favorite trails and his most recent adventure down near Santa Cruz. "Just south of here, off the highway you are in the Redwoods, surrounded by some of the tallest trees on the planet. It's unreal."

"Is it a long hike or something we could do?" Dad asked.

"The entire trail is a little over 14 miles," he answered.

"That's more up to Lindy's speed, not mine," Mom said.

John turned to me. "You hike?"

"Used to," I responded, telling him some of the places I'd been on the Eastside. "I hope to take it up again when this is all settled down."

John provided my parents tips on the best spots for leisurely walks and views of the city and outlying areas. After he left, my parents gave me the space I needed. No questions, no intrusions. Dad helped me to the bedroom and I read until my eyes started to droop.

After I turned off the light, my prayers included giving the Lord thanks for giving me impressions, along with the courage to follow them.

CHAPTER 24

My father waited an entire day before bringing up my romantic life.

"So, are you over Patrick?" Dad asked on Sunday afternoon, his demeanor calm, his voice even.

"Do I look like I'm a bereaved divorcee?"

"On the contrary, you look happier than you've ever been. Are you going to wait for a while, to date I mean?"

"Mom!" I yelled, ignoring Dad. "I need an intervention."

When mom came in the room, Dad looked as guilty as the Grinch with his hands full of stolen Christmas gifts. "I was just about to tell Lindy to not cut herself off from finding a good man because she had a singular bad experience and her self-esteem has taken a hit." He was looking at mom who good-naturedly shook her head in mock disapproval.

I finally found my voice. "Just so we are crystal clear, John came over because he thought I was hungry, that's all. He was being nice. Regarding Patrick, the ending was so abrupt, I don't know how I feel about him."

"You feel better about yourself don't you?" my dad pressed.

"Yes, because I don't believe I'm an inherently worthless person, and that's what I'd been feeling like for a while now."

Dad didn't need to hear about Patrick anymore. His daughter was happy, and if John was going to be a temporary distraction or evolve into a permanent fixture, that was fine. As a father, he liked it.

At 6:30 a.m. Monday morning, I woke with a start, remembering I hadn't called Joseph to tell him about my thoughts about the hedge fund. After I ate, I sent emails to him, Vanessa and Ann. Not long after I heard the shower in the second bathroom, I got a call.

"I'm glad you emailed," Vanessa began. "I went through with it, and Arlene hand-held me through the process. First with my parents." Vanessa described how Arlene appealed to their inner sense of justice and not wanting this to happen to other women. "We'll be going to court," Vanessa said with a false courage. Her real estate agent had orders to sell the house as is and her job with Hermes in Paris was to begin the next month.

"I'm going to miss you," I said, subdued.

"No. You are going to miss the notion of me," she corrected. "Let's face it. You are having twins, and while I want to be around, it's not like you will have a lot of time to be with me."

"Well, I'll give you a credit card to purchase special outfits for the kids only available to Parisians." She willingly agreed, and I turned serious. I told her I was sorry for the friend I hadn't been, and that I wouldn't have the chance to be the friend I always wanted to be.

"I'm sorry it took my life being ruined to help me realize I had it all wrong."

"Lindy, we both had it wrong. We just got our wake up calls in different ways."

I watched television until Mom came in to ask about lunch. I updated her on Vanessa's life changes and my scathingly inaccurate judgment of Arlene based on her job and appearance. Mom told me it was like driving on the freeway and being cut off by another driver.

"It's easy to assume the person is just being a jerk with no sense of discipline or self respect," she said. "But in reality, that driver might be a single parent rushing to pick up a child from daycare or someone who has just been told he or she has cancer. You just never know, and looking back with regret doesn't help you for the future."

I took a long shower, sitting in the plastic chair Dad had purchased. The water drizzled over my head and I knew she was right. Yet it felt like one more scab of my prior self being ripped off. Nothing was going to change the fact I was losing one of my best friends.

When Joseph returned my call, we spoke of the potential buyer of my company in more serious tones. It was enough for me to place a call to Alan.

"The point isn't to tell you I've made a decision, because it's not really my decision to make, at least not alone. It's to catch you up on the events."

"Thank you," Alan responded, exhaling on the last word, relief clear in his voice. "For a minute, I thought my tenure was going to last thirty days."

"Alan, if you had complete autonomy and made a ton of money every month, would it be so bad?"

He chuckled. "No, not really."

"You're going to be hearing from Joseph in the next few days. Just don't let his crotchety manner put you off. He's a sweetheart underneath it all."

The next morning, it was 10 a.m. before I woke. I yawned, turning to my right, and saw Mom had set orange juice and food by my bed. I was so thankful to be relieved of the burden of guilt about Mom being my cook and cleaner and errand runner. If she had been anything but completely and utterly thrilled at being so useful, I'd be doubly stressed, unable to relax.

I ate and read my emails, starting with the most important. Alan confirmed client activity was stable and two new prospect discussions were under way. Were the companies reputable? In good industries?

Oh, get over yourself. Alan has already done the work and made the deals. You have no input and shouldn't pretend to have any.

Sam had created a first pass of the publicity efforts and Kay had come to the office for a meeting to discuss the plan and Alan informed me the IRS confirmed the release of our funds in nine days. By then, I'd be that much closer to knowing the sex of my babies.

I finished my breakfast quickly, my goal as clear as a point of light. I had to get busy, occupying myself with adapting our existing documents, spreadsheets and presentations into template form. I might not be in the office but that didn't preclude me from adding to the value of the company or its future.

The hours flew by as I continued through lunch, after an afternoon nap and up until dinner. Where we served eight or nine clients with a full staff, soon, hundreds or thousands of people, small business owners or entrepreneurs, whomever, could use the same informational materials for a small fraction of what our clients paid. If they wanted personal consulting, they could hire the firm directly.

I was giddy with my altruism. I closed the computer and texted Mom I was going to bed.

Saturday morning, I was in a deep sleep and dreaming of knocking at the door when somewhere in my consciousness I realized it was real and not a dream. I looked at the clock. 8:37 a.m.

Marina and her husband. I'd completely forgotten. I texted Mom to keep them in the front of the apartment until I was ready. Ten minutes later, I emerged, smiling at my mother's scowl. Olivier was in the hallway, immediately saying thank you in an effusive, awkward way. As he did, the guilt I'd kept inside began dissipating. Mom shooed me back to my room, following me with food on a tray. I sat and ate, then worked nonstop until I heard the front door open and shut again. I made my way back into the living room, turning on the gas fireplace as Mom played the piano.

I loved fall in the city. It was backwards to the rest of the world—the fog cleared and the days were bright and cold. The rain that was already pummeling the northwest wouldn't reach us for two more months.

It only been a week since I'd been in this same room with John, enjoying his concern for my well-being, feeling the touch of his fingers on my shoulders, but it seemed longer.

I sighed, pragmatism eliminating any real disappointment. I needed to stay the course, focus on my personal needs. I took a break for lunch with my parents, then we resumed our separate activities: mom reading or playing the piano or talking with her sisters, my father working on the computer and making calls from the second bedroom. We reconvened for dinner, and then watched old movies, the only type we could all agree on. An easy, comfortable pattern was developing that gave me peace and comfort.

On Tuesday, I received the first complimentary words from Dr. Kustin I'd heard.

"You've done well," he complimented. I was now twelve weeks pregnant according to his calculations. "You are getting ready to turn the corner. But this isn't a license to start walking around. All this," he said, pointing to the black around the two little dots, "needs to be white."

It was the first good news of the week. The second came in the form of a call from Darcy.

"I got pictures of Charlie," she said, her voice betraying pleasure, not dissatisfaction. "He's as handsome as you are beautiful."

If only looks were the litmus test of a relationship, I thought, but I said not a word.

"I did the same, of course," she continued, "and sent him a full body shot. He needs to see I have a whole lot of lovin' to give." We laughed. He probably back-flipped over the photo. Darcy then revealed they'd started emailing, then graduated to Facebook and finally were now talking on the phone.

"No wasted time, I see," were the only words I could eke out. John would be so smug.

"For our first date, I'm driving down there." After my surprised exclamation, she calmly told me she was interested in seeing Charlie in his home environment, not one concocted in a nice restaurant in the middle of the city. "That's not real life, Lindy. Real life is a home that needs to have the trash taken out and a kid who hasn't had a nap."

"I'm speechless," I admitted, while telling her to have a fun time and drive safe. "But now I'm going to have to eat crow in front of Dad and John."

"John?" she asked. I updated her on John and his parents.

"Oh, John. Joseph did mention him," she said. "Sharp and good looking was what Joseph said."

"Yes, he's both."

"Changing subjects, I'd like to host a baby shower."

"We're a few months away from that, but certainly that would be great. Until then, go have a love life for me so I can live vicariously through you," I suggested.

Darcy promised she'd do her best, and we signed off. My fears about Darcy and Charlie were unjustified. Thankfully, Dad and John had seen what I could not, and acted when I never would have.

CHAPTER 25

The following day, I received a reminder from Dr. Redding's office about a final follow-up appointment. I'd completely forgotten about it and had already committed to spending the afternoon with Vanessa. I called her, expecting her to be disappointed with my oversight but she was thrilled.

"Can I come?" It was an unexpected surprise which I eagerly welcomed.

"On another note entirely, I'm wondering if you have a theme for your baby room yet?" When I confessed I'd not given it a thought in the world, she scolded me. "Has your fashion sense completely left you?" She asked if she could design a room fit for a celebrity. Without hesitation, I said yes. It would be months but I knew this would give Vanessa a distraction for her remaining time in the city.

She arrived well before the doctor's appointment, books in hand along with two sacks full of colors swatches. Mom joined us in the living room and as I felt as though we were in the front row of a fashion show where the designer was giving us a presentation.

"What if I move?" I asked her.

"I'll come back and do it all over again," Vanessa answered, not missing a beat.

At five minutes before 11, the doorbell rang. Mom opened the door to a delivery man who held a bouquet that started at Mom's waist and stopped over her head. As we looked at one another, Dad smiled and Mom's eyes stayed wide open, but she said nothing

"Alan?" Vanessa asked me. I confessed ignorance. Whoever it was had spent a few hundred dollars.

"Hold on, I have one more package that goes with it," said the delivery man. When he returned, he handed my father a large basket. It had intricately woven green-and-yellow straw threads that were soft neutrals.

"Good for either gender," observed Vanessa critically, who stood, retrieving the basket and bringing it where I sat for closer inspection.

"No card here," Mom said after she signed for the delivery. Vanessa peered through the top of the basket, oohing and ahhing at the contents. She brought it closer, placing it to my right side.

"Still no card," Vanessa said, inspecting the outside of the box. "Well, are you going to unwrap it? If not I will," she threatened.

Within the pale yellow silk bow and cellophane wrapping were books, organic French lotions, foot salts, a scalp massager, and belly oil specifically designed to improve the elasticity of the skin and reduce stretch marks. I frowned in dismay over the notion of my perfect tummy getting stretched like a tiger, along with edible cures for nausea.

"I've heard those are useful," Vanessa said, pointing.

"Whoever put this together knew what they were doing," Mom said. "Have you found the card yet?" We went on a search mission and found it on the side, protected between a glass container of lavender salts and an herbal eye gel-pack.

"Kay," I predicted. It had to be. She had the money, the time and the reason.

"For the mother to be," I read out loud, six eyes all watching my reaction. "Dear Lindy," was at the top, then a hand-written note, in block letters.

"For all that you are,

For all that you have done,

The best part of life,

Is that which is yet to come"

"Nice poem," Vanessa commented.

"There's more," I said. "I hope you are staying put, staying warm and letting your mom feed you great food. If you're up for a visit later in the week, let me know. Me and Janaye will drop by. John."

"John? Who's John?" Vanessa demanded.

I giggled. "It's not like I've been holding out on you," I said defending myself.

Sitting down, I proceeded to fill in the gaps. When Vanessa learned we had only seen each other a few times, preceded by the unfortunate first meeting, and that my discerning parents approved, whatever concern she had disappeared.

"You will meet him," I said firmly. When Patrick entered my life, she'd only had a few interactions with him before I'd fallen hard. This time around, she deserved to have some input and I told her so. "You might see what I can't."

Mom and I continued to inspect the gifts. I lifted my shirt and tested the belly oil on my stomach.

"Is it odd for John to bring his daughter here?" I asked them both, worried.

"Oh please Lindy, really?" said Vanessa. "He's going to introduce her to you and the situation. If she vomits on you completely, then you both know right away what the situation is."

"Mom, you agree?"

"Yes. Doing it this way means no one's feelings are going to get hurt, or if they are, you know what you're getting yourself into."

"Which is a lot more than what you had last time," Vanessa added. "Besides, even if he's a passing fancy, he gives good gifts."

On the way to the appointment with Dr. Redding, I called John and left him a voice mail sincerely thanking him for the basket. I told him that he and Janaye were welcome to come over and meet the troops any time.

As Vanessa guided her sports car along the inner streets of the city, I asked if we could stop for a hamburger on the way. She watched in amazement as I gobbled down a bacon cheeseburger with onion rings and a shake, and put a hand over her fries when I look at them longingly.

"It's the progesterone," I explained, shamelessly stuffing several more fries in my mouth. "I'd like to tell myself to stop, and I've tried, but it doesn't work. I'm helpless."

"They're yours," Vanessa said, handing over the basket.

"All those times I've mentally condemned pregnant women who have blamed weight gain on the drugs, thinking it was a justification for overeating." She nodded, right with me. "And now I'm in it and realize I was so completely and utterly wrong and judgmental." I sighed, feeling depressed at my previous attitudes. "I'm beginning to wonder if all this was the universal law of Karma coming back to kick me in the butt."

"Perhaps," she said. "I'm just really glad to have my friend back."

"You are a friend that I don't deserve, Vanessa. You are the friend that I wasn't for years. I'm so sorry. Again."

Vanessa gripped my left hand with her right. "You're right. You don't deserve me," and she awarded me a wink and a laugh as I bit my lip in regret.

We finished and soon we were in the underground garage. "Here, take my arm," she said, putting it out. The minute we exited the elevator, she made a bee-line to the front desk, requesting a wheelchair.

"Unbelievable," I hissed.

A woman brought the metal chair on wheels and Vanessa pointed. "Get in," she said, more military than girlfriend. I sighed, resigned.

As we rolled by the cafeteria, I heard a familiar male voice call my name, and turned to see Dr. Redding. I smiled and greeted him with enthusiasm. He scanned me head to knee, nodding in approval before the look on his face changed. He was not going to believe all that had happened, and I couldn't wait to tell him.

I introduced Vanessa, expecting him to give the instant, all-encompassing look of wonder that most males gave my tall, beautiful friend, but he didn't register anything but polite interest. I was a patient. She was the friend of a patient. Period.

Vanessa relinquished her wheelchair driving duties to him. "Wait, what's the wheelchair for?" he asked, his voice anxious. I told him it had to do with the pregnancy, not the accident.

"What's she's not saying is she's been put on bed rest and she's not real happy about it."

"Ahh," he chuckled, relieved. "And you're the enforcer."

As we made our way past the gift shop and the blood lab, winding our way through the maze-like corridors, he asked about my general condition.

Once we were in the room, he pulled out the chair next to the examining table. Vanessa was quickly on the opposite side of Dr. Redding, her hands at my elbow.

"Can't I just stay in the wheelchair?" I said plaintively. My answer was a raised eyebrow from Dr. Redding.

"Ready?" he asked Vanessa. They positioned their hands under my elbows and gently lifted me up.

"Seriously people. Vanessa, if you ever leave the fashion world, being a nurse is an alternative career path. Think of it. The first nurse in a Chanel smock."

She laughed. Today, she was wearing navy blue distressed jeans, the slim cut tapering right down to her ankles ending where her leather booties began. Her light brown mock turtleneck poked out of her greyish-green slim cut bomber jacket, taupe shearling on the outside of her cuffs, as well as the collar that opened at the top of the zipper, lying flat across her shoulders. It was short wasted, highlighting her slim mid-section. The entire affect was trendy while still elegant, expensive without being showy.

"Model?" Dr. Redding asked, giving the final adjustment to the back of the table without so much as a glance up at my friend.

"Not for more than a few minutes," Vanessa emphasized. "I knew the end was coming from the beginning so I jumped to the clothing side of things."

"I'm more OP than GQ," he said without missing a beat, moving to the cupboard where he pulled out a pair of gloves.

He reached into the drawer, removed scissors and gauze and placed them on the tray. "Ready?"

Dr. Redding started to ask questions as he touched the top of my head. Was I feeling light headed or queasy? Did I have trouble with my balance or short term memory?

I instantly started laughing, and then apologized. "I'm pregnant, Dr. Redding. I can't tell if I'm light headed or nauseous due to one or the other."

He softly moved back the hair from my face, his own look devoid of expression as he proceeded to move my hair this way and that. "Fair enough. Headaches?"

"Not unless emotionally induced headaches count."

"Vomiting?" On that score, I was lucky. Not a single toilet episode.

"We are getting to the uncomfortable part," he said, warning me that removing the stitches might sting. I felt the tug and pulling of string through skin. "You okay?" he asked, and stopped his pulling. Behind me, Vanessa had crossed her legs, elbow on knee, leaning forward, her eyes alive with thought.

"It feels like a thread of fire was being pulled out of the center of my scalp." He apologized but I told him to keep going.

"How's Alan?" he asked me, probably more to distract me than from a real desire to know.

"Great," I said, holding my breath. "I made him the managing partner of my firm." The hands above me kept working. "I promised to tell you of anything else that happened. You ready?" When he indicated he was I stared at Vanessa, holding her eyes.

"One Saturday night, I had a dream. Then my husband left. Then I got divorce papers and my company almost tanked." I had said it so matter-of-factly that he assessed me, trying to determine if I were kidding.

"Seriously?"

"Vanessa, I can see you're bursting and I'm not supposed to move. Feel free to add your own thoughts."

"The whole thing?"

"Why not?"

"The idiot formerly known as her husband, Patrick, told Lindy to get an abortion when she was still in the hospital. But then it became clear he was leaving anyway. He moved out, took the good art and a cat, and 24 hours later, Lindy gets served with divorce papers. The next day Lindy's bank accounts are frozen because the asshole wasn't paying taxes for years and she gets hit for hundreds of thousands of dollars."

Dr. Redding was speechless.

"True story," I confirmed, telling him he could keep working on my stitches.

"So, here she is, no money and dealing with an unplanned pregnancy and her OB tells her she has blood in her stomach and is going to lose both babies—and yes, that means she's having twins—unless she stays off her feet. She sells all her possessions but keeps the boat afloat."

Dr. Redding stopped the snipping and stood back, looking down at me, searching my face. "Really?"

"I'm living proof that truth is much stranger and more horrible than fiction."

"You look so…calm," Dr. Redding remarked, resuming his task.

"You wanted to know if I had any more 'beyond this life' experiences." I began, a little slowly. "I did. Vanessa glossed over the part where I had a dream the night before my world changed. I was dressed in white and sitting on a white chair in a square, all-white room. I was visited by my dead grandmother and other relatives who came in one at a time. They told me the same four words, 'You must leave him.' The next morning, all I could do was ask Patrick if he loved me, and he said no. I called Vanessa, she came and got me and when we returned he was gone. If it hadn't been for that dream, him leaving and the divorce papers being signed within twenty four hours, I would have been on the hook for $300,000 of back taxes plus penalties. It was a miracle but if didn't feel like it at the time."

The pulling finally stopped and Dr. Redding placed his tools on the tray.

"I've heard of a few incredible experiences similar to yours. A man meeting his daughter who had died years before. Another women talking to her deceased husband and choosing to come back to take care of her family."

"She found God," Vanessa said pointedly. "He had to take out the big guns." Her cell phone rang and she looked at the number, excusing herself.

"I had another woman come in one time, a Shaman," Dr. Redding continued. "That's the person in an Indian tribe who sees spirits. In their world, every living thing has a spirit, from trees to animals to people. One time when she was here, she pointed out to me that a young girl down the hall had seven spirits hovering over her, while her mother had three. She called them the person's ancestors."

Vanessa returned just then.

"Vanessa is one of my drivers," I said, looking her in the eyes. "At least until she leaves this fair town of ours."

"What makes you want to go?" Dr. Redding asked.

"I have an issue I'm dealing with. We are working through the process of the judicial system."

"Not that I'd try and tell you otherwise, but women like you and Lindy are like pillars of light in this sometimes dark empty town of ours. I for one, would find it a much happier place to live with the two of you in it." He said the two of us, but his glance rested on Vanessa a split second longer than it was on me.

I told him Vanessa's plane tickets to Paris were booked.

"Paris is overrated," he said dryly.

We said our goodbyes, and we were quiet until we got into the elevator.

CHAPTER 26

"He was nice," Vanessa muttered to me, the minute the doors closed.

"Yes, he is," I responded.

The elevator door opened and she pushed me through the double doors and parked the wheelchair at the front entrance. I could have imagined it, but it seemed to me that Vanessa stood taller and her gait had a smoother glide than it had on the way in.

During the drive back to my apartment, Vanessa told me she hadn't lost faith in men or the possibility of love.

"Are you attracted to him?" she asked me out of the blue.

"Who?" I asked, looking at her. "Dr. Redding? No chemistry," I said simply, "though he is seriously handsome."

She agreed he was good looking, and smart and personable. "Never in a million years would I ever have given him a second glance," she told me, her comment weighted with remorse.

"Ugh," I said out loud, causing her to turn to me.

"Does your stomach hurt? Are you going to be sick?"

"Of myself, I think. When you said that- I realized that you and I have always gone after the sexy, glamorous, always on the move type of guys. The players."

"Because that's the life we were living."

I rolled my hand on my belly again and looked out the window. "Not anymore. Not for me anyway." Somewhere, someplace, legitimate, hardworking men were waiting. Men like John.

"You want to come inside for a while and meet John?" I asked her when we arrived at the house. "I told you I wanted you to meet him."

She'd been standing with her hand on the car door, ready to shut it. "Are you kidding me?"

A car was parked on the street that I didn't recognize. It was a blue BMW convertible. I'd place a bet it was John's.

"Hi, girls," Dad called.

"Hi everyone," I said calmly.

"John, this is Vanessa." He gripped her hand.

"This is my daughter Janaye," he said, pointing to teenage girl standing next to him. Janaye's dark brown was a mass of curls, spreading out past her shoulders like the wavy threads on a mop.

"I'm Lindy," I said, waving as I walked towards the couch. Don't smother. Don't try overly hard. Just be. No shaking hands. "Been here long?"

"Not really," Janaye answered. "It's early release Friday. We've been hanging out."

"Which means we've been shopping," John answered. Janaye nodded her head, smiling with pride. She was poised and aware, and very observant, looking between me and her father, as if to ascertain what was going on between us.

"And we're a pit stop between malls."

"I did want to come," Janaye interjected. "I'm really grateful for what you have done for Grandma and the center."

"Mom has done nothing but talk about you like the apostles talk of Paul walking on water," John added.

"Paul fell in," I reminded him, the remark garnering a quirky smile from his daughter.

Vanessa sat down beside Janaye, asking where they shopped and what they were looking to buy. In minutes, the two were talking fashion and faux paus committed by young women in the world of San Francisco clothing.

"How do you feel, really?" John searched my eyes, as though they'd be the tell-tale signals of my overall health.

"My doctor said that if I keep on track, I could be up and about in less than a month. Maybe even two weeks."

"Sam told me I won't be long for this life if I tell you anything that causes in any activity on your part," John said.

I grinned. "If you don't fill me in on what's been happening, I may kill you myself." This garnered a smirk from Janaye, who I could tell was listening to every word while carrying on her conversation with Vanessa.

"Apparently, Sam helped write the description of the center, the contribution to the city and potential for the future, one paragraph at a time. While that was going on, Erwin and I took to hammering out the fine print of the contract."

"All this happened in four days? How was that possible?"

"I never saw him," Janaye broke in.

"And wasn't it worth it?" he shot back. She gave him an "of-course" look. "By Thursday it was done."

I couldn't find the breath to say much more than thank you to John, and he put up a hand, pre-emptively warding off the compliment. "This is not my doing," he said.

"Oh, please," I said. "Without you being a part of the deal, I'm sure it wouldn't have happened."

Vanessa held up her hand. "Can you two modest people split the credit for this project already?"

"I only started it," I said, under my breath. "You finished it."

"There wouldn't have been anything to start if it weren't for you," he retorted.

Mom reminded us of the time. "Are you three interested in staying for dinner?"

John gave his daughter a questioning look. "Why don't we take a rain check," he said. Smart, I thought. Take it slow and easy with the daughter.

"I'll stay," said Vanessa, "and I promise I'll eat enough for the both of them."

As John and Janaye rose to leave, I thanked him again for the gifts. "Drop by anytime, you two. I'm stuck here for, oh, the next three weeks at least, and visitors are always welcome."

When the sound of footsteps faded, I cocked my right eyebrow at Vanessa.

"Honest. Gorgeous. Down to Earth. The fact that he's evidently in the "seriously-liking-you" mode is helpful."

"What??"

She grinned. "You heard me. That man is all over you like a hunter who has spotted a deer."

"She's right, sweetheart," Dad said. "It's pretty clear."

"As if the amazing gift basket wasn't enough of a signal," Vanessa added. "You are as blind with him as you were with Patrick. Did you see how he looked at her?" Vanessa asked my father, who nodded, a smug, Cheshire-cat smile plastered on his face.

"Like how?" I asked.

"Like a man taking care of the most important thing in the world," she stated. My parents echoed her comments.

"You can smile, Lindy," said Dad. "It's OK. I approve. And I think his daughter is on board, for now."

"Yes, but this could all change pretty quickly," I noted, not wanting to dwell on what-if's. "In a few weeks I'll know the sex of the twins!"

"Have you thought of names?" Vanessa asked.

"Not at all."

"Then let's start, because if I'm going to have input, I want it to be big."

We spent dinnertime discussing names until I yawned and Vanessa left. I was filled with little more than thoughts of colors of the room for my unborn babies.

That night, I received an email from John, thanking me again for the work and glad I liked the basket. He said he had one question and he didn't want to offend me.

Is your business able to financially sustain a project of this size?

I tapped my fingers on the keyboard considering the right response.

Didn't your mother raise you right? I typed back, smiling as I did it. Let me just say that I was very pleased the timing worked out so that we were able to start another client project around the same time. That helps, but wouldn't have mattered. It was the right thing to do, and we are proud to be part of such a great program.

There. That should shut the drawer on the topic.

CHAPTER 27

I began the following day by slathering my belly with the body butter John had given me. The directions on the container advised starting before the belly became pronounced to 'soften the skin.' *Soften, soften*, I mentally chanted, willing my skin to expand like a balloon resulting in a smooth and lineless ball instead of the white tiger-like stretch marks.

My cell phone rang. It was Sam. "I've been trying to give you your space, but I couldn't resist. I'm definitely going to apply to graduate school." She told me all about the programs as USF. I congratulated her, and she anticipated my next question. "And yes, it does have a little bit to do with my boyfriend."

"Will you be starting soon?" I asked, hoping it would be delayed a few months.

"Not for at least a year, which is fine. Right now, I'm completely focused on the youth center." She was also curious about "any visitors I might have had."

"How did you know that?"

"John called me for your email, so of course I asked why he wanted it." The girl was shameless and I told her so.

The following week, the IRS released the hold on my credit and bank accounts. When my accountant gave me the word, I sent Alan an email, requesting he cut a check to himself for the temporary loan. He refused to add on an interest payment, telling me he was the managing partner and had the deciding vote.

"Pulling rank on me?" I teased him.

"Absolutely. Now I have some more news for you. I've had two conversations with one of the hedge funds called Trident Capital Partners, or TCP. Suffice to say we have piqued their interest. What I didn't get in the first call was the real reason they are interested in us. It's our stocks, Lindy. All the shares in privately-held companies we took as partial payment. Where else can a company purchase a portfolio for cents on the dollar without running into SEC violations? Nowhere."

Now it all became clear to me. "Buying us is like purchasing the golden goose, except the goose comes with the basket already full of eggs."

"Yep, and all completely under the radar," he confirmed. "Given our hit with GeorgiaLiman I wouldn't be surprised if we have an offer soon."

"What's the rush?"

"We will only get more expensive. They want to buy our future wealth before we've made it."

After dinner, I checked email again and read a note from John. He'd found a few apartments in the city my parents might want to consider, free of charge until a paying tenant comes along. I thanked him and forwarded the links to my father. Let reality kill the dream, I thought to myself. If Dad wanted to say no, that was his prerogative.

During my next visit with Dr. Kustin, he told me that the blood had completely vanished and my uterine wall had thickened.

"Does that mean you're kicking me out?" I'd grown to like his blunt style.

"I specialize in infertility and high-risk. You are neither of those now."

I got it. My departure would make room for others who needed him as badly as I had.

"Try this one," he said, giving me a card for a traditional obstetrician. "His bedside manner isn't as good as mine but he's very capable."

Dad had been waiting for me in the office and we walked side-by-side down to the car. An incessant buzz was coming from inside my purse and I saw it was a voicemail message and text from Vanessa. I listened in the car, my thoughts whirling as I heard her dilemma.

"Everything OK?" Dad asked.

"It will be in a minute," I said to him. I looked up Dr. Redding and placed a call. It took a few minutes for the nurse on duty to track him down, and when he got on the phone, he sounded rushed.

As quickly and as calmly as I could, I told him the situation Vanessa had described. When I was finished, Dr. Redding was on board.

"I don't know if she'll go for it," he said, "but I'll give it my best shot." There was no mistaking the determination in his voice.

"That was nice and creative," Dad complimented when the call was over.

"Let's see how Vanessa reacts. She's either going to hate me or thank me."

When she called me back, I'd just positioned myself on the couch.

"I trust you, and I trust your judgment," she told me, raising my gut of nerves from the ground and back to my belly. "And as important, I trust Dr. Redding. What in the world inspired you to call him?"

I closed my eyes and silently exhaled in relief. Someone above or around me most likely.

"I knew I couldn't go with you to the prosecuting attorney's office, and who better to stand by your side than a doctor who's tall, imposing and articulate, and has dealt with a lot of these trauma patients?"

Vanessa expressed worry that it was taking time away from his schedule.

"If he didn't want to do it, or if it would have put his patients in jeopardy, he would have said no, Vanessa." But I knew the truth: he hadn't wanted to say no. He wanted to say yes.

"I'll let you know how it goes," she promised.

Late Friday morning, my mother asked if I'd be ok with company on Saturday night.

"Anyone special?" I asked her.

She told me it depends on who I defined as special. "When John was here, he asked your father and me if the three of us would be interested in coming to his mother's home for dinner. Your father declined, inviting them here instead." She turned to the kitchen and tittered to herself, magnificently pleased she had pulled off a little trick.

"You don't think this is a little premature?"

"As Vanessa said, you might as well know early on whether this has a chance to work or not. Don't be afraid of dipping more than your toe in the water. Jump in. If you start to drown, we'll throw you a life vest."

"That was nice and poetic!" I complimented, and she tried to swat my butt as I walked by her.

I called the office of Dr. Michael Lawler and got an appointment for the following day. Apparently, Dr. Kustin had pull with the front desk, as they had been holding a spot since the referral.

I was so excited I called Ann, who patiently answered all my questions about what constitutes a good doctor and what questions to ask. It was then Ann's turn to ask about my life, and specifically, John. I gave her the update, then voiced my skepticism about a potential future with him.

"Ann, is it was possible he could have serious intentions?"

Ann pointed out my naiveté. "Lindy, at our age, people have baggage. The pickings for heterosexual females or males in this town are pretty slim." Ann maintained that when he showed up to notarize my papers, he made a decision on the spot. "Don't overthink it."

I tried not to.

Dr. Michael Lawler was the exact opposite of Kustin. Whereas Kustin was big of gut, loud of mouth and gruff, Lawler was tall, regal and trim. He formally addressed me by my last name until I told him to call me Lindy. As I patiently waited, I asked him about his family. Did he have children? How old were they?

"Four children," he answered, his head still down. "Three graduated from Harvard and the fourth is a Navy Seal." I took the hint and remained silent. He'd spoken with Dr. Kustin, knew my history and asked me the most basic of questions and then pointed to the gown. He left, I changed, and when he returned, he was accompanied by a quiet, kind-looking nurse who greeted me by name.

"First time mom?" she asked, her face registering an excitement that mirrored my own. As I tried to relax, Dr. Lawler readied the computer keyboard and monitor that was beside the bed. He sat on a stool, facing the monitor, his left hand on the keyboard, his right, moving a rolling device atop my abdomen.

Click, click, he tapped. "I'm taking measurements," he said, just as Dr. Kustin had done, adjusting the screen after each picture was taken. He stopped and clicked, then stopped and clicked many more times. Dr. Lawler scanned the data again. "According to average growth cycles, you're a bit further along than originally diagnosed. I'd say closer to five months."

"I can give you another type of progesterone that will accomplish the same goals without all the weight gain." That would be a bonus.

"Can you tell the sex?"

He nodded. "Yes, and I can tell you now if you'd like. The next appointment is when it's usually done, because it's a 3D view with our neonatal specialist here at the office and you get incredibly accurate, full color view of the babies. It's your choice."

Mom. She'd love to be here, and I'd only hear the news once. "I'll wait."

"Do you have a journal?" he asked abruptly. I shook my head no. "Get one and start writing. If not, be sure to have it the day you have your next appointment. You will want these memories later." Without further explanation, he left.

At the checkout counter, the receptionist asked me if next Friday morning at 9 a.m. would work.

"I'll be here."

On the way home, I told Dad about the journal suggestion and he made a bee-line to Chestnut Street where he picked out a leather-bound journal and three ham and cheese croissants at the bakery next door. When we were at home eating around the table, Mom asked me what I was going to wear.

"For what?"

"Dinner of course." I was perplexed and amused.

"Do you know how long it's been since I had a first date? Scratch that. How about we skip right to a date with a daughter, and with my parents?" We both giggled as I sat on the bed as she went through my closet, garment by garment.

She pulled one out with tags. "Never worn?" She clucked.

"I know," I mumbled, a little embarrassed.

After trying various cardigans with the dresses, she found one that worked, a dark blue top that cut around my ribs with a tie in the middle.

"It accentuates your full chest,'" Mom said slyly. The dress itself was white with a flower print pattern, green stems and red rose petals, with black accents. I turned in the mirror, the A-line cut swirling slightly. It was as flattering as I was going to get in my present state. My belly had exploded in the last two weeks.

I curled my hair, applied more makeup than I had in the past month, and joined Dad in the living room. I had a couple of hours left, and I called Vanessa to see how her conversation had gone with Dr. Redding. When she didn't pick up, I retrieved the journal Dad had purchased from the bookstore.

The wraparound brown leather cover was stamped with an image of a tree. The petals were heart-shaped, some attached, others dropping to the ground. The tree itself extended down, and the roots moved outward and around the spine to the back, making it appear alive and thriving

I unwound the leather and reverently turned the first page. It reminded me of my book that resided elsewhere, the gold calligraphy continuing.

The words came, and I didn't censor the content. I started with the day of the accident. I filled page after page, my small words at first looking like an inkjet gone awry, becoming larger and easier to read. Curls at the bottom of my y's started to appear, and the l's were taller. It was as though a seed of emotion and thought, long buried under the surface, had been placed in fertile soil, provided safety and light, and given the chance to grow.

CHAPTER 28

I wouldn't have noticed the passage of time had it not been for Mom finishing one piece of music and starting the next. When the doorbell rang, Dad stood, pushing his hand to the ground; the universal signal for "stay put."

Dad greeted John warmly. He wore a navy blue linen jacket over a taupe sweater and jeans. His left arm dropped and disappeared from sight, before reappearing on the back of his daughter Janaye.

Mom greeted her, taking the young woman's hand in both of hers, "Nice to see you again, Janaye." I called out a greeting and received a pageant wave in return. They didn't know I'd been given clearance to stand and walk about, which made the welcome less awkward than it might have been.

Mom asked Janaye if she wanted to help in the kitchen and she was game.

"How are you feeling?" John asked me, sitting in the armchair by my father and opposite me. "What's the latest?"

"The doctor told me I'm five months along, not four."

John's eyes brightened with anticipation. "Wow. Over halfway and you'll know the sex of the babies soon."

"What's new with the center?" I asked him, not wanting this to be a conversation only about my pregnancy.

He crossed one leg over the other. "We are working on first phase layouts. Erwin essentially asked Janaye to be his youth consultant on the project." She emerged from the kitchen, a spoonful of dark pudding in her hand.

"What's that?" John asked.

"Chocolate silk," she said with a smile before returning to mom.

"Young girls have the best insight," Dad told John. "When Lindy was in high school, she started acting out a bit and I thought a trip to Texas would do her good, so I pulled her out of school, put her in the co-pilot's seat, and told her she was going to start learning how to fly."

Janaye emerged again, this time sitting by her father.

"We paid a visit to a Houston-based release estate developer and Lindy sat silently until the conversation turned to his planned outdoor mall. He's wearing this enormous cowboy hat and smoking a cigar and up pipes Lindy, who says it's not going to work. 'Excuse me?' he says, and she thinks he's serious and repeats herself. He is so stunned with her comment, he invites her to tell him why she thinks it will fail. After that, I sat back and listened to her give her not too subtle thoughts on his layout."

"What did he do?" asked Janaye grinning with mischief.

"He asked her questions for over an hour. Then three months later, he sends me the final drawings and told me he'd used most of her suggestions."

John put his hand on Janaye's shoulder with justifiable pride. "Same here. Janaye will be looking at it all, from rooms to colors. I, on the other hand, probably won't get to see it until the walls are up and the paint is dry."

We moved to the dining room and my mother talked about operas and how she was looking forward to going again.

"I'm really trying to get Dad to go to more musicals with me but he's not interested," Janaye moaned. "He was permanently scarred as a child by too many replays of 'Annie.'"

"That little freckle-faced, red-topped kid screaming "The sun will come out tomorrow!' It's like Chucky with vocal chords instead of a knife."

"The truth is," continued Janaye, "he wants to be home on the weekends, not going out. He likes board games," giving us the information with all the excitement of a funeral director.

"There are no secrets here," John noted.

"It doesn't sound like you have any," I quipped.

My dad pointed a fork on my mother. "Lindy's mom got us both going to musicals when she was eight."

John gave a pretend groan. "I'm surrounded."

"If you don't like indoors, what about the outdoors? The coast line is great around here. Scuba diving is something you two could do together," I suggested. "Although I think you have to be 12 to learn and 16 to get oxygen tanks. When's your birthday Janaye?"

"February twelfth."

"You will definitely appreciate that date when you are older," I remarked, earning myself a smile from Janaye and a groan from John.

The conversation moved easily from one non-threatening topic to another. My parents talked about growing up, and how Charlie and I were born in Costa Rica and lived in Honduras and other parts of Central America. Janaye was alternately fascinated with the stories of the tobacco plants and iguanas. She asked if I played sports.

"Soccer."

Her eyebrows raised. "Do you still?"

The group chuckled. "My career ended once I finished college. There weren't any pro teams back then."

"You were that good?" she asked.

"As good at playing forward at USC can be," I replied evenly.

"They're still one of the top three aren't they?" Dad asked and I inwardly thanked him for setting me up.

"Number one the last two years," Janaye said, her voice a notch lower, and her tone holding a hint of reverence. "Maybe sometime you'll come to one of my games. My coach says I need to improve my footwork but he's not giving me specific pointers."

I sympathized. "It's hard for a single coach to give personal tips to every player, and worse, coaches on school and elite teams give conflicting advice and use different styles for different girls."

"Exactly!" she hissed, her frustration clear. As we continued to talk about her sport of choice, John's eyes met mine several times. He was glad she and I had a topic in common and I was relieved I had something useful to provide.

We talked of soccer until it was time to leave. Janaye gave hugs to both my parents and a half-hug to me.

It was strange, I thought after they left. It was so obvious we'd just had a group date, the three of us testing each other out, all in the confines of my apartment, yet we pulled it off.

I mentioned this to my mother as she was doing this dishes. "Should I be embarrassed the ink is barely dry on the divorce paperwork?"

"Honey," she said, using her professorial tone. "From what you described, the love had gone out of your marriage years ago. Keeping house with someone doesn't equate to emotional intimacy." If that were the gauge, I'd have been divorced for a long, long time. And from what I'd seen of John, he hadn't had someone in his life since his daughter was a baby. "The timing is right on this one, and as Vanessa said, there is no rush, but there's no reason to artificially deny a connection either."

"I'm not denying anything," I said archly. But I wasn't going to get my hopes up either.

The following morning, a 9 a.m. call woke me up from a sound sleep. It was Saturday, and I was momentarily grumpy until I saw who the caller was.

"You didn't tell me your brother was so engaging," Darcy laughed impishly. She recounted the walk on the waterfront with Charlie and his son Max, the Greek food that followed and a movie.

"Wasn't this supposed to be a meet-and-greet, then lunch and that was it?"

"Yeah," she said and nearly giggled. "Eight hours later."

"You don't seem worse for the experience," I remarked, rubbing one eye.

"On the contrary. I'm fabulous. He's coming up here next time."

"Really? Is he going to bring Max? And if yes, would you be able to share him enough to have them visit us? We'd all love to see them."

"Charlie told me you'd say that, and he also said you're the most generous, giving and patient person he's ever known."

"Aww, Charlie. I love him."

"I know, and so I have to ask you one, very important question. Are you OK with me dating your brother?"

"What?! Oh. My. Gosh, Darcy. I don't know if he deserves you, or if you can handle him, but more power to you. You are both fabulous."

With my blessing, she then gushed in a way only a woman who had been on a fantastic first date can. From the nature of her comments, I imagined Charlie holding the doors open, pulling out her chair, asking her what she wanted for dinner and then ordering for her. He might have had a substance problem, but he'd never lacked in manners nor mistreated women.

After Darcy and I hung up, I showered, thinking that this was proof that the random pattern of dots that connected, weren't random at all, but now were laid out in a seemingly straight line.

I texted John. *Reality didn't kill the dream—it made it better.*

My parents were off to the flower mart, an activity that had become their Saturday morning routine, while I made the most of the quiet morning, reading the papers and leisurely reviewing my product line until my stomach growled. Fortunately, the new pills Dr. Lawler gave me had dramatically reduced my food cravings but I still had a healthy appetite. On my way to the kitchen, my phone rang and I hurried back to get it, guessing the caller.

"Aren't you supposed to be at a soccer game?"

"It was over long ago. She had two of the four goals and we won. Right now she's in the shower and I'm calling you."

"Does that mean this is an illicit phone call?"

He chuckled. "If only. Did you get enough sleep?"

"You know, I don't really need my own mom with you around, but yes, thanks very much for asking, I did."

"Good, because I was wondering if you'd consider going out with me on an adult-only date."

"I don't know," I drawled. "These chaperoned events with my parents have already become the norm."

"True, but we are ready to graduate. When can you be up and walking?" I grinned at his hint of impatience.

"If you must know, I got the clean bill of health the day prior, but thought the whole coming and going thing would be easier if I was sitting. Sorry."

"I'm not offended. By the way, you did good."

"You mean with Janaye?" I was glad to hear it, but… "John, this whole thing—us—is unexpectedly great, if I may be honest, but it's also completely strange. I mean, me pregnant, you with a pre-teen. Are you really sure now is the time for us to get together?"

"Can I match your honesty?"

"Absolutely," I said.

"When I saw you, I wanted to know you much better, but the timing wasn't right for reasons I learned later. Is it perfect now? No, and in six months, you'll be overwhelmed with babies and the rest of us will get very little of your time." He'd thought this through, the fact giving me an inner joy. "How long does a person wait to try and achieve some level of personal happiness? Janaye may not be totally on board, but she's not jumped ship either."

"You're willing to give it a try."

He laughed. "Aren't I already doing that?"

"Very much so."

"So, continuing that approach, how about we have a date night, tonight?"

"Are you kidding me?"

"What? You have other plans?"

"Where's Janaye going to be?

"It just so happens she is staying at Grandma's tonight for a cousin-only sleepover. When dealing with the schedule of a single parent, one must be ready to go on the fly." He suggested I give him a few options for dinner.

The one place I didn't want to go was Fog City Diner. As much as I loved the food and the people, I wanted our first real date to be a new location without history.

"You know where I've never been? There is some famous restaurant, the Cliffs of Cliffside or something…"

"The Cliff House? Done. See you at 6."

I put the phone down, the smile cracking my face wide, and it rang again.

"Lindy, I've got a car full of samples I want to bring by," Vanessa announced. "What are you doing?"

"Thinking about the date I'm going on tonight."

She squealed once, told me she was coming over and hung up. Between the time she arrived, Mom and Dad had returned home.

Vanessa appeared minutes later. "I knew you'd be home with nothing to do!" Both her hands were full of bags brimming with fluffy items in yellows and pale greens, similar to the color of the items in John's basket.

"I'll set these down and make another trip," she said, placing the bags on the inside of the hallway, by the piano before leaving as quickly as she came. Dad got up and followed her out. Mom and I started looking at the bags, but Vanessa caught us and told it was off limits until she could do show and tell. After the third trip, Vanessa closed the door with an exaggerated display of effort and Mom laughed, telling her she had gone to extremes.

"That's normal for her," I said. "She doesn't do halfway."

Vanessa lined up the bags in a particular order, drawing things out piece by piece as if she were in Paris gearing up for the runway. She started by showing us the fabrics she'd selected and then started with pillows, shams, crib-sized comforters and throws for two cribs.

"Green, French-country?" I asked, unsure.

"It's timeless and classic, and goes great with this," Vanessa explained, showing us a chenille throw in an off-white. The fabric was so soft I wrapped it around my shoulders, rubbing my cheeks against the material. Before long, every available inch of space on the couch, chairs and floor in the living room was covered. She told us how she found this boutique with a tagline she loved.

"Luxury for little ones," she said. "Isn't that great marketing? They had this recliner called the Versailles, which looks like an elegant Marie Antoinette-type of thing but is really a nursing rocker." The three of us stared at her. "An upgraded Lay-Z-Boy," she added, showing us pictures. "It's two grand, but you can afford it. What else are you going to do with all your newfound money?"

"I'm a reformed person and I am certainly not going to be putting a $2,000 chair in my registry. How do you find this stuff?" I asked her. "It's not like you run in a circle full of moms."

"I'm in fashion, girlfriend. This is what we do." It was over the top, and I loved it.

"Very elegant," Dad said behind me, leaning over my shoulder. Mom eventually followed him out of the room and Vanessa closed the door behind them.

"I'm never going to say thank you enough. I'm going to miss you so much when you leave."

Vanessa rewarded me with an appreciative smile and a sigh. "Well, I better get this over with then," she said, coming to my side, grabbing my hand. "I'm not leaving this weekend."

She began talking about Jake—not Dr. Redding—and their trip to municipal court.

"Just before I was going to leave for the courthouse, I asked if he'd mind picking me up. I wanted him to know more about what was going on before we got there, rather than showing up and saying 'hi, let me point out my rapist.'" I gasped that she said the words so pragmatically and harshly, but then, it was Vanessa. "Because he'd had to testify in court on cases, he went into his doctor mode, summarizing what I was going to encounter, helping me prepare. It calmed me down to have him be so clinical about the process. There was no judgment, but no sympathy either. It was really like, 'You are going to experience this, this and this, and then they will ask you that.'"

Thank you I thought to the small voice that had put the idea in my head. I hoped I'd continue to act on these quiet impressions, the ones that seemed so absurd and meaningless in the moment, yet turned out to have so much impact on another person's life.

"He was the perfect person to have with me," she continued. "No offense."

"Did the hearing itself go well?" I asked tentatively.

"As well as it could. I provided my version of things and picked the guy out from a lineup. And Jake, he told me that he was going to be by my side throughout this process whether or I wanted it or not, but he said, 'I hope you want it.'"

"What did you say?"

"I told him I did."

Once Vanessa left, I showered and figured I'd skip straightening my hair. It was humid today, we'd be on the coast, and my hair would frizz out regardless. I was spraying my hair with a second coat of hair shine when Mom knocked.

"Can you come here for a minute? We have something for you," she said.

Dad held a large package on his lap. It had a thick, brown ribbon with an unmistakable name on it. Barneys. He had the smug look of a mischievous kid.

"What did you do?" I muttered.

"You'll see," he said, the glimmer in his eye betraying his absolute delight in what was about to come.

Slowly and carefully, I pulled back the white, embossed paper and lifted up the dark brown shearling jacket that was inside. The wide, triangular collar exposed the soft lamb's wool inside the jacket, all the way down to the upturned cuffs on the sleeves. I held it up, wondering how in the world they had pulled off getting the same jacket that I'd had during my time with Patrick, that had somehow "gotten lost" at the dry cleaner.

"Is it the right one?" Mom asked me, a twinge of worry in her voice.

I nodded, speechless. It had the same square pockets in the front and hung to mid-thigh, the perfect length for cold walks on the beach. The collar also turned up and the right lapel flap had a small dark-brown hook that latched to a near-invisible leather chord on the adjacent side.

"But why? I told you Patrick said it was at the dry cleaners." I'd not told them about my dream in which I saw his girlfriend wearing it at Fog City. Just on the off chance it was…well, wrong.

Mom's eyes glinted with anger, an uncommon emotion for her. "He's a liar Lindy."

Dad spoke. "I went to the dry cleaner you mentioned, and they never saw the coat. I called every dry cleaner this side of the valley. Nothing. So, put it behind you like everything else. You're starting over now, and we're helping you."

I walked to the full-length mirror and turned this way and that. It was indeed, the same coat. "Okay, it's behind me. But how did you manage this?"

"Barneys had one in their Seattle store. It arrived just in time for the big date."

I didn't spend much time on my make-up, deciding less was more. A few errant eyebrow hairs were removed, and a thin line of dark top-lid liner was all I added to my eyes. I didn't even bother with mascara. The progesterone and multi-vitamins had done the same number on my eyelashes as they had with my hair; they were thick and dark, pushing together in a mass that reminded me of dark sprouts of upturned grass.

When I came into the living room, I cleared my throat. Dad was sitting on the couch, flipping through a magazine on exotic cars. I went behind him, draping my arms around his shoulders, kissing him on the cheek. His day-old stubble pricked my skin and it felt good. "Thank you, again."

The late afternoon sun was still bright, but it wouldn't be long before the fog started to roll in from the ocean, making its way up the lowlands of the Sunset District, and then up and over the low hills where I lived before settling in on the Bay.

Was I ready? I asked myself. I hadn't answered the question when I heard the thudding of footsteps on the stairs. A smile involuntarily drew the corners of my lips up. The steps weren't slow or light. It was a quick pounding. Was he really so excited to see me that he was taking two steps at a time? A giggle rolled up my chest, and I pressed my lips tight, the sound stopped and the doorbell rang.

I'd soon find out.

CHAPTER 29

John came in, saying hello to my mother. Rather than rushing out to greet him, I peeked into the bathroom one last time to check my hair to make sure my teeth were free of lipstick. I felt the excited flutterings of anticipation as I walked around the corner.

"There she is," he announced, turning towards me, one hand in his pocket. He held my gaze as his arms went up, as if to alert me to the fact he intended to wrap his arms around me unless I signaled for him to stop.

I inhaled slightly as my smile extended wide. His fingers touched the center of my back. "You look gorgeous," he whispered in my ear, the wave of my hair tickling my ear and I mumbled a thank you. He smoothly turned to my parents, letting his one hand on the center of my back linger as he asked if I was ready to go eat.

"Absolutely," I said.

I got my small clutch and jacket, which he offered to carry. Mom and Dad wished us a good time, and we were off.

As I settled in the car, John pressed the buttons on his left door panel, adjusting my seat.

"That's perfect, thanks," I told him. I smoothed the top of my pants with my palms, looking up at him.

"You alright?" he asked, leaning over me. I nodded. "You sure?"

"It's my first date in over five years. I'm a little nervous! Now go feed me unless you want a rabid, pregnant woman on your hands."

John headed us west, toward the Sunset District. "What's on your mind?" he asked me.

"I was wondering about the old men I see, opening car doors for their wives, who look like they've been married a million years. They do it with so much love, like it means the world to them."

John laughed. "Am I the old man in this equation?"

When my own laughter died down, I told him I was serious. "I mean, have you ever kept opening the car door for a person you were dating after you'd been together for a while?"

"Sure, until the woman I was dating told me to stop doing it. Women don't like it," he maintained. "It's like they are being demeaned. What they don't realize is that a man needs to be allowed to treat a woman right, and it doesn't lessen their independence for a man to be polite."

"Not that I've hit a nerve or anything," I said in jest, though I felt hypocritical. His comments meant that my own actions had contributed to the demise of Patrick's shows of affection. After we were married, I vividly remembered times when Patrick had attempted to open the door for me and I told him not to bother because we were in a rush, and later, waving him off when he'd come to my side after a nice dinner.

"I can always stop if you want me to."

"No, it's all good. You get to have the role until I get old and wrinkled."

He turned to me with a look that brought heat to my face. "Really?"

"Sure," I said, the laugh catching in my throat. Another look, another moment of connection.

John pulled the car into the restaurant parking lot and shut off the engine. He gave me a questioning look that was also a partial challenge.

"I'll be waiting right here," I said. My sassy comment was rewarded with a smile, as John got out and walked around to my side of the car.

John helped me out of the car and held my hand, giving me an additional tug for which I was thankful for. He held up my new, shearling coat and I gratefully slid my arms in. The setting sun had taken the day's warmth with it. I slid my hand under his elbow, resting my hand on his forearm. It was my first intentional touch of his body, and it felt as natural as it was exciting.

Inside the building, John led me through the grand entrance and down the hallway to the dining area.

"This place looks so much smaller than I remember," he said under his breath.

"How long ago was that?" I asked.

"Prom. Bad memory. Halfway through the dance she dumped me for a guy who got into Harvard. Around here, UCLA doesn't mean much."

"Oh," I said, laughing at his heartbreak. "Why didn't you tell me? We could have chosen a place without bad mojo." He shook his head, leading the way. "Well, if it makes you feel any better, my prom date ended hours early, when he realized he wasn't going to get my lace dress undone because it had a row of 100 buttons from of the top of neck all the way down to my waist."

"Your Dad pick that out?"

"Of course! But I loved that dress. I felt like a princess."

We were seated by a window so our table was like being perched on the edge of the cliff. The waitress came by and took our order for drinks.

"Mind if I order a few starters?" he asked me, "I know exactly what to get and what to avoid." I closed my menu and listened. Beef sliders, butternut squash ravioli, a bread fondue and an Asian crepe.

"Is that dinner?"

"The portions are bite-sized, so don't worry. We'll have a little bit of everything."

The drinks came and we raised our glasses of Coke and juice to our first date "as adults." I asked him if he lived nearby.

"As the crow flies. I stayed in our home after my wife left, not wanting to change the environment for Janaye, and frankly, I love the place. What? Is that look one of scorn for staying next to my parents?"

"No, not at all. I think that's wonderful. I was thinking about what it's like living with a girl becoming a young woman."

"Ahh," John reached for a piece of bread. "That would instill fear and trepidation in any normal person. But I'd like to talk about that with you for a minute." I waited, taking a drink. "Since you brought up the subject of my daughter, do you have any other fears or concerns you'd like to share?"

I took the moment to swallow. "You sound like a shrink on a follow-up appointment."

"I'm being serious."

"Well, if you must know, it's not Janaye-specific. It's the whole stepmother image." I suspected she feared the notion as well and said so.

"I think she's been more embarrassed I haven't dated at all, like something may be wrong with me." My hand unconsciously raised to my open mouth. "True story. The truth is far more boring. It's just disheartening believing a woman is strong and smart, only to find she's intellectually limited and somewhat shallow."

"Shallow?" A flash of dread did hit me then. I'd been so shallow as to have been attracted to Patrick, and him me.

"It's more like the woman comes in thinking our relationship was going to be one thing, and then found out it was another."

"They didn't know you are a soccer dad?"

"Funny you say that, because soccer was and is a big barrier to a relationship. Going to a single game is miles away from understanding that every Saturday morning, and two nights a week, plus weekends for the foreseeable future, belong to, and include someone else."

"Ah," I said sympathetically, understanding the issue. I'd grown up with it; it was normal to me.

"But it's not just the sport," he went on. "In the winter is indoor training and Friday night games, so that's out, then spring is conditioning, followed by summer league. You get the point."

"My Mom had a hard time with it as well. It never changed as I got older and it didn't end until I left for college."

"Tell me."

"It started when the scouts came during my junior year and I went through the recruiting process on my own. Mom had no idea how hard I'd worked and the value of a scholarship. She didn't care really, and to be truthful, still doesn't. She just seriously hates being out in the cold."

"But I bet she knows all about what it takes to play the piano at Carnegie Hall."

"Exactly! Oh, sorry," I said. I'd stretched out my legs under the table and had brushed against his.

"I don't mind," he said, his eyes bright as he leaned his foot against mine, leaving it there.

"So, the women you date start out believing soccer is just another sport," I interjected, "then bolt when they truly get what it means?"

John nodded. "Then at the other extreme, I've dated a few women who are totally into the outdoors, but who approach Janaye like an abandoned orphan who needs cuddly protection."

I thought of her demeanor when we first met. "She's eleven, not two."

"Exactly. They are emotive and want to bond so she rejects them outright."

I thought of John's predicament. He was handsome and successful, his family well-known in the local community.

"It's really not surprising that women have a preconceived notion of what life with you would be like. What do you think Janaye wants? From a woman who's with you, I mean."

John confessed he didn't have a clue. "We are all a bit trapped in what we don't know. I'd like to spend the evening getting to know you. Is that possible?"

"Of course," I replied, ready to do what mom had recommended and not run away. "Where do you want to start?"

"Tell me about Patrick." The name brought a reflexive swallow in my throat, like bile was going to come up.

"And here we were, having such a nice dinnertime conversation," I said, knowing it was perfectly normal that he'd be interested in knowing more about my former husband.

"I think the best summary would be to say I married someone who everyone tried to warn me against and I was blind to it all." I told him how the roof got blown off the marriage, the affair, the charging of the meals, the taxes, up to and including the selling off my possessions.

The appetizers had come and gone as John had ate, listened, and had given me mixed facial expressions of disbelief, disgust and outright shock.

"So, who do think has it worse? Your wife leaving when Janaye was a baby or me? Because I'm thinking you."

"No, you, because you might be experiencing some minor trust issues."

"You think?" We both laughed.

"Your friends, like Vanessa, what did she think of the way it went down?"

"The few friends I still have jumped for joy the moment he was out of my life. Vanessa, who you met, and Ann, my cousin, being the most important."

"She must be pretty surprised I'm in your world."

"Ann was, but you will be gratified to know that Vanessa gave you the thumbs up." As if that's all it took to win me over. John then asked me if I knew what caused the breakdown in the marriage.

"The day he left, he told me he never loved me. He wasn't even sure he had loved me when we got married."

"That was harsh."

"Maybe it was because the success of my company outstripped his own job as a vice president. I'll never know and really, don't care very much about it now. It's all come to a good place."

I fiddled with the food on my plate and took a bite of asparagus. It was time to tell him the other part of the story. "I'll tell you how it all came about if you promise not to laugh," I said.

"There's more?"

I nodded. "Quite a bit. It didn't start with him leaving. That was the last part. It started when I was on my way downtown to pay a parking fine …"

The retelling of the last few months of my life took the next hour, because John kept asking questions. When I'd finished, he stared at me thoughtfully.

"You look like you've seen a ghost," I said uncomfortably. It had felt so right to take him through the more important part of my journey, but now…his look was so intense, I second guessed myself.

"I hope you're not offended, but it doesn't sound like you were headed in the right direction before this all happened."

Was that all? "How can I be offended at the truth? The infuriating element for me is I didn't see it."

"No one does. My bet is that with the increased success in your business, he felt inadequate. You didn't notice because you were and are so damned good at what you do, your business kept sky-rocketing upward, keeping you focused elsewhere."

I remembered being featured in Fortune Magazine. The article had caused our phone to ring off the hook for days. The next time Patrick and I ate at Fog City, more than one member of the wait staff had commented on my newfound fame and congratulated me. I never thought for a moment he'd been bothered. In fact, I'd given him credit for being so modest. Hearing about it from a male perspective, what had been flattering for me had probably been unbearably emasculating for Patrick.

"You think he felt dismissed to the point of irrelevance?"

"Nothing shakes up a man's sense of self than to be overshadowed by a woman who is more successful than he is, especially if the roles were reversed in the beginning. That's hard on any relationship." There I was, enjoying every moment of going out to eat and shopping and living my life, completely oblivious, thinking he was so proud of me. "If you hadn't literally been hit by a truck, would you have learned to see life any differently?"

"No. I'd have gone merrily along my way, for who-knows-how-long. I guess you could say that death saved me." Saved me from living a life with priorities out of order, one of missed opportunities.

John told me I was fortunate. "How many poor saps are forced to meander through life without a wakeup call? You had yours. Mine was my wife leaving."

It was my turn to eat as John told me how he was blindsided.

"The difference was that I was full of myself, thinking I was really was the greatest heterosexual male in San Francisco. Janaye's mom wasn't just pretty, she was drop-dead beautiful. Came from a great family. We had a dream wedding with hundreds of our closest non-friends. We went to Cabo on four-day weekends. When she got pregnant, I thought, 'This is it. I'm going to have the world's most beautiful family and we're going to live happily ever after.' To me, that meant going out on my salmon fishing derby weekends with the guys, flying off to North Carolina to golf at Pinehurst. All the things that successful, family men do in this town." John's smile began to fade and his fingers went for the glass.

"But, unlike you, Janaye's mother didn't want to be pregnant and hated every minute of it. I was like how you were with Patrick, hoping she would change her mind and come to love the little baby she carried once it was born. That didn't happen. She disliked nursing and the change to her schedule. She didn't like being tired. There was nothing about the entire experience that she did like. In hindsight, she probably could have sued me for abuse on the grounds I made her carry Janaye."

"Now *that* is harsh," I remarked. To listen to John describing the experience of going through a pregnancy and having his spouse reject her own child after she'd given birth definitely sounded more heartbreaking than what I'd experienced.

"When she finally announced she was done with the family unit, it didn't come as much of a surprise. I didn't hire a nanny. My parents agreed with me, but at the same time were incredibly compassionate towards

Janaye's mom. I think they knew well before I did that she wasn't going to be in it for the long haul." He gave me a half-smile when he made that comment. "So, to wrap up a very long story, she was thrilled to set herself free of any obligation to Janaye, and didn't want much more than some cash, her clothes and jewelry."

"She felt guilty," I concluded.

"That's the first thing my brother Paul said. You'll like him by the way," he said as an afterthought.

"Does Janaye ever bring her up?"

"No. When Janaye was eight, she told me she didn't want anyone in her life who didn't want her just as much."

"That's profoundly wise and scary for an eight-year old."

John looked me deep in the eyes, his gaze drawing out my insecurity and replacing it with confidence. "You'd be the coolest stepmother ever. Of course, you have to fall in love with me first, then me you. Little things."

A burst of air escaped my mouth at his words.

"Speed dating as single parents is really weird isn't it?" he asked. I nodded, reaching for the water. "But good, right? If I was half this efficient when I was dating pre-marriage, my entire life would be different."

"Do you regret anything?"

"No," he said soberly. "I love Janaye. Having her got me to grow up and focus on the right things."

I looked out the window to the water. The sun was setting, covering the horizon in reds and oranges. I wanted to be on the beach. Patrick would only walk along the Embarcadero or over by the marina, ever concerned with ruining an expensive pair of shoes.

"Would you take a walk with me on the beach?" I asked him.

"Love to." I made a mental note to never compare this man to Patrick again. It was time to put him in the past and leave him there.

CHAPTER 30

The wind was mild, nothing more than the usual, evening breeze from the Pacific Ocean, but chilly nonetheless. John put on his windbreaker and we walked down the paved steps to the waterfront.

I pushed up the collar and fastened the clasp on my neck, tucking my hands deep into my pockets. Despite the lore about being hot and pregnant, I was cold, and told John I wasn't sure how long I'd make it.

"We don't have much daylight left anyway," he said, noting the deep red on the horizon.

"Do you think that all the events you've experienced in the last few months have been divinely inspired?"

"Absolutely," I answered. "I also now wonder about the inspiration behind what happens every day, about most everything."

An image came to mind then. Walking on a beach with a person I couldn't see. The emotions I felt when I was with the dream figure were as real as what I experienced now.

"What is it?" John asked me.

"Grandfather told me that you don't ever stop having feelings. He said you carry them with you; joy, sadness, anger, regret." I glanced at John. "I'm just trying to be a better human being, you know? Because clearly I wasn't before."

"You aren't giving yourself enough credit for who you were then, or, if I may say, who you are now. Like with that guy Monson. No one told you what to do."

I inhaled the cool air. "I'm just consumed with regret. There have been so many times I've felt like I should or could do something, and I didn't. I just went on with my life."

"Since you are already struck with remorse, this is now the perfect time to tell me why you acted the way you did when we first met."

"Oh, that's a hard one to swallow," I replied. "You surprised me, of course, when you wanted to talk business, I should have handled it better but…"

"But…?"

"Look. This is going to sound utterly pathetic and there is no other answer. I just felt inadequate."

Back came the Cheshire cat grin. "Are you telling me you were attracted to me?"

"Yeah, but only a little." I rubbed my shoulder against him as we walked, with no intention of moving away. In response, John removed his hand from his pocket and draped it over my shoulders, drawing me an inch closer.

"You didn't think you were attractive enough?" I lifted my shoulder slightly. "Being with Patrick clearly took its toll. Well, let me shatter the image your former husband helped create. Just open your eyes and see all the men, and women, who have given you a second glance as we'd been walking down the path."

"They have not," I said with little confidence.

"Trust me, I don't mind. Had you been more like Janaye's mother, you'd be seeing and relishing every look and glance that was thrown your way. Your complete ignorance is wonderfully refreshing."

"And your willingness to give me lovely compliments is much appreciated. Now here's an odd one. Do you really like to play board games?" It was a bit of information Janaye had imparted over dinner.

"Yes, because I'm competitive by nature, but I don't usually have any takers and end up playing Call of Duty."

"The on-line game?" That was a solitary pursuit, one that I likened it to Patrick sitting in the second bedroom listening to music for hours on end.

"Don't panic," he cautioned. "I'm not a 14-year-old staying up until three in the morning. Board games require players and I don't often have people over to the house."

"What's that all about? Anti-social?"

"You haven't been divorced long enough or with a child to fully appreciate this. My married friends want activities where the entire family can participate. If the men my age aren't married, they are on the prowl. The divorced ones, when not with their kids, are also on the prowl. In either case, I'm ten years past that."

"Even in the beginning?"

"Janaye was in diapers and I was working, trying to keep it together. The minute she was walking, I was there, then she started Kindergarten and first grade, which meant plays and in-school events for every holiday known to man."

"That sounds exhausting," I said, considering what lay before me. "But now it's a different sort of busy, right?"

"Yep. I doubt I'd have pursued you had I not had an actual need driving me. Plus," he shared a quirky smile, "your rejection made you unforgettable."

"Probably because no one had ever rejected you before."

"No one I wanted. Physical attraction aside, I had you pegged entirely wrong, and I'm sorry about that."

"I was probably coming across the way I felt inside; not all that great."

"It worked out. Ironically, Janaye told me what I had needed was a good take-down. She's been relentless about bringing up your name ever since."

John's arm dropped from my shoulder and he put his hand through mine. "When I showed up at your house, I had no idea what to expect, and the fact you were in your pajamas and your hair was crazy, I have to tell you, only made you more sexy."

"I still can't believe you came over."

"Well, you worked miracles with the center. The least I could do was say thanks in person. After I got over my disgust at your former husband, I wanted to stay and get to know you."

The sun had nearly set by now, the red glow touching the edge of the water.

"That's beautiful," I said, referring to the horizon. John stopped walking and turned to me.

"And amazing, like you." With a tender touch, he lifted my chin to him. His lips were warm and soft, the skin a velvet softness on my own as he pressed lightly at first, then harder as I responded. I snaked my right hand over his shoulder and around his neck, resting my fingers just below his hairline. Emotion I'd not allowed myself to feel came out as we moved in and out of kisses, finally stopping when the red eye on the horizon had finally shut.

"We better get going," he murmured. My lips curled up against his and I rubbed the side of his nose with mine.

On the drive home, I yawned.

"You're tired," he said sympathetically, placing his hand over mine, curling his fingers underneath.

"Yeah, these babies take the life out of me." Still, I didn't want the night to end. He raised an eyebrow as though he knew there was more. "I want to stay in the car and kiss you."

"That means I have the green light to ask you out again." I lifted his hand off the stick shift and up to my lips for a soft kiss, then placed it against my cheek. I let go, and he slid his palm behind my neck. "I'd ask you to come over tomorrow but Janaye has a birthday party and I'm doing driving duty for a group of 11-year olds. How about next weekend?"

He walked me up the stairs and to the landing, and I had visions of being sixteen again with my dad waiting just on the other side of the door.

John must have thought the same thing, since he leaned into me and whispered, "We'd better keep it 'G-rated." He placed a soft kiss on my lips then another on my cheek. He stepped back, and I knew that was my cue to open the door.

#

Monday morning at 9:30 I was on email when a pop-up box appeared in the lower right-hand corner of my computer. "Need to Know," was the subject line, and it was from Alan. Intrigued, I clicked on the box and scanned the email. The next instant I'd picked up the phone and was dialing Alan's number.

"I knew that'd get you,"' he said, a victorious note in his voice.

"I can hardly believe it. I just wish he'd been sent to jail."

"That might still happen, but it appears Patrick got himself a really good attorney."

"OK, so tell me everything."

"Patrick had been ordered to pay $300,000 but got it negotiated down to $247,000, and payments are going to be made over a dozen years or something. Of course, the only reason we have this information is because the imbecile showed up at the Fog City, had too much to drink and started spilling the beans to Dave."

People like him, slimy and dishonest, but good looking and blessed with a knack of presenting well, would invariably land upright.

"Did he pay for his own drink?" I asked.

"According to Dave, he did, in fact, pay for the drinks. You're better off without him, Lindy, by a long shot." I agreed, though I'd been hoping for jail time.

"What's the latest with the acquisition? You've been completely silent on the subject."

"In truth, it's been pretty busy around here. Word of your work on behalf of the center has spread, and as Sam predicted, the benefits of taking on a project pro bono has opened a number of doors I'd never considered."

"Such as?"

"The Opera House. The Landon Foundation." Those were big, prestigious names.

"You think that's all because of Kay?"

"Maybe more so because of her son. Maybe I shouldn't say anything."

"What? Why not?"

"Let's just say I'd like to think we earned a spot at the table, but it's now accelerated beyond our current capacity. I'm weighing the benefits of hiring more people or starting a backlog of business. Lindy, I know you are supposed to be taking a break, and I hate to say this, but keep doing whatever you're not-supposed to be doing. It's working. And PS. I approve. You have my blessing."

Alan's laughing drowned out my response and he was still going on when he hung up.

Whatever will happen is out of my hands. It's in His. It wasn't a pithy statement. It was the truth.

I was passing through the living room when something caught my eye and I looked back to the table. The most enormous bouquet of red roses was in an equally large vase, and it didn't look like cheap plastic. It looked like crystal.

"That's a whole lot of interest, right there," Dad said in his driest tone yet. I counted three dozen. "Lead crystal."

"He has good taste even if he is a tad excessive," Mom said, giving me a good morning peck on the cheek. "Just like your Dad."

"He's not going to last long," Dad intoned.

"What in the world are you talking about? You think I'm going to burn him out?"

He calmly smelled the roses. "On the contrary. I'm saying he already knows it's over. You're the one." Dad shrugged in his know-all way. "I knew your mother was the person I wanted to marry two weeks after the first date."

"And you Mom. Do you subscribe to Dad's way of thinking?" A sly smile tilted the corner of her mouth upwards. "That's a yes," I interpreted. "So what did you do after that infamous first date where you slayed him with your amazing-ness?"

"I'll tell you what she did. She played it cool," Dad answered for her. "Which is exactly what you should do. You play it cool."

I informed them I was going to 'play it cool' by calling him to say thanks.

"How'd you like to return your thanks by coming up to Sausalito with me on Wednesday?" John suggested. "I have to look at a building complex project. We could grab lunch on the way back, or even there. Or," he paused, "is your social calendar booked?"

"The roses effectively wiped out my prior engagements," I responded, thinking that my Dad would be disappointed. That was about as cool as a hot coal jumping back in to the fire, and I was burning.

CHAPTER 31

Tuesday morning, Mom and Dad surprised me by announcing we should start looking at alternative living arrangements.

"I wasn't super interested in the apartments John sent you," Dad said, "but that doesn't mean there isn't something out there. Regarding your own plans, you could stay here for the first year or two, but the truth is the city doesn't have a lot of parks around."

I called Charlie. Might as well get his input on the matter, especially if he was going to start coming up for visits. Charlie thought that any place with an extra room for Max and him was enough for now. "Don't want to get ahead of myself," he said, though his optimism was clear, "but I don't know what I'm doing down here if the three of you are up there."

When I called John, I conveyed dad's lukewarm response to the apartments, hoping that other options were available.

"You can help me out by getting on line and get an idea of what's appealing to your parents. We can discuss it over lunch."

Dad and I spent hours side-by-side, laptops open, swapping links of home sites until it was time for dinner. We showed mom our top picks.

"You'll have a lot to go through on your date," Mom said.

"At what point did it go from lunch to a date?"

"When I saw that big smile on your face."

An hour before the 'date,' I received an email from Alan. The subject title was Acquisition Proposal. The offer was ten million, not including bonuses for employees to stay on with the company. I'd have a scaled payout, in accordance with the hours I worked. The employees were bound to stay for 12 months or forfeit bonuses and any stock grants.

I thought of Sam and her desire to attend grad school in a year. This would mean she'd keep all her stock, vesting her further. By the time she left, assuming she chose to do so, she'd be set for another five years. My response to Alan was short and to the point. He had my approval and full support.

John arrived and he had the convertible.

"Top up or down?" he asked me.

"Down, definitely." The wind felt exhilarating as he drove through the streets, up and through the districts and then across the Golden Gate bridge. Traffic was light going out of town and the view was breathtaking, made all the more so because I was with a man who enjoyed my company.

We made it to the building complex in less than twenty minutes. During John's meeting, I strolled along the waterfront, stopping in a bookstore and then a boutique kitchen shop. I received his text when he was done, and we met at a Tapas bar. Over authentically wrapped tamales and sweet corn breads, I told him about the acquisition offer for the business. He asked questions akin to that of a board member. The returns, payouts, employees and transition.

"It all seems to be coming together," he surmised. "But you don't seem overly enthusiastic."

"I'm not *unenthusiastic*," I clarified. "But it's impossible to see around a blind corner and I'm afraid to guess how I'll feel when I get there."

He shook his head, loading up a chip with guacamole. "You're moving on. How could you possibly anticipate how you will feel? You've essentially turned the business over to Alan."

"Yeah. I was so sure about it, and still am. It's just uncomfortable."

"Of course it is. Going back to working as an individual consultant. The upside is you can set your hours and engage as you want to. For a person in your position, it's ideal."

On the way back, John drove along the waterfront, the view of the city different from this side of the bay. "What's this?" I asked as he pulled onto a dirt road. "Are these things legal in such a sophisticated town?"

"It throws off the casual trespassers." The road ended at a large, Nantucket style home with a view that stretched from the Bay Bridge to the south and east, and the city of San Francisco across the Bay. "It's our family home, a place we come to on the fourth of July to watch the fireworks."

"Impossible," I disputed. "It's always foggy on the fourth."

"That's not the point," he said with a laugh. "We have a bonfire and sit around eating all night long, over there."

We sat on the grass at the edge of the beach, watching the massive cargo container ships move through the treacherous waters. I learned that neither of us had a desire to be on a sailboat, unless it was of the luxury kind and it was somewhere warm with an island in sight.

John lay back on the dry grass, his arm outstretched. The invitation was in his eyes. I lay on his arm, closing my eyes as he stroked my hair, the sun warming my skin. His fingers moved to my face, touching me as carefully and respectfully as if he were feeling the skin of an angel.

"This is awfully intimate for a second date," I murmured.

"I like it, and I like you." His thumb touched my lower lip, back and forth along the rim. "You're beautiful and kind and forgiving and funny. I want to kiss every square inch of you, and at the same time, I want to protect you and take care of you. It's unreal, in the most real way."

After a few moments, he moved slightly, rolling on his side, my head still on his forearm. He slid his palm down my hip, lingering.

"May I?" My answer caught in my throat, but I nodded. He extended his fingers, his touch so light I barely felt it. I watched his eyes as he positioned it in the center of my stomach, feeling the warmth of his energy. It seemed to seep through my layers, warming me to a core. "Can you feel anything?" he asked me.

I nodded. "It's just started a few days ago."

"Sometimes the babies will move when they hear sounds of familiar voices. Or when you stop moving, because motion rocks them to sleep."

His hand was still on my stomach, his face and lips now closer to mine. "I'd so like them to know my voice."

"John, may I ask you something that might be a little late in coming, and for that reason, odd?" He lifted his hand, keeping only his fingertips on my skin. "No, that's okay. Don't move. So, here's the deal," I said, inhaling my fear. "You're gorgeous, intelligent, single. But me..." John drew small circles on my belly and hips. Keeping my gaze, he lowered his lips and lifted my shirt past my belly button. Lightly, his brushed his lips against my skin, closing his eyes while turning his head back and forth.

"I think your real worry is that we are going fast, you are uncomfortable with it and wonder if I feel the same way."

"Yeah."

"I know it's fast but I'm not uncomfortable, as you can tell." He tenderly drew my shirt over my belly, covering it, switching his touch to my inner arm that he slowly stroked. "Before we first met I knew of you. I'd seen you at Fog City a few times and you struck me as intellectually aggressive, which was unbelievably sexy, but I also saw glimpses of your bright smile which indicated how upbeat you could be. When the time came for us to actually meet, I was mentally close to you when you turned me down because I thought you were single. Janaye pointed out to me later than I was put off because I had some expectations about how it might go—"

"Because you are so handsome and debonair," I teasingly interjected. He tilted his head in confirmation.

"Then later, well, you were in the middle of hell. Once Patrick was excised like the cancer he was, I felt more than ready to move forward." It was his turn to look unsure. "Should I have played it out?"

"We skipped right over dating convention, whatever that is," I remarked dryly. "I was obviously terrible at it before, which is making me second guess myself now."

His look gently teased me. "Really?"

I touched his chin. "You know, I do like this clean-shaven look best. It's how I first saw you."

"Changing the subject won't work." I brushed the tip of my thumb over his lips then dropped it, turning serious.

"Put yourself in my shoes. Your dream date enters your life just as it's shattering. Any and all sense of self-worth is gone, along with confidence in your ability to trust your own opinion. What would you do?"

"I see your point."

"And on top of it, you have this inexplicable interest in my pregnancy. I don't understand how you can seem to be excited as I am, but you are."

"You think that's strange?"

"Sort of." John shifted position once more. He was directly above me, shielding my eyes form the sun.

"When my ex was pregnant, I was working and didn't attend many of the ultrasounds after the first. She made them sound uninteresting, not even telling me of the big appointment to learn the sex. The baby shower and nursery were done without my involvement and at the time it didn't occur to me things could be otherwise. It was only after a few of my friends had kids that I saw how involved they'd been, and how damn happy they were. Heck, I didn't even know a joint baby shower was possible until it was too late."

"It's exciting for you, then?"

John kissed my fingers. "It's special being a part of this."

I'd always taken it for granted that he'd gone through the pregnancy process once when it truth it was like the first time for both of us.

"I'm glad you're here with me and sharing in this too," I said sincerely. He placed his hand on my belly again and hummed at the same time. My belly moved, he laughed and kissed me. The intellectual, rational side of me said it was coincidence. The rest of me knew I was in harmony with the little, growing beings inside me, joined in mutual adoration of the man who was covering me with his affection.

CHAPTER 32

"Thirty seconds," John called to Janaye. She nodded her head. It was four in the afternoon a week later and we were at Sunset Park. Janaye had her cleats on and was warming up with high kicks, pulling her knees to her chest, limbering up her shins, ankles and thighs. John set out the portable goal and dumped the soccer balls from the net bag. I sat on the berm watching.

On the way over, we'd talked about Janaye's stats, her strengths and what she saw as her weaknesses. She also described the issues with her coaches, one who wanted to play an offensive game and the other a defensive.

"John, pass Janaye some balls. Janaye, rotate between using both feet for scoring." As she kicked the balls back to her father, it didn't take me long to spot a few areas of improvement. I waited until she came over for a drink of water and asked if she was ready to hear my thoughts.

"Of course. That's why you're here. Well, one of them," she snorted, looking at her dad.

"Janaye, you seem to be favoring your right leg, but the outside kicks need more strength and precision when using the outside of your foot."

She nodded. "That's what coach says, so I practice kicking a hundred times but it doesn't improve." I stood and walked beside her. It was really the only way to show her what I meant. John was on the other side, observing.

I used my right foot to place the ball between my legs. I was wearing flats, not ideal for the circumstance, but they were comfortable and the best I could do with my expanding feet.

"I can only do this once or twice, so look carefully," I told her. She watched my feet intently as I showed her how she needed to alter her footing. "Do you see the difference?"

She shook her head, never looking up from the ground.

"John, kick me that other ball will you?" He did, and I repositioned it between my legs. "I'm going to describe what I'm doing and then show you two different techniques." Placing the weight on my left foot, I lifted my right foot and slid it behind and around the left of the ball, slightly tilting down my foot. "See that angle? It allows you to lift the ball up, giving it the force it needs to stay in the direction you are kicking. You can then flick your toe as you lift up on the outkick. See that? I'll do it again."

Janaye's concentration was complete as she observed me execute the kick two more times.

"Now here's the other technique. It requires you to jump over the ball, and again, using the outside of your right foot, kick sideways or forward. It's a lateral pass and best for short distances. You aren't going to try and make a long-distance goal with this, but in a short game, it can make all the difference.'

"I'm going to do this twice in slow motion because I don't want to jump." I asked John to kick the ball to the outside of my right foot and when he did, I stopped it, then immediately moved my right foot on the inside of the ball and hit a swift kick back to him.

"Why hasn't the coach taught me that?" she wanted to know, clearly annoyed.

"He doesn't have to," I said. "That's what individual coaches are for, and trust me, a lot of parents hire them for their kids who are on the elite teams. But practicing these two moves will really help your game. Now, I'm going to go sit down and watch for a while."

"Can I practice the left side too?"

"Absolutely. Every player has a stronger side, a kicking foot, but the objective is to be equally strong on passing and footwork. In tennis, conventional wisdom is that it takes 500 balls to get the foundation for a good swing. I don't know if that applies to soccer, but I guess it's somewhere in the range."

"Five hundred??" mouthed John when Janaye wasn't looking. I grinned back, waving him to the field.

We didn't leave until the sun was going down, draping the edge of the water with glorious orange rays.

Friday morning, I was totally silent as Dr. Stanton, the neonatal specialist in Dr. Lawler's office sat on his stool near my right arm, his hand on the plastic, T-shaped ultrasound device, already smothered with a line of warm gel. Mom sat to my left, on the other side of the examination table. Her eyes were fixed on the screen. She'd been commenting on the clarity of the images, amazed at how far technology had come from her days of childbearing, when a stethoscope was used to hear the heartbeat and the images only provided the outlines of the bones and heart.

"We are looking at the two hearts," Dr. Stanton remarked, his left hand turning up the sound. The frantic little sounds were rapid, overlapping one another and then separating, like two balls bouncing off a wall. He compared that information with the rate of growth of the organs.

"Yep. 21-22 weeks now," he said. That puts you at around Valentine's Day for delivery, but expect to deliver before."

Mom and I looked at the screen, both waiting for his next comment.

"I can see the sex of one clearly, not of the other. Do you want to know?" I looked at Mom, excited and nervous.

"Yes."

He turned to the screen without so much as a blink. "Look right here," he said, pointing the sonogram wand to one of the babies. "The legs are spread, and it's clearly missing an appendage. This one's a girl. She's going to be your little daughter."

The words rang in my ear. Your daughter. To hear him say it — my daughter — made my lips quiver.

"Hold on a minute. This one's just turned over and I want you to see this yourself." He pressed on the side of my belly in an attempt to get the baby to roll over.

"That's what I want." He placed the wand where he wanted it. "What do you see?" he asked me.

"Nothing."

"Exactly. That means you have another little girl on the way. Your thriving, growing, healthy daughters." He looked me square in the eye and smiled. "Congratulations."

My throat tightened. I felt the zing of an emotional hit to my brain. The doctor was quiet, as though he knew I wanted to savor the first few moments after learning I had little girls inside me.

Mom and I made eye contact again, this time hers were covered with a glassy sheen of tears.

"Grandma will want a few photos I imagine?" Dr. Stanton hypothesized.

"Grandma does," Mom said smiling. The small, palm-sized black-and-white photos started printing, connected like lottery tickets. Once we were with Dad and shared the news, he gave me a big hug.

"Let's call Charlie from the car."

The first 15 minutes in the car consisted of speed talking, laughing, crying and more talking with Charlie. Once we were on our way, I texted Vanessa, John, Darcy, Sam, Alan and Ann.

Girls - 20 weeks-Approximate due date: February 17th

Sam requested to be an honorary Aunt, Darcy asked about the baby shower. Vanessa reserved the right to name at least one girl.

The image of two young women not much older than Janaye standing beside a book came to mind. They had been beside a white pedestal. They had to be my daughters and they were waiting to come down, to be with me.

Dad looked at me, touching my leg. "You alright?" I nodded my head, my voice cracking as I told him I was just perfect.

That night, the prayer wasn't just about me and the health of the children I carried, or about Mom and Dad or Darcy and Charlie. It was also about Arlene and Vanessa, Ann and her husband, Alan and Sam, and even Ronnie and Jackson. I thanked the Lord for giving me the experiences to be mentally and emotionally ready for John, and also what he was more than ready for me.

Then my heart and mind wandered to another place, one I never thought would be possible for me to go.

Patrick. It couldn't have been completely his fault that he'd fallen out of love before he bailed on our marriage. The reality was that he wasn't ready for a life with a family. I consciously or subconsciously pushed him away. And I wasn't smart enough to see the signs, or if I had, to know how to communicate with him and discuss our differences of opinion. The gratitude I felt for John was matched by the compassion I now felt for my former husband and the father of my twin girls.

I also understood something else. I recalled flattering Patrick about his looks, but not his job or his accomplishments. I saw how I had become consumed with my clients; the next deadline or product launch. I hadn't tried to minimize his importance, it had just happened. I felt all the weight of my responsibility and the consequences of my own actions.

I prayed for Patrick, fervently hoping he'd be happy in whatever he was doing. I prayed for God to forgive me for treating Patrick less like a man than he deserved, though I didn't feel compelled in any way to call him up and ask for forgiveness. What I'd done was unintentional, and I would have tried to work it out if I could have, but that wasn't the plan.

I finished my prayer asking for the strength and the insight to understand John's daughter, and to be aware of her needs without sacrificing my own. I prayed that I could treat her the way my mother treated me; with love and affection.

Saturday morning, Dad and I talked through the acquisition again. As I told my father, after all I've been through, and the little promptings and feelings I've had, I was expecting to feel assurance, like a warmth in my belly.

"Instead, I feel nothing."

"Lindy, sometimes the answer is neutral because it's not going to make a big difference in your life either way, or it won't impact you negatively. A third reason for the neutrality is that you already know the answer. I think you knew this was the right thing to do when Joseph first brought it up." I thought back to that moment in time, when I was on bed rest, listening to a complete stranger asking about my business.

"You know, at first I thought it was crazy, but then almost immediately it made sense, both for me and the business."

"Exactly."

"Whew, okay," I said, nodding my head. "Learn something new every day. Now, what do you think of those homes John sent over?"

"I liked them. If you stay in the city and don't select one, I just might. The flats for Charlie are also pretty nice. We might try a high rise for a few months and see what we think."

I about choked on my blueberries. "You're not serious?"

"I'm getting my mind around the idea. No lawn. No trash. Might be a nice change. Plus we'd have the portability to pick up and leave if you decide to move to the East Bay."

I looked at mom. "I think there might be an issue with having a piano in an apartment." She shrugged, smiling. She was still over the moon about the twin girls, plus she was in the same city with her daughter and her son had a romantic interest that was going to bring him and his son in to town. Turning back to dad, I told him he wasn't the person in control here.

Dad shook his head no. "Of course not. The person controlling our lives is a lot smarter and probably has a lot better knowledge of real estate prices."

The remainder of the day was lazy, full of relaxing. Mom and Dad had taken off for Santa Clara. It left me and Remus, lounging together.

A little after one, John called. "Your coaching was in full view today," he began. "Janaye tried the new moves, and she didn't get a goal, but she came pretty darn close. She wants me to start coaching her a few times a week after school."

"Shall we all go out for a celebratory dinner?" I asked him, "for Janaye's newly acquired soccer skills, the twins and the fact that it's a Saturday and I want to see you again."

"How convenient," John answered. "I know the perfect place."

"You do?"

"Yep. With Grandma and Grandpa. Janaye's already over there helping Grandma make dinner." That didn't sound threatening and was certainly convenient. I'd love to see where he grew up and the famed Abrahms' house on the coast.

John showed up in a black leather coat and jeans, baseball cap on his head. He assessed my straight hair. "I'll keep the windows up and the seat heater on."

"Are you kidding? Sunny days are to be treasured. Top down."

After I was settled in, he told me he had a few hats in the glove compartment if I wanted, and I picked the Simms hat. I adjusted it the mirror and then looked at John for approval.

"Do I look like a fisher-woman?"

He pulled his head back for an instant and opened his eyes wide, looking pleased, noting, "You are a rare woman who looks good in a Simms hat and you are doubly attractive because you know the brand. Would you go with me?"

I nodded. "You find me a lake and I'll fish it with you."

John rubbed my cheek with the back of two fingers. "Unreal," was all he said before starting the car and pulling out.

The sky was a cloudless blue, the wind moving across the top of my head, protected by my cool hat. The heat from the car seats warmed my back and legs, making the drive pleasant and fun.

A kiss. That's what I wanted. I carefully placed my left hand on the arm rest between us and leaned towards him. He glanced at me, then looked back at the road, concentrating…waiting. I put my right hand on the middle of his upper thigh. Without a word, I slowly slid my lips from his cheek to his ear, pressing on his thigh as I made my way to his ear, which I nibbled, rubbing my face to his.

"I'm so sorry. I just couldn't wait any longer," I whispered, continuing to his hairline and then down to his neck. I breathed in, smelling his cologne as I explored the crease under his ear and down to the collar of his shirt. My hand pressed on his thigh, giving me stability and a connection point to reality, for I felt as though I were having an out of body experience.

John said nothing but I felt the rumbling in his throat, and I could tell he'd slowed the car down. He curled his right hand around my arm, gripping it with a force equal to his pleasure.

"About five more minutes," he said softly. I worked my way back up the length of his neck, under his jaw and towards his lips. Finding what I so wanted, I brushed my lips against his as he focused on the road in front, removing my right hand from his leg and using my thumb to trace the other side of his lips that I couldn't reach. Gently, I pulled on his chin, spreading his lips apart, just enough to place the tip of my thumb within and curl down his lower lip. I absorbed it into my mouth, kissing and sucking, ever so softly as my hand stroked his face.

I hadn't been counting the minutes and didn't try. My head was delirious with a craving I'd never felt in my life. I slowly drew my hand back down and slid my lips from his, giving him one long, last kiss on his neck.

"That might just hold me," I said, smiling as I pulled back and saw his face. It was flushed and his eyes were fierce, full of the fire a man has when he wants and feels something so badly, but is exercising control of almost super-human proportions.

John downshifted and I congratulated myself on the timing. We drove up a hill and turned right in to the old community. The place looked so familiar, I was sure I'd driven past it many times.

John quickly pulled to the side of the road, unbuckled his seatbelt and collapsed the distance between us. The ache I'd felt was now a full-bodied yearning. As he spread my lips with his own, I had felt it was possible to be more satisfied with a single kiss from this man than ever being intimate with another.

He gave me a final squeeze. "You might want to check your hair to make sure I didn't push anything out of place. The house is up a few more."

"Sneaky."

We pulled up a large house I recognized. He walked around to my side of the car and helped me out.

"Welcome to the home where I grew up. Soon enough this place will be a zoo with all the grandkids, so enjoy the quiet for the time being." He led me up to the veranda and then around the back on the left side of the home.

"Wait a minute," I ordered, gripping his arm. "You only said your parents!"

His face was lit up with a wicked smile. "Surprise. Time to meet the whole family."

With my mouth still open, he turned the nob on the door, called out to his mother, and gestured to me to come through.

CHAPTER 33

Although John wouldn't know this for some time, I recognized the entryway, kitchen and living room from my dream.

John pulled out two bottled waters and invited me to follow him through a set of sliding French doors. Janaye was laughing, and I heard Kay speaking.

"I know exactly what you need," he said, as he leaned in and drew me toward him. He kissed me with all the passion in the car, although this time he exercised more discretion.

"Nice, Dad, in the kitchen." Janaye's dry comment didn't stop John from finishing what he started. She'd already left when he drew back.

"A smooth beginning," I remarked, but wasn't worried. Janaye sounded amused, not irritated. He held me tight and we stepped through the doorway. Kay was sitting on the couch beside her husband Adi, who I'd met at the Gala.

"Hi Mom. Adi, you remember Lindy from the Gala."

"Of course," he stood. Kay was first, embracing me, squeezing me with as much appreciation as she felt a pregnant woman could take, and when she released me, Adi took my hand and then put his arm around my shoulders.

"I'll give her back," Adi chided his son. John was hovering like a helicopter mom at the first day of school. Janaye stayed on the perimeter until I was free then she gave me a one-armed hug around the waist.

"Thank you so much for all the work you've done on behalf of the center," Adi told me. "It means so much to all of us."

"We have a little while until the others join us. Would you like to sit down?" Kay offered. We moved into the living room, which had a stunning view of the ocean. John took a seat on the couch beside me.

"Dad's being mean to you by bringing you today," Janaye warned me. Her easiness with the situation perplexed me, until I recalled my own words. She's eleven. She isn't looking for a replacement mom. Maybe I'd be more like an older cousin endowed with some amount of disciplinary authority.

"You will wow them over with your warmth," Kay predicted, and Adi seconded her opinion.

"And my eating capabilities," I said, expressing a hope that she'd made enough. "Janaye, are you going to help me keep everyone straight?"

"Now that I'm at the big table, yes."

Kay left to work on dinner, and then called for Adi to help bring in some vegetables from the cold storage room. John got up as well, kidding his mother that her list was longer than one man alone could manage. Suddenly Janaye and I were in the room alone.

I shifted in on couch, struggling to find a good position. My Buddha belly had grown so much my lower back now had a curve that hadn't been present two weeks prior.

"You ok?" Janaye asked, eyeing me with concern. "You've gotten so…"

"Big?" I laughed. "And just wait. I'm told I'll double again." Her eyes were already wide when I exclaimed. "Oh!" Startling myself and Janaye. We both waited expectantly. "It-they- something moved—hard!" My hand shot to my mouth. This felt like the edge of a rolling pin.

"Is this the first time?"

I nodded. "Like this," I answered, nodding and exhaling. Her eyes glowed. "You want to feel it?" She nodded, coming to my side. I smoothed out the fabric of my top. "Touch here," I suggested, and she placed her hand on me so lightly I barely felt her. She watched my stomach expectantly. I shifted a little, and still nothing.

"Why isn't it—" was all she got out before her eyes lit up at the movement I felt. She went quiet, and it stopped. "Can you—" and we both felt another faint bump.

"Wow," was all I said.

"What's going on?" John asked, looking at his daughter with her hand on my stomach.

"I felt them, Dad. Two times."

"That's great," he said, coming over, placing his hand on my stomach as well. His warm hand was next to Janaye's, both of them looking at me and each other with a sense of wonderment.

"John, does anyone know I'm coming today?" I was wearing a black and white Victorian top that gathered below by chest, and skinny jeans. My stomach felt large to me, but I knew that most people wouldn't assume I was pregnant. I just looked big in the middle.

"Yep. The whole family," he admitted, a smile coming to his face.

"I felt it again," Janaye whispered. "When dad spoke."

"The two of you have been the only people around other than my mom and dad and Vanessa. That's pretty cool they seem to know your voices."

The sound of feet outside the front door announced other arrivals.

"Here they come," Janaye said looking at me. "You ready?"

"No!" I whispered back, feeling like I was a part of a conspiracy.

Dinner was a lively affair--loud and noisy, but intelligent and interesting. I met all the siblings and their respective spouses with the exception of Paul's wife, who had gotten called in at the hospital. He told me it was an unexpectedly busy afternoon in the maternity ward.

"Women have schedules to keep and men have to get back to work on Monday," I said to Paul sitting to my left.

"Precision birthing is what that is," he agreed. John sat across from me, and Kay was to my right, all three determined to keep me feeling at ease.

"It's all those soccer games," chimed in Greg, John's brother in law.

Lisa, his wife, ran the family's foundation and had greeted me warmly, but her countenance was drawn. Scott, John's other brother, was a software sales executive, and married to Alice, a chief financial officer for a biotechnology firm. The two struck me as unassuming while exuding the strength of character of natural born leaders. All knew about my company long before today.

Paul told the group John had tried to hire me. "But you turned him down," Paul asked me, "or did Janaye tell the story incorrectly?"

"Shot down," Janaye piped in from the other end of the table, causing the adults to laugh.

"Perseverance wins in the end," said Alice.

Janaye was between her two cousins, Alex and Mark, both of whom looked a few years older than herself. I heard Mark telling her I couldn't be half-bad if I played soccer at USC.

"So Lindy, he's making you walk barefoot over hot coals by meeting us," said Paul. "Have you thought about how you're going to get him back?"

"He's already suffered through all I can give, being barefoot and pregnant and all."

"A lovely euphemism for making him suffer," said Paul. I shook my head.

"It's not a euphemism at all. It's reality, except for the barefoot part."

Dead. Silence.

Kay patted her mouth with her napkin and I saw her shoulders moving up and down, her eyes twinkling, but she too, kept silent. At the end of the table, Janaye and her cousins had gone quiet, their eyes wide as though we were going to have a Jerry Springer moment.

John put his fork down, wiped his mouth with his napkin and. "I guess now is as good a time as any." I wanted to explode with laughter, because this moment in time was going to go down in family lore. "Lindy is pregnant. With twin girls."

The eyes looked at each other, at Janaye, at John, at me.

"I always knew you had it in you," said Paul, lifting his glass. "You could have done a lot worse. Cheers!"

I broke out laughing, unable to hold it in any longer, and John did the same. I ventured a glance to Janaye and saw the two boys were pressing her for the details.

"Wait, wait," I said, asking for a moment when the laughter died down. "Lest you think that John was out scatting around, this is not his doing. I have been married for the last five years. When the man I was married to learned of the pregnancy, he elected to leave. One day, we can share the gory details, but I'm just starting a wonderful meal with new acquaintances, so we'll save that for the next dinner. In the meantime, Greg, can you pass the potatoes?"

I heard Mark tell Janaye he thought I was funny, but if she gave a response, I didn't hear it. Scott clapped his hands, and Paul put his arm around my shoulder.

"Eat up girl," said Paul.

After dinner, we moved to the veranda. The sun was starting to set, casting the deep blue ocean in red, making the water darker and the beach a blood orange. The conversation was easy and varied and while I enjoyed it, eventually I found myself stifling more than one yawn. John, who had been sitting on the veranda bantering with Paul, caught my eye. I nodded. He walked over to Janaye and leaned into her, and she nodded her head. John gave her a kiss on the cheek and went for my coat.

Paul gave me a hug. "You'll be my guest when my wife isn't around." Alice and Scott were as congenial as they were in the beginning, saying how they enjoyed meeting me. Lisa was gracious as well, while Greg smiled and wished me luck with the pregnancy, his tone clearly expecting never to see me again.

Kay and Adi extracted a promise that I would come back soon.

We waited as the soft-top automatically rose behind our heads and over us. When the lock clicked in place, we moved at the same time.

"I hope you don't mind," he whispered as he started kissing me. "And the way you played the pregnancy thing…" he stopped, laughter cutting off his kisses.

On the drive, I checked my phone. No messages. It reminded me of the glitch I'd had since the accident. When I told John, he requested the device at the next stoplight. "Who said they called but you didn't hear from?" I gave him the list of family and friends. His fingers deftly moved over the keypad, grunting, then he turned the screen to me.

"Your settings were messed with. They were all blocked, each one. Right here. You never would have known they called, texted or left a message." Seeing my fury spark light a fire John clicked the phone off and put my chin in his fingertips.

"It's fixed. You are with me, and that will never happen…again." He sealed his promise with a wonderful kiss, quelling the heat of my anger like a soft rainstorm over a burning field.

We arrived at my home too soon. I was grateful the landing had a privacy wall or the neighbors across the street might have blushed at the departure scene that took place between us.

I'd settled on the bed with Remus wedging himself between my legs when the phone rang.

"You can't be home already," I teased John, thinking he might have turned around, my heart thudding a bit stronger at the idea.

"Not quite, but I am wondering if you are up for another soccer game."

"I hate to make it a habit of asking you this, but did Janaye approve?"

"She was the one who told me to ask you." I was so happy Janaye had asked me to come to her game that I called Vanessa. After listening to me, she shared her own news.

"Jake taught me to surf today!" She exhaled with a ruffle of clothing in the background. "I hated the cold water, let me reiterate, hated it. But we paddled out and I got up on the second time!"

"You're too skinny," I deadpanned. "Get some more fat on you and the water will be warmer. Still, I'm proud of you." The real bravery was occurring each moment she was alone with another man.

"I have more news," she said with excitement. "Hermes gave me the option of staying and running the Union Square store if I want to wait until February when the position becomes available."

"Seriously?" I didn't need to ask if she was going to do it because she was speed talking through her change of plans. "But where will you stay?"

"My parents of course. It's been like high school all over again, except no curfew."

I told her about the dinner with John's family, and we laughed about dropping the pregnancy bomb to the point where we were in tears.

The next week, John arrived to in a black SUV that looked more Presidential escort than dad minivan. "It's required for all the kids."

"Hey Lindy," Janaye greeted from the back.

"I'm sorry if I took your seat," I told her.

"So'kay" she said. The next instant, her earphones were back on and she was in the zone, staring intently at her phone screen but no doubt hearing every word we'd say.

"We're picking up some teammates on the way down anyway," said John.

I looked at him from the corner of my eye. "Carpooling?" I mouthed. He nodded, a wicked look that told me I was getting the full experience.

The girls were alternately rowdy and quiet on the drive to the park and paid me little attention, or so I thought. It wasn't until we arrived and they piled out of the car, grabbing their balls and bags, that I heard the giggling and questions about 'the new girl.' John grabbed the thermos of hot chocolate I'd made which he carried to the field, along with two chairs.

"I can't believe I'm here," I said under my breath. "At a soccer game with a father and a gaggle of girls."

"You're doing pretty well so far."

"I'm a pregnant soccer mom, except I'm not the mom of anyone playing, and you didn't get me pregnant. It's a new reality TV series."

John gamely gave me a kiss on the cheek then left to warm up with the girls. Janaye's footwork had dramatically improved since I saw her last, and I told her so when she came over to check on me.

"Thanks to you," she said, wiping the sweat from her face. I was touched she came over to me, but as Dad reminded me time and again, I knew to play it cool.

Janaye scored half-way through the first period, and again right before the half. During the five minute break, she asked me if I had any recommendations.

"Keep on the inside line when number five is on you," I told her, watching the players on the field. "She keeps kicking to her left, at nine o'clock. I think you can steal it from her if you come from behind."

Janaye nodded, took a gulp of Gatorade from her water bottle and ran to the field. It wasn't until three minutes left in the fourth that she got a chance to execute a steal. I felt my heart speed up as I anticipated her actions. Just as the girl passed to her other foot, Janaye dropped back and behind her opponent, slipping her foot between the inside of the ball for the steal. She kicked it to the left forward who took it and straight-lined it into the goal.

I erupted as did John.

When Janaye came to us, her smile was wide, and the others girls could talk of nothing but her skills on the way home.

"Lindy told me to do that," she informed her friends. I caught John's look of satisfaction at the remark.

"Can she help me?" asked one girl.

"You're not going anywhere, are you?" asked the other girl.

"She does have a life, hello," Janaye drawled.

John dropped the girls off in the same order they'd been picked up, then it was my turn. He pulled the car in my driveway and hopped out. As he came around to my side of the car, I told Janaye to have a great week at school.

"Will you come to my game next week?" she asked me.

"Seriously?"

"Well, yeah. I'd like you to. If you can."

"Sure I'll come. But I gotta be honest with you; my body is not happy at getting up this early so I don't promise to always look fresh and put together."

"No worries," she replied, then put her earphones on again.

John helped me out and walked me up the stairs. "I was wrong. You're not amazing. You're super-woman," he said, kissing my cheek when we got to the landing. "Talk to you tonight."

The house was empty, just as I'd expected. I gratefully slid into bed after having a snack and woke three hours later. The first call I returned was the one from Vanessa.

"You sound tired," she said.

"I am. I just woke up from a nap."

She told me to get it in gear. "I'm coming over and bringing our favorite doctor. Be ready."

I had barely enough time to slip into my pregnancy jeans and a cashmere sweater and wipe a line of lip gloss on my lips before they arrived.

Dr. Redding greeted me warmly, giving me a hug and telling me I was beautiful. He also told me I was no longer allowed to call him Dr. unless we were in the hospital.

"I can't!" I protested. "You're the one who saved me. You deserve a title."

Vanessa gave him a squeeze around the center. "He does saving really well." She positively beamed and he put a protective arm over her shoulder.

Dad got a firsthand account of how Jake had brought me back to life. Dad and Mom were seized with tension as they relived the play-by-play and Vanessa glowed brighter in the ancillary pride of the man who sat beside her, holding her hand.

Vanessa then requested the update on John and I gave it the group.

"Dinner at the house and the soccer game?"

"Tell us and we'll try to make it," Vanessa said, turning to Jake who nodded. "We could surf in the morning, hit the game as a show of solidarity and then go shopping in Stanford. I could call it reconnaissance for work."

John called me after dinner, informing me that he and Janaye were having a popcorn and movie evening, although she had wanted to spend the night with friends.

"The minute you were out of the car, she called up her girls and I heard their take on you all the way home." The comment made me feel as if I were sitting outside a board room waiting for a decision to be made. "Don't worry. It was all good. They want you as their new soccer coach."

I smiled. It could have been a lot worse. "Vanessa and Jake want to come to a game if that's alright." John responded by telling me he looked forward to meeting the man who saved my life.

"Next Saturday right?" I suggested.

"Yeah, but I can't wait that long. Feel like another mid-week lunch date?"

"Absolutely."

CHAPTER 34

Sunday morning I reviewed the final paperwork from Trident Capital Partners. It included the section for the employees to sign, confirming they would receive a signing bonus for staying on board for 18 months. I imagined their elation would be like saying the White Sox won the series after 89 years.

I started to dial Alan, then stopped and dialed another number instead.

"This is a nice way to start a morning," greeted John.

"Yes, and I'll give you a very sexy visual of me in bed with paperwork across my lap." I told him that he was going to witness the final nail in the coffin of my former life of grandeur. "I've become an asterisk in the paperwork."

"Lindy, the way it's structured, you always have the option to change your mind. Maybe you'll be like Alice and go back when the kids hit grade school."

"Maybe," I said, the thought of changes to come raising the subject of homes for myself and other members of my immediate family. "Found anything for Charlie?"

"In fact, I did. We can check out a few places this Wednesday before lunch."

Immediately after we hung up, I called Alan with the idea of opting out of the consulting part of the agreement in return for less money. Whenever I thought of my little girls, Janaye kept coming to mind. It was silly, I knew, to worry about her as much as I was doing, but I couldn't help it. The illusive, mysterious 'mother-gene' that I'd read about had kicked in, and kicked hard.

Early afternoon Alan called me with news.

"A million eight hundred thousand is what they wanted to shave off the price for you not being in the office, but I got them down to a million two. That's how much you're leaving on the table. Can you handle that or do you want some time to think about it?"

That was a lot. The great unknown was scary but I wanted one thing more than money: flexibility.

"Alan, you did great. Thank you so much. Were they ok with the idea?"

"Oh sure. To be honest, I think they were relieved you weren't bagging out entirely."

"I'd never do that."

"Which means I'm as proud as hell of you. What does money matter if you don't have a family to spend it on?" He said the money would be transferred this Friday.

As I thanked him again, he reminded me it wasn't charity on his part.

"I'm getting a million for staying, remember, which I'm not even sure I'd have it weren't for you getting killed." His laughter had a serious undertone. If it hadn't been for the accident, he'd not have had the chance to lead. If not for the accident, I wouldn't have had to sell my things, call Darcy, talk to Joseph, find a buyer for the firm…The trickle-down effects had brought forth so many amazing and wonderful events, it completely erased the pain Patrick had caused.

When I told Dad about the final agreement, he beamed. "You need to celebrate," he said.

"Great. Where are we going?"

"No. Not with me and your mom. John."

"But I was just with him."

"So? This is a milestone moment in your life. Do it with the right person. Go call him," he encouraged, jerking his head towards the bedroom.

I called John, who was all for it, but had business and family obligations until the weekend. "How about the day after the money hits the account?" I suggested.

"Awesome, and this doesn't take away from seeing you on Wednesday."

"No it doesn't," I said, which got John to chuckle. He'd heard the excitement in my voice.

On Wednesday, we arrived at the building of townhomes, I admired the marble floors and modern metal and crystal chandeliers. "This is glamorous," I told John.

"It appeals to the international crowd who want a waterfront location and easy access to either bridge" John said, leading me to the bank of elevators. He slipped the key into the slot at the top, above the buttons for the other floors, and pressed penthouse.

"You have got to be kidding me," I said.

When the elevator opened, I realized he definitely hadn't been kidding. The floor to ceiling windows took in the bay and Oakland to the east, and then the marina on the south. The other side of the floor was a view of the city, and not as appealing as the site of the water in my opinion.

"You could put two families in here," I observed.

"That was the original idea until a buyer from Russia expressed interest in the entire floor. When the financial crunch hit, the deal with him fell through and we never changed the lay out. We'd have to add another kitchen and it's not worth it, at least now. The market is soft for this kind of luxury condo."

I went out on the veranda and ran my finger along the railing. "I might have to come down and stay with Charlie." On the south side was a deck with an extended patio. I sat down on one of the oversized sofas, leaning back in the plush fabric, stretching my legs out in front of me. The noon-time sun was still warm, though it was tinged with a crispness of fall. "Too bad we can't have lunch delivered."

He raised his eyebrows. "Why not?"

"What? I was kidding."

John pulled out his phone and lay beside me. "Let's pick," he suggested, scrolling through the list of restaurants downstairs and within the next block.

"More Dim Sum," I suggested. He laughed. "What? The last memories were really good!" John's look of interest went well beyond a memory of good food. When he put the phone to his ear with his left hand, he lifted his right arm up, and I slid underneath. He proceeded to order as I snuggled next to him. I was in heaven.

He placed the cell phone on the table beside the lounger. "We have about a half-hour."

"Is that all?"

The next day, Cranston Davis, the CEO of Trident, called me.

"I know you are stepping aside, but I wanted to speak with you nonetheless." The twenty-minute call was more formality, as he spent most of the time complimenting me on my hiring capabilities. "If, and when you decide you want to go back to work full time, just let me know." I thanked him, soaking up his flattery like a dry sponge under a water faucet.

Mom prepared for Charlie's arrival with his son Max, who showed up at four p.m.

"Hey beautiful sister," he said, hugging me from the chest up, carefully avoiding my belly. Max came in full of life and energy and promptly asked if he could play with the cat.

"If you stay really still, he'll sit on your lap," I told him. The rambunctious three year-old instantly became the human version of an Egyptian sphinx, stone still. Tentatively, Remus crawled right up and stretched his fat, black self the length of Max's legs. He was still there when John made an impromptu visit.

Dad opened the door and invited him in.

"Hey!" I called, standing and simultaneously catching Charlie's eye.

"I'm not going to stay long, Janaye's waiting in the car, but I have to swap out cards to the place downtown."

"What? He's already been downgraded?" I asked. Charlie was on his feet, hand extended to John, who was quick to explain.

"We just got an offer on the penthouse today, sorry. But we have another one two floors down. It also has a balcony and a great view, but these places have a catch. They are dead space to us until they sell or get rented, so it's temporary housing, although glorified to be sure."

"I'm grateful to have a roof and running water," said Charlie. He clapped John on the shoulder. "I'll take you to the Redwoods on a personal tour if you are ever in my part of the state and won't have any hard feelings if I get kicked out after a week."

Just as I expected John to leave without a show of affection towards me, he came over and kissed me on the top of my head. "See you Saturday."

After the door shut, Charlie turned to me. "Nice guy."

"That's it?"

Charlie sat beside his son, stroking the cat. "I could have said that it's about time you hooked up with a guy who could afford to properly feed you and house the rest of us, but I thought that might be a little much."

Even mom laughed at that one.

"Thanks for the vote of confidence."

"What are the odds Lindy; of you and I, both divorced and with kids, potentially living in the same city?"

"I wouldn't have taken that bet," I answered.

The drive down to the soccer game on Saturday meant Janaye and I tortured John with a random compilation of musicals sung mostly off key. It stopped only after he offered to go to the next Broadway musical that came to town.

At the game, I received more than a few stares from the women on the sidelines, but was also greeted warmly by the girls who carpooled with us the week prior. Janaye was scoreless until the third quarter, and followed it up with an assist in the fourth quarter, but it didn't help. The team still lost and Janaye was unhappy. When she came to the sidelines, she brushed off John's congratulations on a good game and my own words fell on deaf ears.

"It's a competitive thing," John muttered as we walked off the field. Janaye trailed behind with her friends, the group somber.

I knew exactly how she felt, but as I told John, a little good food went a long way to comforting a loss. Janaye conceded she was hungry and had no opposition to Fog City. She'd never been there.

"It has excellent meatloaf and the chocolate bread pudding is to die for," I explained, turning around in the car to emphasize the point. The odds were low Patrick would be at the restaurant on a Saturday afternoon.

Stacy greeted me a huge smile and a hug. She told me how gorgeous I was and how she'd heard life was treating me 'very well.' I introduced John and Janaye as "my dear friends," the comment eliciting a smile of acknowledgement from John and a quiet smirk from Janaye. She sat us immediately, much to the dismay of the lunchtime crowd that was standing in the entryway, placing us in a main booth at the front window, with me facing the door and John and Janaye opposite me. Various waiters I knew stopped by to say hello, touching my shoulder, commenting on how I looked and generally gushing over me.

I soaked it up. I realized now how much I had missed this restaurant and the people here. I would no longer let Patrick keep me away from a place I loved so much.

Janaye gradually emerged from her funk as we replayed the details of her play and assist. I was right in the middle of answering her question about a side-kick when the door behind her opened. Janaye shivered and John put his arm around her, drawing her close. The gap provided a clear view to the man and woman who walked through the door.

My mouth went dry. We were separated by an aisle and the piece of wood between the bar and dining area. I looked down at the menu. If I don't move, he won't look at us. But I couldn't help myself. I looked up, wanting—but not wanting—to see the person he was with.

I inhaled. The blond wore a chestnut-colored brown shearling jacket. *My jacket.* On her shoulder was a light-brown Prada purse with yellow piping. *My purse.* A surge of pure hatred tore through me, from leg to my head. I felt the heat of rage on my face and the sickness of regret in my stomach.

It was like my dream, but worse. It was real. It *is* real.

"Lindy, you look green," said Janaye, squirming out of her dad's arms and leaning towards me. John's countenance immediately changed and he placed his hand across the table, reaching for mine.

"Do you need to go to the doctor?" he asked.

"No, I'm just hot, actually." My voice was flat. I reached for a glass of water.

"Your hand is shaking," Janaye pointed out, and I instantly gripped the glass, but dared not lift it to my lips. I overcame the nausea in my throat to glance at the bar. Dave looked at me from behind the bar and we shared a moment of disgust. He briefly nodded his head in disbelief and a shrug of his shoulders. What could he do? Nothing.

"I'm sorry, what did you say?" I asked John, not recalling his words.

"I said—did you see a ghost?"

"Yes. Over there," I said, barely above a whisper. "At the bar, it's Patrick. With his—date."

Janaye's eyes went wide. "Patrick? That's his name? Your…" she let the words trail off.

I nodded, not wanting her to finish the sentence. "And she's wearing my clothes. Remember I told you my $2,500 dollar shearling coat had gone missing, and that the one my parents just bought me was a replacement? That woman, his date, is wearing it. And that Prada bag? The one I bought and also went missing when it still had the tags on it, Patrick blamed it on the housekeeper. She's wearing that too."

Janaye's mouth dropped open. She started to look over her shoulders, but glanced back at me and stopped.

"It's ok Janaye. Go ahead and look."

As she did so, I stared down at the menu, placing a hand up to my forehead.

"She's butt ugly," Janaye announced, and I stared at her through the slates between my fingers. John couldn't help himself. He had to lift himself up to get a good look.

"Not in your class at all," John said a bit more diplomatically. She wasn't ugly at all, I thought. She was quite pretty in fact. But she was short and blond, very Romanesque and exotic. Even being thirty pounds overweight hadn't given me that curvaceous figure. Her chest looked as high and firm as a bar stool, ready to hold a glass of wine.

Janaye went from neutrality to anger, the reaction so kind I felt tears welling up.

"He has some balls to come here with his girlfriend, wearing your clothes," she hissed.

"Are you allowed to use that kind of language?" I joked, my wavering voice confirming my distress. "One part I didn't tell you, John, was that I learned he'd used my company account here, racking up thousands of dollars in bills. Another tidbit of dishonesty."

"He lied. He steals," Janaye said. "He left you." Her mouth drew back, a perfect picture of a pre-teen ready to take down her opponent.

The bathroom was right behind me and to my left. "I'll be back."

In the bathroom, I sat on the toilet, not bothering to use it. I concentrated on breathing, in and out, touching either side of my abdomen as though doing so could get out my anxiety. What if he saw me? What would he do if I went over and claimed my coat and purse, making a scene in front of the entire bar crowd?

My stomach clenched. I might be good at conflict resolution in the workplace, but I preferred to avoid it in my personal life. How long I could stay in here? Probably until a line formed.

I heard the door open. "Lindy?" asked Janaye quietly.

"Yeah, I'm here."

"You can come out now. He's gone."

"Really?"

"Yeah, we watched them drive away."

When I opened the door, Janaye was nodding her head. She wasn't laughing or making fun of me.

"I feel like an idiot," I admitted, walking out slowly.

Janaye got the door for me and her countenance took on a fierce look, the one she had when an opposing player stole the ball from between her legs. "Oh, yeah. He's gone."

I followed her out and we returned to our table together

"We ordered while you were gone," John told me, matter of fact.

"Apparently, they've known what you want for years."

"It's true," I affirmed, sitting on the soft booth. "Sorry to you both. You'd think after all this time it wouldn't bother me." I took a drink of my Arnold Palmer lemonade.

"Aren't you wondering why he left all of a sudden?" Janaye asked me, a grin on her face.

I looked between the two of them. "Did you do something?"

John fiddled with his glass and shrugged. "Oh, I gave him a little of his own attitude back to him."

"How?"

Janaye started giggling.

"Dad used my cell phone to call Stacy. Told her it was an emergency for a patron at the bar name Patrick. When he got on, I told him he was being watched. That the coat and the purse he'd stolen from his ex-wife were on the woman he was with."

I looked at Janaye for verification. "He said it all," she confirmed.

"I then told him the thefts had been reported to the police by his former wife, and if he didn't want him and his girl arrested, then he'd better leave. I also strongly suggested he not be seen with those clothing items on or around him ever again."

"True story," Janaye said.

I was torn between laughter and awe. "Could you see his face when you were talking to him?"

"No, but Janaye did."

"He kept looking around but he had no idea what was going on. When he got off the phone he walked around, totally paranoid, but left pretty fast."

John could not have been happier. "That probably bugged him out more. He looked straight at me and had no idea who I was. If I were a betting man, I'd say he won't be here again for some time, and I'd also suspect he's going to be removing those articles from his companion."

I was overcome with emotion, and I laughed, an infectious, happy-spirited sound.

CHAPTER 35

Sunday morning I spoke with John then spent most of the day reading and was in bed by eight. When I finally emerged on Monday, Mom had to heat up my breakfast that had long since gone cold.

"Isn't the big event happening today?"

"Tomorrow, actually."

"Shouldn't you be excited? Oh." She said, understanding in her voice.

"Yeah." It was the recollection of Patrick that left me feeling off kilter. As much as I told myself that I was over him, watching it play out in front of me had been like fist smashing into a bruise. It was still there, and it hurt.

Mom and Dad left not long after. They were going for a drive down to Half Moon Bay and if time allowed, would wander through the hills down into Santa Cruz. I started working on the computer but couldn't concentrate. I gave up, trying to sort through my feelings. The anger towards Patrick I thought was non-existent—I'd even prayed for him!—was real and dark like a storm cloud, almost overtaking the bright sun that John had become.

I called Ann, who listened and sympathized with the situation with Patrick, but told me to be optimistic. I was definitely heading in the right direction from all indicators. "John handled it magnificently and if Vanessa approves of him then I'm inclined to do the same, though I still want to meet him in the very near future."

"With all that's going on, I just worry I'm going too fast with him."

"Look, I get it. You are overcompensating for what happened with Patrick, second guessing your gut and what everyone is telling you. Geez, Lindy. You should have done that with Patrick, but not with John."

Her words made sense, but that wasn't it. I wasn't having second thoughts or doubts about John at all. There was something else.

I called Vanessa, the hardest sounding board I had. "You can't see it?" she asked, slightly exasperated.

"See what?"

"What I mean is, you don't see what the loss of your company is doing to you."

"It's not a loss," I corrected. "It's an acquisition."

She humphed. "You can say that to Alan, your parents and the team, but not to me or yourself. You are struggling with letting your identity go. The same identity that has made you very prominent in this town along with a good deal of money. In business, that means the position, prestige and power are all going to be gone in one fell swoop."

"That sounds dismal," I said.

"But it's coming, just like the babies. The balance though is a blessing. You lose a business but gain a family."

A partial family. Nothing was guaranteed in this life, especially not a husband or family unit.

Yet that wasn't an attitude I needed to share with John. He seemed to implicitly agree, or at least understand. As much as we were attracted to one another, shared common interests and I'd bonded with his daughter, a lot in my life was in flux. As he had said one evening a few days earlier, I could up and decide to relocate to another state.

"Why would I?" I'd asked in shock.

"Because you have no reason not to, not after your year of consulting is up." In other words, he had to be realistic himself. There were no guarantees, on either side of the relationship.

"Well, I am making one major decision." My serious tone caught him up short. "I'm getting a new car."

"Just no minivans."

On Thursday, I was driving a brand new Audi crossover.

"I can see Janaye carpooling in this," said Mom, I could too. It was a happy thought, and one that was starting to feel more natural.

John had an out of town wedding that weekend for a cousin and he kept calling me at strange times, which amused and flattered me. Once it was during breakfast and another time from the men's get-together. "Second marriages don't warrant a full bachelor party," he laughed.

"Aren't you supposed to be with them regardless?"

"I'd rather be talking with you," he said simply.

"It would be nice to have you here," I said, hearing the longing in my voice.

"Do you mean it?" The innocence and vulnerability of the question struck me. He sounded exactly how I felt.

"Yes. Absolutely."

"Can I come see you when I get home?"

A giggle erupted, spontaneous and happy. "This living with my parents is such an odd thing."

"It makes it interesting. Like high school."

John wasn't able to see me on Monday as planned. Charlie and I spoke that night instead, and he mentioned that after the first two get-togethers with Darcy went well, they'd started arranging three-day weekends, alternating a schedule for one of them taking a day off. He also summarized his interaction with Joseph.

His recollection of events was later affirmed by Darcy. "Didn't any of my good credit carry over to my brother?" I asked.

She laughed. "Of course it did. But you know Joseph. He doesn't feel satisfied unless he tests someone's mettle by roughing them up a bit."

Between parental duties and work, I'd not seen John the entire week and the game on Saturday was on the Peninsula. With regret and relief, I told John that I couldn't make it.

"Six a.m. and I don't work any longer, but I'll guarantee one thing. The next time you see me you will not believe it. I've exploded."

"Are you ok to be up and about?"

"Sure. I feel great."

Later that evening, I received a call from Jackson. After he was satisfied my health was good and the babies were fine, he asked me if I was interested in talking replacement pieces.

"Like what? For my place?"

"Yes. I can't bear the thought of you living in that hollow shell of an apartment."

"Oh aren't you sweet?" I cooed. "Thankfully, my fortunes have turned around." I told him about the release of the funds from the IRS along with GeorgiaLiman going public.

"That means you can afford what I want to show you."

"Yes, but we have a slight complication."

Jacksons tone dropped when he asked, "Do I want to know this?"

I summarized the options for my parents and a potential move in my future. "Hence the reason that refurnishing my place didn't make a lot of sense for the time being."

"And you have someone you trust? I can recommend quite a few good real estate agents."

"Have you heard of John Abrahms?" I asked casually.

"John? Of course. His family, his siblings, they've all been clients of mine at one time or another." Jackson told me to wait until I had a place and then send John his way. "He always gets pieces to suit."

"Well, he won't be paying the bill, I will, but still." Another thought occurred to me. "Before you go, can I ask, do you like John?"

"Of course. He's a nice—wait a minute. Are you dating him?" he asked incredulously.

"I haven't been in the dating circuit for a long time, but I'm thinking that if I met his family and he's met mine, then the answer might just be yes."

"Ronnie will take satisfaction in knowing that he was right. He gave you less time on the market than I did. I thought you'd be around until you had the kids, but this town and those single, straight males... They could find you out within a ten-mile radius."

"Yes, the allure of pregnancy, that's what got John," I said sarcastically.

"This is going to sound, well, I was wondering if you've ever heard, or know…" I stopped, unable to continue my line of questioning. I sounded so awkward and felt insecure.

"Let me help you out on this one," Jackson cut me off. "John's a good guy and straight up. I don't mean straight up in a heterosexual way, though he is. He's one of the men who we say that if we didn't know he was straight, we'd think he was gay and I mean that as a compliment. It means he's not a skirt chaser. Not once in all these years have I heard even a hint of rumor of his acting in a way I'd consider inappropriate, and since you are now considered in my 'sister status' category, I care about these types of things."

"No better category to be in."

"Ronnie and I have adopted you. But seriously Lindy, as far as a man's concerned, I'm not sure you could do much better than John in this town."

The conversation was comforting. I'd not had the benefit of knowing any of Patrick's acquaintances or friends until a few days before the wedding. To have Jackson give me a good report was another check in the plus column.

When Saturday came, I ate a solid breakfast of eggs and oatmeal and was just putting on my shoes when the door rang. Mom and Dad were already gone on their weekly Saturday outings, which I told John at the door. He stepped in, sliding his arms around my waist.

"Then I can do this properly," he mumbled, his lips vibrating against mine. It broke the moment and we were soon off to the waterfront.

John lucked out on parking, finding a curbside spot at the very end of the south side, near the marina. "We won't go that far," he promised, taking my hand. Bikers, roller bladers and strollers passed us then lapped us again as we made our way past the ferry, then around the bend in front of Fog City, and then down to Pier 39. On the way down, we talked about business, his and mine, and as we turned around, it went to Janaye.

"She's suddenly obsessed with how much money you make," John said, sounding as mystified as I was. "I don't know if that's a good sign she's interested enough to care, or if I need to be worried she's focusing on the wrong things."

"As I've been told recently, don't over think it." He lifted my hand to his mouth. As we walked another thought occurring to me. "Perhaps she's wondering whether you are going to become insecure with me."

"Like Patrick?" I asked.

"Maybe I'm giving off signals my daughter can see that I can't. You're slowing down," he remarked, matching my stride. "Does that mean you are getting tired or you want to be in my presence as long as possible?"

I started giggling, pulling him to a complete stop. My hands around his waist, I felt the warmth of the sun on my right side as I started with his ear and worked my way to the center until I met his lips. It was an image I'd witnessed in a hundred couples on the boardwalk, but never experienced myself.

"That answer your question?" He mumbled an affirmative, but I did ask him to get a cab. I was feeling tired.

On the way, John received a call from Janaye, asking to be picked up. "She's at a friend's, which is convenient. He's a soccer dad, and I actually need to talk with him briefly about an upcoming tournament." When we pulled up, Janaye and her friend were outside the home, lying on the grass.

"I'm going to stretch while you talk," I said, hoping to work out that odd feeling in my tummy. I'd read the skin got tight, which mine had, and that mild movement sometimes helped.

"Holy cow!" Janaye exclaimed, standing up as I emerged from the car. "You are huuuge!"

"I know! Every week I'm expanding like a balloon addicted to helium."

She came up to me and peered closely at my stomach.

"It's super hard, too, and pulling." I warned her, the sensation still odd to me. A few weeks ago it had been firm, but now was taught like the leather on a basketball. John wasn't long, emerging from the home with the father and his wife. Janaye's friend said goodbye and we got in the car while John wrapped up his conversation.

"Can you move very well?" Janaye asked, still in a bit of awe.

"Standing straight up is easy, sitting down is getting more uncomfortable. But I'll try not to hit anything going around a corner."

"Still, I bet it's great being in your position."

"Why's that?"

"You have my dad, who is awesome, totally digging on you. Your company sold. You get to do what you want, like pick a place to move, and have your parents and brother around to help. Plus," she went on without a breath, "you get to name your kids all by yourself."

"There is that," I said ruefully. I turned as best I could. "Janaye, this may seem weird, but I've never dated a person with a child before, or someone who is divorced. And now I'm doing both," I laughed, getting a smile from her. "So for the record, if I never get another chance to say it, thank you. Thank you for letting John see me and spend some time with me. It's really nice to be treated well, you know?"

"I like you," she said honestly.

"That's good, but I'm serious when I say this. My number one worry is that I'll add more challenges by coming into your life at this point, and I don't want to do that, as much as I enjoy your dad and adore you."

Now Janaye shifted in the backseat. "Dad is really cool. I just…there's no one to talk to other than my aunt and Grandma."

"My dad was always gone when I was growing up," I offered. "Mom is wonderful, but we have very different personalities. Because my dad was gone so much, I got resentful, then mad. Very furious, enough to start acting out."

This perked her interest, and she glanced at her father. "How?"

"Boys." One word to sum up the majority of my bad decisions. "Trust me. The adage is true. Girls that don't have enough attention from their fathers seek it from other males. That's why he threw me in the airplane and took me to Houston. Not because some rich developer needed the opinion of a 15-year old. He had to get me away to understand what in the world had gone so wrong with his daughter."

Janaye's eyes darted back out to her father. "But it all worked out," she said, watching John shake the other man's hand.

"Eventually. My dad and I had no relationship compared to what you and your father have, and so we had to start over from scratch. That's not easy to do at 15. It worked for a while, then we had another phase in my twenties which didn't get rectified until my husband left me."

"Wow," she uttered, then shook herself. "Will it last this time?"

"I hope so. I was attracted to the wrong things for a very long time, and it took me losing all of it to learn what's really important."

Janaye touched my shoulder, light but meaningful. "Thanks again for your help with soccer. It's pretty cool you know how to play."

"Anytime."

CHAPTER 36

"Can we see them?" Janaye asked once her father was in the car.

"You mean come to the doctors and see the ultrasound?" I clarified. I looked at John and saw elation in his eyes.

"I'm in," he said. As though her question was a sign, I felt a tinge on the right side of my belly. I lifted my left hand, placing it on my side. "Did you get an internal affirmation?" I nodded, hoping my smile didn't convey my actual discomfort.

"As long as your dad approves of you missing an hour of school in the morning, then you can come to the next one."

At home, I skipped dinner, opting to sit on the couch and talk with Charlie on the phone. This weekend, Darcy was at his home, currently outside in the yard with Max. He was happy and distracted, I was uncomfortable and felt full, even though I hadn't eaten since before the walk.

The following morning day Ann came over for a brief visit with her children. She agreed with Janaye that I looked like I was going to pop, enjoying my moan of mock agony. "But you don't seem very uncomfortable yet."

"I was last night after the walk, but it's fine now." She cocked her head and leaned forward.

"May I?" I nodded, watching as she touched my belly.

"They must be sleeping." I hummed, a happy, contented sound. I shifted in my chair, pushing my back into the sofa. The stretch felt luxurious.

"Did that get them moving?"

"Nope, and you know, I'm glad of it. My sleep has been so awful since they started moving around all night long." She sat against the couch, her elbow on the edge.

"Just wait until they arrive. A person never truly appreciates a good night's rest until it's no longer possible." That night I ate a small salad, more to keep my mom from worrying about me than from any real hunger. I slept like a baby, completely undisturbed, thinking of Ann when I yawned with gratitude the next morning. John was already at the office when he called to confirm the doctor's appointment.

"Janaye isn't talking about it directly, but she's been asking me things like your favorite letters and colors. I should also mention Darcy and Kay have been working with Sam on your baby shower extravaganza."

"Isn't it a little early still?"

He chuckled. "It's never too early for girls to celebrate a baby."

We arrived at Dr. Lawler's office a few minutes late, having splurged on ham and cheese croissants and one filled with chocolate. I excused myself to check in and give my normal sample for the nurse, who complimented me on my outfit. When I returned to John and Janaye, I spoke in an undertone.

"Not to be rude, but I'm texting Vanessa we are here. She'll freak." John put his arm around my shoulder.

About ten minutes later, the nurse called me to the front desk.

"Do you think you can get me a little more?" she asked quietly. "This wasn't quite enough." I took the cup and gave it my best shot, grateful I had a lot of juice that morning.

When the nurse called my name the next time, she held the door open with a file folder, glancing at John and Janaye. We followed her to the examination room and she brought in another chair for John. For the routine exams, I was weighed, measured and my stomach monitored with the ultrasound. I rarely took more than ten minutes, and I almost felt guilty Janaye was missing school.

"Is this as exciting as you thought it would be?' I asked her. She'd been uncommonly quiet, either holding back her sass, saving it for later or was as mystified as a normal eleven year-old would be.

"You aren't going to use those, are you?" she grimaced, pointing at the stirrups. John and I laughed.

"Nothing says intimate like metal foot holders," I muttered just as the doctor came in. John stood, and they shook hands. Janaye said hello and I remained on the table. Dr. Lawler had warmed up with each visit, even allowing a smile now and then. Today, he wasn't smiling, though the nurse who was behind him was a kind as always. She turned on the machines and Dr. Lawler asked me about my week.

"Good," I answered, thinking how I'd been on my fanny most of the time. "Got in a nice, long walk with John over the weekend."

"Your sample came back a little differently than I expected," he said, applying gel to the roller. I lay back, running my fingers along one side of my belly.

"After we walked I was hurting here," I showed him. "It wasn't horrible, just like pulling." Dr. Lawler's eyes assessed me, his neutral gaze disconcerting.

"Did it continue?"

"It got worse for a little while, but I breathed through it. It went away before I went to bed."

The black screen turning multi-colored as it moved over my stomach, showing the heat patterns and outline of the little bodies inside me. It was quiet as he didn't have the sound on.

"Tell me about your sleep," he asked.

"It's been getting harder, as you predicted, and I have pillows on either side now, which helps."

"Have you noticed any change with the movement?"

"They are acting just like you said they would, moving around more at night than day, although I think I wore them out with the walk too, because that night I slept great. Last night too, actually."

"John and Janaye, would you like me to point things out as I go?" They shared a look and said yes, so he began by identifying baby girl one and two, the arms, legs and heads. The sizes were nearly identical. "They won't be identical, because they are in separate sacks, see here."

Janaye was excitedly pointing out the little fingers and toes, with John leaning forward. They'd not noticed Dr. Lawler had stopped talking, and was moving the wand back and forth on one area.

"What's that black?" I asked, squinting. As I spoke, Dr. Lawler's lips moved and he picked up the phone. "Get a room ready at the hospital." He hung up and turned to me, ignoring John and Janaye. "The placenta wall has ruptured. Lindy," he paused. "I'm going to turn the sound on."

"Okay…" I said slowly, looking at John for support. His lips pressed together. Janaye didn't know what to make of it, but she was quiet as the doctor turned up the volume.

He placed the wand over baby girl two, the heart beating clearly and loudly. It was away from the black and red area he'd identified. The pause was long enough for him to tap and click, I guessed to measure the heart beats per minute. He then went over to baby number one. Once, then twice, he moved the wand over and around the little entity.

Quiet.

My throat felt like it was collapsing inward as it closed off my air. I stared at the screen, then at Dr. Lawler as he adjusted the dials and moved the wand again.

"This, right here," he pointed. "The placenta that keeps a baby alive, provides the oxygen she needs—her life support system if you will, pulled apart from the uterus. It's called placental abruption. I'm sorry Lindy. Baby girl number one is no longer with us."

Several seconds of silence passed as I watched the doctor, bit my quivering lip, feeling John's firm grasp on my hand. "I'll give you a few moments, but then we need to admit you to the hospital."

When the doctor left, John took my hand between his and bent over, our hands on his forehead. "I'm so sorry," he whispered, sounding agonized.

"Me, too," Janaye said quietly, touching my leg lightly, then withdrawing, as though her very touch could cause more harm.

"Lindy," John began, his voice hoarse. "I never should have encouraged you to go for a walk—"

"No," I broke in, my voice rasping. "I'm the one who wanted to keep going, who insisted…" We gazed at each other, grief, regret, heartache shared. "I'm so sorry," I choked. I'd been so stupid, and this would be my lifelong price.

"But I let it happen," he continued.

"Stop it," Janaye cried quietly, her face taught with emotion. "It doesn't matter. What matters is that…she's gone." John and I were silent, my eyes as full of tears as his own. He put his arms around me and Janaye joined him. We were still in that position when the door opened. We separated as the nurse technicians came in with a gurney.

"I need to call my parents…" I got out, stopping the instant the familiarity of the words hit me. "John, could you?"

"Of course," John said. "And Vanessa, and Ann. Can I let Sam and my mom know? They'll all be worried. And what about Darcy?"

"Your purse, Lindy?" Janaye asked. "Is that where your phone is?" I nodded at Janaye, grateful. I typed out the password then handed her back the phone. As the nurses directed me on how to move and helped me lie down, John and his daughter were quietly transferring information.

"Will you…" I started to say, unable to finish. My eyebrows crinkled in a pain of a different sort. I needed him beside me, so badly I couldn't talk. And Janaye, with her loving, big eyes, so full of heartache for me.

"Of course," he said firmly, his eyes intense. "All day." In my peripheral vision, I saw Janaye nodding her head.

My eyes were closed for most of the ride over, flashes of my friends and loved ones, all who had gone through dramatic, heart-wrenching experiences. Ann and Monson, both losing a child, Vanessa who'd been through a horribly traumatic experience. Mine would be no different.

I'd get through it, and there was one key difference, I kept repeating as the doors opened and shut, and I was carefully transferred onto a hospital bed. I still had one healthy child inside me. That was what I held on to, as the nurses then attending physician asked me how I was feeling, took my vitals, hooked up the IV and drew the blinds. The moment the door shut, all the self- talk stopped and I did what came naturally. I cried.

The gut wrenching, agonizing racks of pain I felt made what I'd endured when Patrick raised the topic of abortion nothing by comparison. All my previous worries and fears, being a single mother, alone and without a husband to share my world came rushing to the forefront of my mind. The salve on my wound had been the knowledge of two little entities, built-in playmates for one another, not a single child consigned to a single parent, alone in their own sphere.

My cries grew harder as the pit of remorse deepened. John was lovely, is lovely, and had been wonderful, and I knew he liked me. But love me?

My chest heaved from the sobs, the physical pain stabbing through my chest in cross sections. Lights were flashing in my head, hitting against a blackness so real that my mind was closed to all thought other than my desire to die. The thoughts rolled faster, one after another, until my mind cried out to please, let me die again go to the other side where it was warm and safe. I could take this remaining baby with me, and even if that was wrong and awful, at least we'd all be together.

At this decisive moment, the pain eased slightly. I breathed from the dark place in my mind, and that moment a scene unfolded. A bearded man wearing a white robe sat with his arms extended wide. He looked up, encouraging me to join him, willing me into his circle. I stepped forward, instantly absorbed by a love so powerful it stopped my tears.

"Be of good cheer," the man said. Within each word was the knowledge I'd never felt so much love, complete and pure, to heal my wounds, offer a reprieve from pain and give me hope. I didn't recall walking forward, I just did, feeling warmer, brighter and more love as I neared. A snippet—a question from my Grandfather who'd ask me what I'd go through to experience the love I saw envelop Vanessa. My heart and mind had told me then I would. Here, now, I was having that desire answered.

As he held me, my suffering ceased as he absorbed my physical and emotional pain.

I closed my eyes. My life wasn't going to be easy, but it would be what was right for me. Dr. Redding's words were prophetic. I was here for a purpose, but all the reasons I'd previously thought were wrong.

CHAPTER 37

John came in alone. He was hesitant, worried, remorseful and yet there was a look I don't recall ever seeing on Patrick's face, not even when we got married. It was one of love.

"I asked Janaye for a few minutes alone with you. I hope you don't mind." When he came close enough, I felt for his right hand, feeling his skin. It was warm and soft, unlike Patrick's when his cold and clammy hand had touched mine the last time I was in the hospital. His had been moist and cold, like a slug waiting to crawl back under a rock.

Erasing the mental image from my mind, I concentrated on the man before me. The good, kind, steady individual who was interested in me despite my faults, who could see beyond the exterior and had begun to know the real me.

I knew he was wracked with regret and guilt over what had happened, as I had been. "John, we went on the walk because we wanted to be with one another, enjoying life and what we have. I didn't want it to end. Neither did you. I didn't feel any pain at all until the very end, and it wasn't really bad."

"It might have been enough had we stopped."

I moved my thumb slightly, stroking his hand. "No. This was supposed to happen." He watched my face, taking in my composure. How could I possibly describe the experience I'd just had so he could understand what I was feeling?

I saw movement through the small window in the door and knew others were arriving. "Will you come back later so we can talk more?"

He was uncertain, looking as though a little bit of his life had been lost with my own. "You may change your mind. You may never want to see me again."

"More likely I will never want you to leave." I gave him an emotion filled smiled and pressed his hand to my cheek. "Truly. I'm at peace."

"Are you sure?"

"Yes, and I'm sure of one other thing. I'm sure I love you, for the person you have been and the friend you have become. After all this is over, will you still be in my life?" He nodded, unable to speak, bringing my hand to his lips, pressing hard while closing his eyes. His shoulders shook, and I saw the water at the corner of his eyes. He was feeling the grief I'd experienced earlier, and I wanted to take it away.

I pulled him to me and we shared each other's emotions of hurt, gratitude, hope and comfort through the warmth of our bodies.

"I love you Lindy. All of you." I pressed harder.

The door clicked, opened then shut. John drew back, his fingers gliding down my cheek then chin as he stood. He started to smile as he saw what his words had done to me. I felt warm within, the embers of an almost extinguished fire coming back.

"If it's okay, I'm going to take Janaye to school. Everyone I called said they were coming right away." He looked up, nodding. "Your parents are already outside." His warm lips lingered on my lips, then forehead.

After John left, there were a few moments before the door opened again, and I suspected he was greeting my parents or catching others up on the situation. Once again, I was grateful. It would spare me the effort of going through it all again.

I took a drink of water and looked outside. The water of the bay was mostly obstructed by the view of another building, but I saw just enough of the blue to give me an emotional lift. I'd had so many good memories in this town, and recently bad ones, but that was tempered by the knowledge it was all required for me and my journey. I'd always hated that phrase, 'what doesn't kill you makes you stronger.' It was wrong. The last word should be changed to wiser, or compassionate or empathetic.

"Or D, all of the above," I said to myself.

"I see you under the most extreme situations," said a voice to my right. It was Dr. Redding.

"You're on shift today?"

"Later tonight, but I was with Vanessa and she told me what happened. She's waiting outside. I'm so sorry." He came to me, lifting my chart, concern and worry blending with his objectivity of a physician.

"You told me that you'd like to hear about my life, once this was all over," I began. "Not just what Vanessa told you, but the real things. What I saw, beyond. Can I tell you now?"

He sat down and I shared my experiences, the ones even Vanessa didn't know about. When I finished, Dr. Redding's eyes were alight. "You positively brightened as you spoke."

"One of the reasons I wanted you to hear all of this is because you have seen others like me. Speaking from your doctor's perspective, does it last? Does the warmth and love and happiness continue, or…"

"Does it fade?" he finished for me. "I think it depends on the person. I've not had all those I've treated make repeat performances or give me follow-ups," he said with a smile. "But I will be honest. The majority of those I have seen over the years eventually went back to who they were before the incident. The afterglow faded, is the best description. But a handful, three or four maybe, were never the same."

"Yeah," I said softly, more to myself.

"I suspect you will be one of those." He stood up, unnecessarily checking the IV. "And I hope it's not overreaching on my part, but John is a solid guy." I smiled and Dr. Redding winked.

"Many good things have come out of this," I said, my hands already on my stomach, but also meaning his friendship with Vanessa. "So many…" I said more to myself.

"I wouldn't be surprised if many more lives are altered than the ones you have already touched, Lindy. Think of that as you go through the hard days that will come."

I thanked him, grateful for the wisdom and perspective. Closing my eyes, I offered up a prayer. Old wounds had been healed, even as new ones were created. Love had been given where none had previously existed. A birth would bring forth new challenges and affirm that choices have permanent consequences. Above all, I felt grateful I'd been given a second chance. Yes, what I had gone through was worth it to get to this point. I now prayed that knowledge would be enough to carry me into an uncertain future.

ABOUT THE AUTHOR

Before she began writing novels, Sarah Gerdes established herself as an internationally recognized expert in the areas of business management and consulting. Her books have been published in sixteen countries, and two book series have been optioned for film. Follow her on Instagram at sarah_j_gerdes, facebook or download free chapters and subscribe for special deals at her website, www.sarahgerdes.com, Instagram at sarah_j_gerdes or facebook.

AUTHOR'S NOTE

This book is for the very real "Patrick" who made my life misery for a period of time, but who I must now thank. If he hadn't come into my life, I wouldn't have had the brutal and amazing experiences I recount in this (only slightly) fictionalized book. It took me a long while to realize that it was necessary for me to become the person I am today in order to find lasting love with an incredible man and have a beautiful family

OTHER BOOKS BY

Sarah Gerdes

Fiction: Contemporary Women's Fiction

Destined for You, book 2 in the Danielle Grant Series, (2017)

Made for Me, book 1 in the Danielle Grant Series, (2016)

A Convenient Date (2015)

Fiction: Action- Adventure

Chambers, book 1 (2012) – also translated in Indonesia (2014), Poland (2015)

Chambers: The Spirit Warrior (publish date fall 2017)

Non-Fiction

Sue Kim: The Greatest Korean American Story Never Told Authorized biography, (2016)

The Overlooked Expert: Turning your skills into a Profitable Consulting Company (2009)

Navigating the Partnership Maze: Creating Alliances that Work (McGraw-Hill, 2002)